A bump in the road

Gerard byrne

Chapter One

Two in the morning on New Year's Day and Jack was already starting to worry that any chance of pulling that night was growing slim. The nightclub was packed with partygoers and he'd lost sight of his cousins over the last half hour. Didn't bother him too much. They were boring as fuck and dragging the whole tone of the night down. He'd only agreed to take them out, just to get his mother off his back. But besides all that shit, he'd only a few days left until he escaped back down to Cork for another few months. Away from his overbearing mother and goal achieving father. It couldn't come quick enough.

Thankfully the effects of the two ecstasy tablets were still flowing through Jack's body and he was horny as fuck. He needed sex and at this rate, any woman would do. Scanning the poorly lit room, Jack spotted a woman alone at the edge of the dance floor. She was a big blonde girl, who looked well into her forties. But she seemed to be single and time was running out.

Jack forced his way up to the counter beside her. More difficult than you'd expect in a packed nightclub. He couldn't help but check out her large ass as he tried to get her attention, "how are you tonight ?", was all he could come out with.

The woman turned and looked him up and down, with a face filled with disdain, "can I help you?"

He couldn't help glancing down her low cut top and imagine burying his head between those large breasts. Thankfully he snapped out of it quickly enough and stared up into her eyes, "was just wondering what a hot looking thing like you, is doing alone at a bar like this", he tapped the counter beside him for effect.

The woman finally broke a smile and leaned in close, "my husband is getting our jackets from the cloak room and if he comes back and catches a little fuck like you, trying to chat up his wife of twenty two years, I reckon he'll smash your fucking face in. Do you get where I'm coming from Romeo?"

Jack was out of his head. But he still knew a dangerous situation when he saw one, "no worries. Sorry for bothering you", he got one last quick glance at her boobs before wandering on. If he didn't pull that night. He still had a bit of wanking material for later.

He pushed his way through the busy crowd in search of another available woman. It wouldn't be long until the night was over and he'd have to go home for a wank in front of Babestation. That was the last thing he wanted. But the search of the nightclub was not bringing up any other potential conquests. Everyone seemed to be taken, or in large groups of women. Last thing he wanted was to try and charm a group of them, just in the hope of pulling one. Way more hassle than it was worth.

Jack gave up hope and stepped out into the car park, which doubled as an extra smoking area when the nightclub was at full capacity. The lighting was poor and a crappy waist high metal barrier cornered off a small area from the rest of the parking structure. Jack was pretty sure he could smell hash in the distance. A few quick pulls of a joint would have been nice about now, but he hadn't the head to go in search of its user.

Suddenly a voice called out from behind him, "got a light?"

Jack swivelled around to come face to face with a beautiful red headed woman in a very short and extremely tight dress. He recognised her straight away. Just not by name, "you used to be in my school", he pulled out his lighter and gentlemanly lit her cigarette.

The woman took a long drag and rubbed her reddened eyes discreetly, "were you in the same year as me?"

Jack rubbed the back of his neck awkwardly, "no, I was in first year, when you were in sixth. I just remember you to see. The name's Jack by the way"

The woman dragged at the cigarette that hard, that half of it was gone already, "Yvonne, so what's that make you?. About five years younger than me. You don't look it"

Jack saw his opportunity to turn on the charm, "more like you only look about twenty. You're still as beautiful as when you were back in school. You on your own tonight?"

Yvonne's mood dampened slightly, "lost my friend earlier. You know the way it is. Probably met a fella over the course of the night. What about yourself?"

Jack didn't want to be reminded about his boring cousins. Not the type of people you'd admit to being out with, "same shit as you. Just lost sight of them throughout the night. You know the way it gets in this place"

Yvonne stared into his eyes and cheekily smiled, "you're whacked out of it. I can see it in your eyes. What is it?. Ecstasy?"

He hated being called out on his buzz. Especially by people who weren't under the same influence, "yeah, just like trying it the odd time", he lied.

Yvonne's eyes glanced down towards his crotch, "explains that then"

Jack looked down to see his ever growing bulge that was pushing out from his tight blue jeans. He tried to discreetly cover it with his hands, "sorry about that. I wasn't even aware that something was happening down there", he could feel his cheeks reddening with each second.

Yvonne moved in close to him and kissed Jack passionately on the lips. Pushing him up against a nearby pillar. Her right hand wrapping around his side, while her left began to caress his bulge. He didn't want this moment to stop. His head swimming in the pleasure of it all.

Suddenly Yvonne pulled away and grabbed him by the hand, "let's find somewhere a little quieter", she lifted the barrier out of the way and led him towards the darkness of the car park.

Jack was in his element as they turned a corner and Yvonne put her back to the cold brick wall.

She began to open up his tight jeans, "bet you wanna fuck me?"

He smiled goofily, "damn right I do. You're so fucking beautiful"

Yvonne was still struggling with his belt, "keep telling me that"

Jack didn't know why she wanted that. But he didn't much care, "you are fucking beautiful. Like a model"

Yvonne finally got his pants opened and pulled down his boxers. Jack's thick ten inch erection popped out to attention, "fuck me", she gasped, "that's some fucking size you have there"

Jack had always been proud of his appendage. He'd been with many women over the years. Most of them loving the size of his cock, "thanks very much", he replied smugly. He lifted her tight skirt up to reveal that she was knicker-less.

Yvonne just pulled him close and began to guide his cock deep inside her, "I want you to fuck me hard"

Jack had heard this before and knew what was expected of him. He lifted her up by the ass and leaned her body into the wall, while letting the full length of his thick shaft slide deep inside her moist pussy, "does that feel nice?"

Yvonne shut her eyes tightly, "just fuck me"

Jack pumped hard into her. All he wanted to do now was shoot his load. He didn't care if Yvonne orgasmed or not. There was too much cum built up inside his loins, that wanted out. He'd already decided that if she still wanted an orgasm after, he'd just sink two fingers up there and finish the job. Jack had been good at that all through college. When you had a larger than average cock. A lot of women preferred if you fingered them first. But for now, that was the least of his worries.

Suddenly Yvonne's body tightened and she moaned loudly, "oh fuck that was good. Keep going", she ordered loudly.

But it wasn't long until his warm sticky load shot deep inside her, "sorry, I couldn't hold it any longer. Been holding that in for a few days now"

She pulled him close, kissing Jack passionately once more, as his cock grew limp inside her. Jack lowered her feet back down to the ground, "thanks for that"

Yvonne pulled her dress back down and checked for stains, "you don't need to be thanking me. We both helped each other out, when we were in need. Now, I better get back inside. See can I find my friend and get off home"

Jack felt he should say something, "can I get your number or even just add you online?"

Yvonne kissed him on the cheek, "let's just call this what it is, a quickie against a car park wall. Let's just leave it at that and move on", she glanced down at his crotch, "you wanna put that thing away before a bouncer sees it. You'll end up getting fucked out, or even worse, arrested"

Jack began to put away his appendage carefully, "wanna go somewhere after this?. Even just go for something to eat. I'd like to get to know you better", there was a weird connection there, that he couldn't explain.

Yvonne rubbed his smooth cheek, "trust me, you don't", and with that, she walked back towards the crowds of smokers, disappearing into the mass of sweaty people.

Jack couldn't help but feel that he let something special walk out of his life.

Chapter Two

The eighth of June. He'd been dreading this day. For most it meant a little more freedom from their homes. But to Jack it meant having to return home after many happy months away from his family.

Being locked down in Cork, meant partying with his friends for months on end. The only contact necessary with his parents was a polite phone call about how the credit card balance needed paying. It's easy to build up six thousand euros in debt when you're having fun.

But the last phone call for money had not gone as planned. Jack's father had insisted he return home to visit for the rest of the summer. He'd refused at first, quoting government guidelines about only being able to travel twenty kilometres. But his father was having none of it.

So now Jack was on the final leg of his journey as the train pulled into Drogheda station. He grabbed his heavy bag and reluctantly made his way out to the quiet car park. Straight away he noticed his father's pink BMW. An eyesore at the best of times. Jack could still remember all the sneering he got from his friends when his father had bought the antique vehicle, and decided that green wasn't his colour. But the pink was god awful. Especially after a drive in the countryside and it hit a number of muddy potholes. Slightly reminiscent of the time he tried anal on a girl in college and it turned out she had a bad stomach. That was some mess.

Jack's father Michael, struggled out of the car, as his large beer belly got stuck on the steering wheel. He finally broke free, hurting his back in the process, "fuck sake. That's your mother again, always changing the seat and never putting it back properly after. Hard to get it right again"

Jack opened the boot of the car and threw his bag inside. He felt depressed already from just being back in this town, "how's mam?"

Michael lit up a cigarette and leaned on the edge of his car door, "she's pissed that you've been avoiding us for months now. Pandemic or not, you should have been home with us. I know you're mother can be overbearing. But she's still your mother at the end of the day. She does love you"

Jack opened the passenger door as he struggled for a reply, "I was just following government guidelines"

Michael couldn't hide his annoyance any further, "we both know that's bullshit. Now get in and we can get going"

Jack begrudgingly got in the car and kept his mouth shut. No point in opening up old wounds from the very start of his visit.

The drive towards home was mostly quiet. Even though they only lived a mile outside the edge of town, it still felt like you were in the middle of the countryside. Jack had fond memories of walking these roads many a night. Mostly in an intoxicated state or high as fuck out of his head on drugs. Surprisingly he had never been run over in all that time.

The lack of conversation with his father was now starting to bother Jack, "how you getting by without the pub?"

Michael lit up another cigarette as he opened the car window, "it's fucking desperate son. Can't even get out of the house these days. Most of the lads can't come over for a drink because they're self isolating"

Jack let out a little laugh, "you do know you're in the high risk category yourself. You should be self isolating as well"

Michael was seventy five. But he didn't look it at all. His wife Ellen was twenty years his junior. A trophy wife at the time. Not so much now since age had caught up with her. There had been attempts at plastic surgery over the last ten years. Unfortunately it hadn't gone that great and poor Ellen was left with a constant slightly surprised look about her eyes. Her mouth had been botoxed to within an inch of safety levels. Jack always found it embarrassing to be seen in her company. Especially if she decided to wear something a tad too revealing.

Michael took a large pull of his cigarette, "fuck that, if I'm gonna die then I'm gonna die. Why hide from it. I can't live my life in fear. That's not fucking living. I'm gonna go out of this world the same way I came in. Kicking and screaming"

Jack knew better than to disagree with his father. It wasn't worth the hassle. Michael always felt that he knew best and that was that. The only person who could knock him off his high horse was his wife.

They finally reached their destination and Michael pressed the button for the large wrought iron gates to open. They creaked and moaned as they spread wide for them to enter. Jack still missed the old gates. He had personally made them out of disused pallets. He'd sanded them down and varnished each panel to a high standard. All those woodwork classes had paid off. He'd even connected them together to make a good high gate that matched the thick brick walls on either side, in height. It had been his proudest achievement.

But like all good things. Someone just had to tear them down. That came in the form of his brother Oliver. Drink driving once again and he forgot all about the beautiful wooden gates. He plowed into them at high speed, destroying one and knocking the other off its hinges. Of course their parents took a sympathetic view as always. More worried about Oliver's mental health, rather than the psychological damage he had projected onto Jack over the years. Something that would never leave him. No matter how hard he tried to forget the past.

As Jack got out of the car, he couldn't help but stare up at the large three storey house in front of him. His father had built it from scratch thirty years ago. But that's where it was left. He never bothered to modernise the house ever since then. Always too busy with other building jobs to be bothered with his own home. Since Jack had moved to Cork he found his bond to that city growing more and more over time. If he had it his way he'd never come back again. Maybe some day that would be the truth.

Michael opened the door and wheeled his son's suitcase into the hallway, "can you at least pretend to your mother that you're happy to be back here for a few weeks. I know you're loving Cork. But college is over with now. It's time to start thinking about the future. Three years of business studies, better show for something. Don't you agree son?"

Jack stepped into his father's western saloon style sitting room with swinging doors, small bar and cow hides hung high on the wall. Tacky at its finest, "haven't decided on anything just yet. I've been looking around Cork city for full time work"

Michael went in behind the bar and took out two bottles of beer from a mini fridge and handed one to his son, "me and your mother were thinking that you could take over the office section of my company. You'd finally be part of the family business. What do you think?"

Jack took a slug of his beer as an attempt to delay answering. Working with his dad was the last thing he wanted, "I was hoping to do something on a larger scale. No offence dad. But I wanted to start my own business from scratch"

Michael was far from impressed, "don't know why you wanna go out on your own. Have you a woman down in Cork?. It's always a fucking woman"

Jack had been hiding his relationships from his family for a couple of years now. Somehow they always had a habit of ruining them. Either his father would get a bit too sleazy and openly try to eye them up, or his mother would try to outdo the young woman in the style department. While his brother Oliver would make a rather open attempt at chatting them up. His way of showing his dominance over his little brother. Jack liked to keep his love life to himself. But things had been progressing along well over the last eight months and now seemed the right time to share.

"Her name is Denise and I've been seeing her for a good while now", felt good to finally get those words out after all this time.

Michael was unsure how to react to this, "just make sure she's the right one for you. Young love is great and all, but when the sex dries up and all you have left is each other's company. Then you know if she really is the one. So can you say that already?"

Jack wasn't sure how he felt anymore. But he wasn't letting his father know that, "I'm taking it one step at a time dad. Don't you worry. But I reckon she's the one"

Michael's expression stayed somber, "I hope you're right son. Sometimes there's no going back after a few years. Remember that"

Suddenly his mother marched into the room in her large red heels, denim skirt and tight white top. But there was something very different about her appearance. Her large breasts were now bulging out of her revealing outfit. Jack was lost for words.

But his mother wasn't, "glad to see you've finally decided to come home"

Jack was still staring at her oversized cleavage, "what in God's name did you get done now?"

Ellen glanced down at her large breasts and beamed with pride, "got them enhanced in January. Your dad's Valentine's present to me"

Jack wasn't even surprised at his father being behind this. Michael was happy to encourage his wife to keep getting more things done to her body. Anything to hold back the ageing process.

"A Valentine's present for himself more like it", Jack replied.

Michael poured his wife a glass of wine and handed it to her, "there you go dear. May as well celebrate our little man coming home after all this time"

Jack knew better than to say it. But his parents had a habit of using any excuse to have a drink. Their need for alcohol had only gotten worse with age. On the plus side, at least their drug use had eased. Difficult to get asleep at night, when you can hear your parent's bed frantically creaking after a drug fuelled night out on the town with friends. They'd even taken part in threesomes and orgies over the years. Jack could still remember a rather disturbing incident when he walked into the house after a night out, to find his parents on the couch, getting off with a married neighbour from up the road. Mrs Foley hadn't looked the kinky sex type with her tracksuits, messed hair and large glasses. But that night she was riding Jack's father like a cowgirl, while his mother watched on from a nearby chair. Thankfully Jack wasn't seen and he snuck off to the safety of his bedroom to deal with the nightmare.

Jack reluctantly hugged his mother, "wish you wouldn't call me your little man. I'm twenty four for god sake"

Ellen grabbed his cheek and shook it gently, "you'll always be my little man. Now tell us, how's college treating you these days?"

Jack didn't want to get into it. But he had to give some sort of answer, "it's grand. Last few months was weird with everything going on"

"He's got a woman", Michael added.

Ellen suddenly had a new interest in the conversation, "really, and who's the lucky lady?"

Jack was afraid to say much about her. Especially if his mother tried to contact her online. Something she had done in the past with his ex's. One time, when an ex had two timed him. His mother had tracked her down online and threatened to get both her kneecaps shattered with a heavy duty bolt cutters. There was no chance she'd follow through with such a threat. But that still didn't stop a visit from the guards investigating her messages and the threat of further legal proceedings from the girl's family. People tend to get pretty upset when you threaten a fifteen year old girl with physical violence.

"Her name is Denise. You'd like her mam", Jack reckoned she wouldn't. But when was any girl he brought home, right for him.

Ellen put her drink down and attempted to fix her oversized breasts, "hopefully I get to meet her before the end of the year. Do you reckon there will be wedding bells and all that shite?"

Jack had thought about that already. But had fallen short from bringing the conversation up with his girlfriend, "early days mam. We'll see"

Michael had heard enough already, "leave the young lad alone. He shouldn't be thinking about marriage yet. Still many years left to sow his wild oats"

Ellen stared at her husband disapprovingly, "he better not be sowing any wild oats": she turned to her son, "last thing you need is a load of little kids running around to different women. Cost you a fortune in the end. Hope you always use a condom?. Even with the ones that say they're on the pill"

Jack couldn't remember the last time he used a condom. Denise was on the pill. So there was no need there. And as for the numerous flings he had behind her back, he hadn't worn anything on those occasions either. Yes, he knew it wasn't the best idea. But sex always seemed so much more fun, when it was skin on skin.

Unfortunately Jack couldn't share that view with his parents, "I'm always careful. Don't worry about that", he wanted to escape the conversation by any means necessary, "I'm just gonna go the toilet. Might bring my bag up to the room while I'm at it", he got up off the bar stool and headed towards the hallway.

Ellen pointed in the direction of the kitchen, "why don't you use the downstairs toilet?"

Jack kept on walking, "just wanna see my room as well", bullshit!. But it got him out of the conversation.

Jack flung his suitcase onto his single bed and looked around at the bleakness of what was once his sanctuary from the world outside. Black wallpaper and blue carpets. The room definitely mirrored the mood of his teenage years. Something he didn't miss. Framed movie posters still hung on the walls. His mother wouldn't let him just blue tac them on loosely. She said it would take the look off the place.

The next stop on his journey was the bathroom. The whole room was painted in horrible shades of pink with matching fixtures. A large jacuzzi bath that fitted four people, sat in one corner of the room. When Jack was young, he couldn't understand why his parents needed such a big bathtub. That was before he became aware of their sexual exploits with other men and women. It was a shock to find out that his mother had no problem having sex with other women. But when he found out his father was with other men as well, that was an even bigger shock. Both were unfortunately too open about it. Happily admitting that it helped their marriage brilliantly. But it wasn't the image you wanted stuck in your head for the rest of your life. And the bottle of lube on the side of the bathtub wasn't helping the situation at the moment. Jack just forced it to the back of his mind and moved on.

As he headed back towards the staircase Jack couldn't help but stop outside Oliver's bedroom. The door was shut tightly and the numerous stickers to stay out were still covering its wooden face. Part of him wanted to open it up and take a look. But that would only just hurt.

So he moved on further down the hall, passing another door that had a pink unicorn painted in the centre. It stood out in the hallway amongst all the plain white doors. He tested the handle. Unfortunately it was locked. He reckoned it was probably for the best, knowing his parents.

Jack walked back into his parent's tacky saloon to find them kissing behind the bar. He was pretty sure that his father was doing something else to his mother, so he coughed loudly, "sorry for interrupting"

Michael wiped his fingers off his T-shirt and picked up his drink, "you're not interrupting. Me and your mam were talking. We were gonna throw a little get together tonight for your return. Think of it as a mini graduation party, since you're not getting a proper one"

Ellen cut her husband off as she fixed her skirt, "I was gonna go into town and get drink and food for it. You could come help me if you like"

It didn't surprise Jack that his parents weren't taking the lockdown seriously. He hadn't done much socially distancing himself, while down in Cork. But he felt he had to say something, "you're not suppose to be throwing large parties at the moment and you don't have to do it for me. I'm just happy to be home for a few weeks", he lied.

But his mother was hearing none of it, "no way. You're getting a party and that's that. We'll have family, friends and some of the neighbours over. Mrs Foley is always asking for you and you used to be such good friends with Paul. Might be nice for you to see him again"

The only memories that Jack had of Paul, was of a weird young man who didn't like to hang around most people. They had been good friends as kids. Always playing together and going on adventures out in the adjoining fields. But as they both entered their teenage years, Jack had discovered women and a social life. While Paul had just retreated into himself and stayed out of the public eye. Except for school time, were he was regularly bullied by classmates. Jack was glad that they had gone to different secondary schools. No way had he wanted to be associated with the fella. Everyone considered him a weirdo and that even went for anyone that chose to be in his company.

Jack didn't want to share any of his views with his parents. Especially since they were a little too close to Paul's mother, "you don't have to do this. I'm happy just to be back"

But Ellen was hearing none of it, "no, my son is getting a party and that's that. Now get your jacket, cause we're going into town. We're having a party tonight"

Chapter Three

A cold wind blew through the long shopping complex and out the other side like a poorly built railway tunnel. Jack was starting to wish that he had of listened to his mother about bringing his jacket. But he wouldn't dare admit to that.

Unfortunately the queue outside the supermarket was longer than expected. Ellen had been expecting a few ahead of her. But when they had arrived, the line was going down one wall and up the other side. She had tried to keep her temper as they slowly approached the entrance after three quarters of an hour.

Ellen glanced at her watch for effect, "this is fucking ridiculous. You'd think they'd be letting more in the shops after all this time. Hasn't been that many people dropping dead over the last few weeks. You'd think they'd lighten the restrictions a bit"

Jack hated it when his mother started off on one of her rants. Even worse when it happened in public. He glanced around in the hope that no one had heard her, "please mam, don't start this again. I'm only home and the last thing I need is for you to start causing a scene"

Ellen looked around at the other people in the line, "no one else seems to care what I have to say. So why are you so bothered?. I'm just vocalising my anger. You should try it sometime. Great way of venting your stress. That and sex"

The woman in front of them turned around with a disgusted look on her face, before turning back forward. Thankfully Ellen hadn't noticed because she was too busy admiring her reflection in a nearby shop window. But Jack had seen the look and hoped it wasn't the start of many. Because when his mother got started on someone verbally. It was pretty difficult for her to stop.

The queue finally started to move and Jack was quick to catch up, as his mother struggled to drag herself away from her reflection. But then they stopped as quickly, as the queue came close to the front door.

Ellen struggled to bottle her annoyance. Only thing she could think of to distract herself, was to ask about her son's new girlfriend, "so tell us then. What's this Denise one like?. Is she from a good family?"

Jack could see this was an attempt by his mother to see was his girlfriend good marriage material. Denise most definitely was. But he didn't want his mother knowing the full extent of her family's financial history, because there would be a strong chance that she'd involve herself in his love life.

Ellen had done this several times in the past with ex girlfriends of Jack and Oliver's. Appearing supposedly accidentally at certain events or days out, that had been planned by their ex girlfriend's families. It always ended with embarrassment, as his mother would say something that would ruin the day. Normally about sex, or prying too deeply into the girl's parent's private life. No way was Jack going through that again.

The line started to move again and they were finally at the front of the queue. Now he had no choice but answer. Just not fully, "she's from a good family. I'll bring her up sometime for a visit", he lied, "maybe after all this is over with the virus"

But that wasn't enough for his mother, "okay, but what does her parents do for a living?"

It was only then that Jack realised that he hadn't a clue what his girlfriend's parents did for a living. He'd never even thought about it until now. But that left him with a big decision to make. Should he admit the truth and give his mother fuel for the proverbial fire. Or come up with some bullshit to keep her happy. He chose the latter, "he works in business or something along those lines and her mother runs a clothing boutique". Well, he thought she did. She was definitely a manager of some description. But he never bothered to probe his girlfriend any further. Thankfully the security guard ushered them on with a stone faced nod of his head.

As soon as they were inside, Ellen headed straight for the drinks section and started to fill up her trolley with a mixture of spirits and beer, but mostly spirits. Jack had always been concerned with his parents drinking habits over the years. But he was pretty sure that it had escalated in recent times, into higher volumes of alcohol content. Even though he didn't want to comment on it.

Jack's mouth still disobeyed his common sense, "do you and dad only drink spirits these days?"

Ellen placed another two bottles of vodka in the trolley before staring him out of it, "don't you start and all. Get enough shit off your grandparents already. I'm not a feckin alcoholic before you start. Me and your father just like to enjoy ourselves and there's fuck all else to do with this lockdown"

Jack knew he was moving into stormy waters with his line of questioning. Last thing he wanted was to get off to a bad start on one of his rare few visits home, "I was only asking mam, because I care. That's all. But I know what you mean. The last few months have been tough. Just don't want to see you and dad having any liver problems. Especially after what happened with uncle Steve"

Ellen loaded another two bottles of vodka into the trolley, "don't even start comparing me to that nut job. He's locked up in a home now. Totally lost his mind. But me and your dad aren't even close to that yet. So don't even bring it up to him. He's cracking up enough not being able to work. I've asked him to retire at the end of all this and let Lofty take over the business. But you know him. He loves to be hands on all the time"

Jack knew Lofty all too well. He was closer to his mother's age and had taken part in many of his parent's sex parties over the years. Now, in Jack's opinion, everyone had a right to live out what sexual fantasies they wanted in this life. Just as long as they didn't hurt anyone else. But Lofty had a young Thai bride, that he had brought home from one of his many holidays to her homeland. He'd basically turned the poor young girl into a baby making factory. But he wasn't happy waiting for her to pop out another child before having sex again. So he was getting it elsewhere. Not just Jack's parents. But he had other women on the side, which he'd parade around at social events, while his poor wife was stuck at home with the kids. It was strange because nobody seemed to say anything about it and just left him to carry on with his abusive behaviour towards the poor young woman with even poorer english.

They arrived up at the tills with two shopping trolleys full of alcohol. Even though Jack had noticed it many times before, he was still fascinated by the clear Perspex screening that had been put up to protect the staff from virus carrying customers. Somehow he had a feeling that the screens would stay in place, long after the virus was dead. A new norm, far from the way of life they once knew.

It was only then that he noticed who was sitting behind the till on her little chair and wearing a poorly fitting dark uniform. It was a rather disgruntled Yvonne. Her eyes didn't gaze up, as she began to scan the stuff through like a well worked zombie.

But Ellen had noticed something and couldn't help asking out straight, "when you due?"

Jack hadn't noticed, but suddenly his eyes were drawn to Yvonne's stomach, which bulged out slightly through her tight top. Could it be his?.

Yvonne looked up and was about to answer, but her eyes met a panicked looking Jack. It had been months since she'd last seen him and honestly she had hoped that New Year's would have been the last time as well. But she played it cool as always and turned to address his mother, "five months now"

But Ellen was only starting with her line of questioning, as she worked up to what she really wanted to ask, "I'm surprised they're letting you work with the current crisis still going on. Doesn't the government expect you to be at home through all this?"

Jack hated it when his mother pushed her opinions and values on others. But this was ten times worst than that. And all that kept running through his troubled mind, was if that child was actually his, "please mam"

But Yvonne didn't need any help from anyone, as she answered anyway, "it's up to the employee if they want to work and I couldn't imagine being stuck at home for months. Besides, I haven't heard of it affecting young pregnant women just yet, so fingers crossed", she mockingly crossed her fingers and put on a dopey grin for effect.

Ellen was visibly unimpressed. But thankfully her phone rang in her handbag. She quickly pulled it out and saw the name flashing across the screen, "I better take this. Can you deal with this on your own?"

Jack was used to getting dumped with an entire job to do on his own. But this time he was relived to see his mother walk away from the awkward situation. Now he finally had the opportunity to ask the most obvious question, "is it mine?": his voice was low and discreet.

Yvonne didn't even look up from her job in hand, "surprised you even remember who I am. You were fairly whacked out of it that night"

Jack was slightly insulted by her comment. But he made sure not to show it, "I wasn't that bad and I can still remember clearly what happened between us. So please just answer my question. Is the child mine?"

Yvonne looked him dead in the eyes, "I'm not sure. There's a chance it might be"

That's the last thing he wanted to hear. He could barely look after himself, let alone a child, "what do you mean by might me?. How many other men did you have sex with that night?"

Yvonne was visibly annoyed. But she kept her voice low, "what kind of girl do you think I fucking am?. I just don't go around fucking random fellas"

Jack was quick with his comeback, "well you fucked me quick enough in that car park"

Yvonne checked to make sure that there was no other staff members nearby, "didn't hear you complaining at the time. And you were quick enough to stick that oversized sausage of yours inside me. So don't start trying to make out it's all my fault. It takes two to tango"

Jack noticed that nearly all the alcohol had been beeped through the scanner. Which meant that the time to discuss this was running out. But he needed to know more, "look, can we meet up to talk about this further?"

Yvonne scanned the last few bottles of vodka and handed them to him, "what do you wanna talk about?. You can walk away from this and never bother with me again. I was planning on dealing with this on my own. So go on then. Go back to your perfect life and forget about this conversation"

Jack noticed the final price on the till display and even though he didn't want to, he handed over his own credit card. Anything to keep his mother away for a few more minutes, "I'm not that type of fella. So can we meet up and discuss this?"

"Rejected", Yvonne was deadpan in her expression.

Jack was finding her a difficult woman to deal with. Far from the perfect fantasy he had in his head over his teenage years, "why can't we just meet to talk this out?"

Yvonne handed him back his credit card, "it's not that. I was just telling you that your card was rejected. Think you'll need to call your mammy over to pay. And as for meeting up, I'll be in the memorial park on Shop street, tomorrow at four, if you really want to meet up and chat. And I won't be waiting around ages. So when my poetry group is over and there's no sign of you, i'm out of there. So the ball is in your court now"

Jack was still finding it difficult to believe that this rough voiced girl was involved with a poetry group. But he felt it best to keep his opinions to himself, "I'll be there. Don't you worry about that", now he had to embarrass himself further by calling over his mother to pay.

Ellen was flustered as she attempted to carry on her conversation on the phone as she struggled to understand what was wrong. Jack held up his credit card and mouthed the word rejected. It didn't take her long to get the hint and she took out her own card and handed it over to Yvonne, before walking away to continue her call.

Yvonne ran it through the system and Jack typed in the pin. Thankfully it went through this time. Yvonne couldn't help but make a joke of the situation as she handed him back his card and the receipt, "lucky your mother is here. That would have been really embarrassing"

But that was the least of Jack's worries, "so I'll definitely see you tomorrow?"

Yvonne pulled her tight top back down over her bump again, "I'll be there either way. So if you wanna talk, be there. Because I ain't waiting around for a no show"

Jack was growing more annoyed with her flippant attitude, "I'll be there alright", and with that, he headed off with his two packed shopping trolleys full of alcohol.

Thankfully it wasn't long until his mother finally got off the phone and took her own trolley once again, "that was your aunt Danielle. She's coming over tonight for the party. She wanted to bring that waster of a husband of hers along. I told her no out straight. That bastard would drink us out of house and home. Now there's an alcoholic if I ever met one. Speaking of wasters. Seen you getting on a little too well with that one behind the counter. Hope you weren't planning on asking her out?"

Jack was insulted by this for several reasons. But he tried not to reveal the full extent of his annoyance, "I wasn't chatting her up. I'm with Denise. But what would be wrong if I wanted to date a girl like that?"

Ellen wasn't one to hold back, "for one thing, she is pregnant with another man's child and looking at the head on her, she's probably not even sure who the father is. And the other thing is, that I know about her family. Heavily involved in drugs. Definitely not the type of people you wanna be around. So don't even go there"

Jack hated being told what to do. Even though he had no plans of going there, it still annoyed him, "she seems like a nice girl and you shouldn't be making up your own opinions about her, without much to go on"

Ellen noticed the queue was a lot shorter than when they had arrived. She internally cursed herself for not coming an hour later, "I can judge a person by a short conversation and I'm telling you now, that girl is trouble. Only a matter of years until she's locked up for something. Now let's forget about all this for now. We need to get this stuff home and get the house ready for a party"

Jack knew better than to keep pushing at the current topic. Better to let it go and just move on. Tonight was gonna be hard enough. Stuck in a room with a load of his parent's so called friends for the night. The sooner they got this party started, the sooner the night would be over.

Chapter Four

House parties could be a wonderful thing. Loads of fit young people partying the night away, as they danced, fucked and got whacked out of their heads on something or other. Those were the type of parties that Jack enjoyed. But unfortunately his parent's idea of a house party was much different.

The ground floor of the house was filled with neighbours and family friends. Most of them in their fifties and sixties. Social distancing was well out the window, as they huddled in tight groups, laughing and joking. Jack couldn't help but wonder how this party was for him. He had the offer of inviting some of his own old friends. But a large part of him wanted to leave them in the past. He'd changed too much over the last few years to even try and go back there. The wild drug fuelled party animal he once was, had turned into an intellectual drug taker who liked to discuss life's bigger problems while snorting coke off his girlfriend's breasts.

By god did he miss Denise's breasts. Those beautiful perky nipples that defied the laws of gravity. And the sexual things she could do in and out of the bedroom. Even sucking him off in a toilet cubicle in the train station before he left for Drogheda. He could still remember Denise's cute smiling face looking up at him from the toilet floor, as she wanked the last of his cum out onto her face. Denise knew what he liked sexually and was happy to fulfil his every need when necessary. He couldn't wait to get back down to Cork.

Suddenly his mother nudged Jack roughly, "I want you to meet my new friend Becky. I was telling her all about you"

Jack turned to come face to face with a near carbon copy of his mother. The only thing that seemed different was the hair colour and outfit. Becky had the enhanced large breasts, botox lips and overly stretched facial features. Jack shook her hand and made his introduction politely. Now he hadn't a clue what to say next.

Ellen always had an ulterior motive, "Becky runs a local computer company and is always on the look out for managing staff to help run the different departments. I was telling her about your college training and she was interested in talking to you", she suddenly noticed someone arriving, "I better go make an introduction to my new guests. You two talk between yourselves", and with that, she rushed off through the crowds.

Becky suddenly got a little closer to her young prey and flicked her red hair to one side, "nice to finally get to meet you. Your mother has spoken so highly about you over the last few years, that I had to meet you in person. You definitely don't disappoint in the looks department", she toyed with the straw in her drink suggestively.

Jack had been in this position several times before. Older women looking for an easy fuck behind their husband's back. He'd even improved his grades in college when he'd slept with Mrs Hamilton. A lecturer who had given him shit for most of his first college year. Jack knew that he was being singled out and decided to confront Mrs Hamilton in her office. That had ended up with him fucking her on the desk and suddenly his grades went up. This seemed to be another one of those moments.

"You know the way parents are. They're always gonna big up their kids achievements. I like to get by on my own merits", Jack knew how to talk the talk when necessary.

Becky moved in a little closer, "either way, I like what I see. Do you like what you see?", she purposely held her drink close to her ample cleavage and roughly knocked the ice around inside the glass, as if trying to draw his eyes down there.

Jack knew where this was going and was quite happy to accept the offer, "do you wanna find somewhere a little quieter to talk?"

Becky jumped at the opportunity, as she grabbed the young man's hand and led him down a nearby corridor towards a darkened part of the house. Jack knew what was expected of him. He wasn't impressed having to go there. But sex was sex and he could already feel his cock growing large in his pants. Better to make the most of the moment and worry about the consequences later.

Soon enough, Jack was going through the motions in one of the downstairs bedrooms that thankfully had a lock on the door. Letting Becky open up his pants and get the usual shock as her eyes spotted the size of his erection. This was were a lot of women differed. Separating the experienced from the novices. Some would just wank it gently. Others would try to lick and kiss the tip of his long, thick shaft. While a few would chance the deep throat. Thankfully Becky was the last one, as she placed her mouth down around it and sucked hard on his throbbing cock. She'd definitely dealt with large cocks before and knew how to work the situation. Her lips locked tightly as she sucked hard on the purple tip with delight. She stared up at him through the whole process.

Jack was fearful that he was gonna blow early, but his mind started wandering back to earlier that day. He could still remember the large baby bump that Yvonne was showing off. What if the child was his?. He wouldn't hear the end of it off his parents. Jack looked down at Becky still sucking away. Thankfully there was no chance of getting her pregnant. Didn't matter how much plastic surgery Becky had gotten over the years. It was still obvious that she was well into her sixties.

Jack was still holding back from shooting his load when Becky suddenly stood up and pulled down her tights and knickers, before firing them onto the floor. She straddled his half naked body and slid his long cock deep inside her surprisingly tight pussy.

Becky moaned with delight, "only after getting my fanny tightened recently. Worth every cent. Not even my husband has had the pleasure of feeling how tight my pussy is again. You're one of the lucky few"

Jack wasn't sure how to reply to that, except by saying, "thanks"

Still didn't mean there wasn't a load of other one night stands in there as well. May have been a tight fanny, but somehow it didn't match the elderly body that it was attached to. The thing about having an abnormally large erection was that when friends complained about a woman being loose during sex, Jack would normally end up with the same girl at some point down the line and find that they weren't as tight as suggested. He wasn't sure was this because his cock was a lot thicker than most men, or were some of his friends just assholes who liked to belittle women sexually. He figured it was the latter.

Becky rode him like a cowgirl until she orgasmed several times. Jack liked to satisfy a woman sexually. It had always been important for him to leave a woman fully pleasured. Thankfully it looked like his job was done here and he shot his sticky load deep inside her with a small moan.

Becky stumbled off the bed and fixed her skirt back down again. She picked up her underwear and threw them at his face, "think I'll go commando for the rest of the night. You can keep them to remember me. Especially if you need a wank later", and with that, she unlocked the bedroom door and headed back to the party.

Jack pulled up his pants, before throwing her underwear in a nearby bin. No way was he wanking over some old women's dirty knickers. She was grand for a quick shag, but Becky was far from wanking material. What he needed now more than anything, was a fag.

The large back decking was packed with smokers who were laughing at stupid jokes that Jack couldn't understand how they were funny. He smiled and nodded as he made his way through the crowd. He needed peace for a bit and there was one place he could be sure of it. A place he used to go when the world was getting on top of him.

As Jack drew close to the old picnic table that sat at the bottom of the garden, he suddenly got a strong smell of hash lingering in the air. Then the outline of a person sitting with his back to him, came into view. He'd no idea who it was. But that smell of hash was strangely appealing, "any chance I could get a smoke of that?"

The figure turned around with fright. Only then did Jack recognise him as his old friend Paul. But he'd changed a lot in appearance. He was scruffy looking with long hair covered with a dirty baseball cap and his clothing would be more suited to a tramp. Paul had definitely gone down hill since Jack had last seen him.

"Is that you Jack?", Paul asked nervously. Hiding the joint as best he could.

Jack sat down on the opposite side of the bench and quickly became aware that the seat was wet, "the one and only. You must be sick of this party as well. This was never your thing"

Paul started to act a little less awkwardly, as he took another pull of his joint, "still isn't. My mother dragged me along. Said it would be good for me to get out. I've been here hours already", he passed the joint over to his old friend.

Jack took a large drag of the joint, "how much of that time was spent out here?"

Paul looked a little embarrassed, "I've spent most of that time out here. Remember when we used to have a camp around here somewhere?"

Jack had forgotten all about that memory until now. But the image of their poorly built hut came back to the forefront of his mind. He pointed at a particular area of the tree line that bordered the large back garden, "it was right over there. It lasted pretty well until that big storm hit. Wasn't much left of it after that"

Paul laughed to himself, "remember when you dropped that weight on my head?"

Jack hadn't thought about that in awhile. Wasn't a nice memory to have. Dropping an old and extremely heavy window weight on his best friend's head, "pity you weren't better at tying knots"

Paul nodded in agreement, "that's true. Think I put a shoelace bow on it. Probably not the best idea. Where the fuck did we get that weight in the first place?"

Jack shrugged his shoulders, "haven't a fucking clue. We never even had windows that used them. Think we just found it. Lucky I didn't kill you that day"

It hadn't been a fond memory or one of the worst that haunted Jack's thoughts. But for some reason that day, both of them had decided to build a treehouse. And it seemed totally reasonable to make a pulley system to get the materials up into the tree. They'd hoisted up loads of timber, nails and a hammer. But for some strange reason, that was lost to both of them now, they felt a heavy weight was necessary as well. So Paul had secured the dense metal weight to the thin piece of rope and Jack began to hoist it up into the tree.

It was about half way up when the knot loosened and the weight fell back down to the ground. Jack could still remember that view from above, as it fell down towards his friend's head. It always seemed to be in slow motion when he thought back to that day. Then it struck Paul's head roughly and the blood began to pour out onto the ground.

Jack had panicked, climbing down from the tree quickly, hurting his ankle with the final jump to the ground. Paul had already run off around the garden crying for help. It definitely seemed like a hospital job at the time. But

Jack's father had heard all the shouting and screaming. He rushed out into the garden and took control of the situation. Checking Paul's head to see how bad the damage was. He shouted for Ellen to get this special medical powder he put on all injuries and a bowl of water. Ellen had always joked that if someone's leg fell off, her husband would probably just cover the stump with his special powder and he'd say everything would be grand. But thankfully that day, it actually worked. No hospital visit required. Mrs foley arrived and brought Paul home. That was the end of that. Wouldn't be the case these days with all the lawsuits being served around the world.

An hour later, the two old friends were still getting stoned in the garden and catching up on old times. Jack was already badly stoned, but something seemed comforting about talking to such an old friend. It was like they were picking up from were they'd left off. He knew this was only a temporary situation until life got back to normal. But he welcomed it all the same.

Suddenly a sense of guilt washed over Jack's stoned mind, "I'm sorry about the way I treated you after primary school", he'd been a cunt and he knew it.

Paul just began to roll up another joint, as if he wasn't too bothered with the past, "we went our different ways back then. You became pretty popular in your school. Maybe it was for the best. I would have just dragged you down"

It didn't make Jack feel any better, "I still was a prick", some part of him needed to talk desperately about his current problem, "do you remember that really hot girl I used to tell you about in first year?. The red head with the short skirts. She was in sixth year at the time"

Paul struggled to remember, "think so. What about her?"

Jack looked down at the badly scratched table in front of him, "there's a chance I got her pregnant"

Paul's shocked face said it all, "when was this?"

Jack still had fond memories of that brief moment of madness, "met her New Year's Eve and fucked her in the car park. Didn't even know she was pregnant until today. I'm meeting her tomorrow to talk about it. My parents won't be impressed about this. They want me to end up with someone whose family is well connected. Don't even think they'll like my current girlfriend. Let alone Yvonne"

Suddenly Jack's mobile rang and unfortunately he had no choice but answer. After an interrogation from his mother, he hung up the phone, "I have to get back inside. Sorry about this. Maybe you'd like to come in with me?"

Paul shook his head as fear filled his eyes, "no fucking way. I'm happier out here. Can't be arsed trying to make conversation with a load of strangers. My parents love it. Especially my mother. She can't get enough of your parents. Always wanting to hang around your house, while my father just sits at home. Think that's where I get it from. I'd rather be reclusive with my hash plants"

Jack was quick to pick up on this, "you grow this stuff?"

Paul couldn't understand what the big deal was, "yeah, you can call around tomorrow if you like. I'll show you the set up"

Jack quickly remembered his future plans, "I have to meet Yvonne at four. But I can call around tomorrow night if that's okay?"

Paul's face lit up at the idea of company, "that'll be great. Just knock the back door"

Jack said his goodbyes and as he headed back towards the house, he couldn't help but feel that he'd finally rebuilt a bridge that he thought was long demolished for good. Hopefully it was a positive sign of what was to come tomorrow. But for now he had to finish out the night and try to avoid the advances of any more of his mother's friends. Easier said than done.

Chapter Five

The local amateur poetry group had fallen upon hard times, thanks to the virus. They used to attract large numbers of up to twenty people. But since they had to move outside from their usual spot in the church building, members had started to drop off in numbers. Most likely due to the fact that most of them were elderly and at high risk. So the remaining members of the group, had started to meet in the memorial garden next to the church.

It wasn't the largest of areas. But it was enough for the dwindling numbers that still attended, while allowing for social distancing. The numerous cement benches accommodated the small group. While the constant flowing waterfall effect had the unfortunate habit of making poor Yvonne want to pee. She wasn't one to get easily nervous, but waiting to recite her new poems, had that affect on her. She could feel the sweat running down her back. Yvonne had been coming to the meetings for three months now, but they still didn't get any easier.

As usual, Evan took control of the whole meeting. There wasn't an official leader of the group. But somehow he always took over the whole event. He was a frail old man himself, but somehow he didn't seem worried about catching the virus. Not even wearing a mask throughout the meeting.

Yvonne listened on as each person recited their poem and waited for the comments from the rest of the group.

That was the part she wasn't too sure of. Constructive criticism was never her thing.

Suddenly Evan turned his attention to her, "now young lady. What have you brought for us today?"

Yvonne loved it when he called her young lady. No one else addressed her in such a polite manner. Yes, he may have been flirting with her. But it was still nice to hear those words.

Yvonne struggled up to her feet and fixed her short top back down over her baby bump, while making a mental note that she had to invest in new clothing. Coughing gently to clear her throat, she threw herself into one of her offerings for the day, "this poem is called love"

She looked around once more at the faces of the few members in attendance. Each one waiting to hear her words. It was equally exciting and nerve wracking at the same time,

"Watching and waiting,
For that little spark,
A connection with someone,
More than jokes and a laugh.

Common interests,
shared views,
Touching your soul,
In ways that they should.

As life goes by,
It becomes more than just sex,
A deeper connection,
Emotional and respect.

A strong long bond,
That touches you both,
Mostly never acted on,
Another of life's lost hopes"

Yvonne sat down quickly as the silence around her went on for too damn long for comfort. She had been proud of that poem and was hoping for at least some encouragement.

Evan sat forward on his bench, "you could really feel the emotion in those words. That was definitely from the heart"

A rather eccentric woman called Margaret, whipped her multi coloured hair to one side, as if she was about to make a one woman performance on stage, "amazing how the want of love always seems to crop up in people's poetry over the years. It's such a strong emotion that affects us all. Either we want it, need it, or are just afraid to lose it", she turned to Yvonne, "take it you yearn for that feeling. You can hear it in your words"

Yvonne hated to share her emotions with most people, even family and friends. She knew the poem was a tad revealing of the person she tried to hide. But she hadn't expected to share so much of her innermost yearnings.

Now there was a reply expected of her. She hadn't been expecting that, "I just wrote how I was feeling at the time"

Evan shot back in with his own opinion, "I thought it was a beautiful poem. You wrote from the heart. That's what matters most. You can hear it in your words"

Yvonne had a strong suspicion that they were only trying to be kind. She didn't see her work as being in any way spectacular. The words would just come to her and all she did was write them down on paper. It never seemed a struggle. She'd heard other members of the group complaining about struggling over a poem for days. That just wasn't her. If it didn't flow out instinctively in a few minutes, then it was discarded just as quickly.

Another elderly woman called Bethany, who had long bleach blonde hair that just didn't suit her, suddenly spoke up, "love will come someday to you dear. Sometimes more than once if you're lucky"

Yvonne found her words strangely ringing true, "I'd be just happy with the once"

Evan quickly steered the session back on course, "right then. Think it's my turn now", he stood up and cleared his throat quite dramatically.

"Excuse me. Is this the poetry group?", Jack felt kind of stupid saying it. What else could this group be and he could see Yvonne at the far end of the garden.

Evan was pleasantly surprised by the interruption. He always liked to see new faces arriving, "yes it is young man. Are you a poet yourself?"

Jack had written a few pieces, when he was a lot younger. Nothing to write home about and quickly forgotten. But there was no point in mentioning them, "no, I'm just here to meet Yvonne when she's finished. I'll just sit over here and watch", he grabbed the nearest bench that was a good distance from the rest of the group.

"Well, you're welcome all the same", Evan wasn't put off from the job in hand. He held up his extremely small piece of paper and attempted to read his own poorly scrawled words. It was his usual style. All visual flairs and style, but very little true emotion at the back of it all. When he was finished, Evan sat back down as his faced beamed with pride

Yvonne could see that Jack was bored out of his mind as each member of the group took their turn. She was enjoying watching him look uncomfortable throughout the whole thing. Gave her a warm feeling inside. That was until it was her go again. Part of her wanted to lie that she hadn't brought anymore poems with her. But that wasn't gonna work since she'd already told the group at the start, that she'd brought two new poems with her.

Yvonne stood up and tried not to look Jack's way. Her hands were clammy with sweat as she tried to moisten her lips, "this one is called depression", she looked around the group once more and even though she didn't want to, her eyes lingered over in Jack's direction. He seemed to be waiting to hear her, just as eagerly as the rest of the group,

"A loch gate of emotion,
Explodes inside your mind,
Some of it irrelevant,
Some of it denial.

Problems that you make,
Out of situations that don't exist,
Littering your mind,
Like a landmine filled football pitch.

Shutting down,
for hours at a time,
Lost in your thoughts,
Going out of your mind.

Climbing a ladder,
Through shit and dense mud,
Fighting to escape it,
Wondering if you should.

We can't escape our demons,
We can't outrun our past,
But we can learn to live with our actions,
And live our life at last"

Yvonne sat back down quickly and waited for the groups comments.

Margaret was the first one to speak up, "you really write from the heart"

Yvonne smiled nervously, "thank you"

Evan leaned forward on his bench, "what were you going through at the time when you wrote this?"

But Bethany cut him off, "you shouldn't ask her that. The reasons for writing is an extremely personal thing and not everyone likes to share. Me being one of them"

Evan didn't back down, "I'm only asking because I'm fascinated by the construction process of a poem", he turned to Yvonne, "hope I didn't offend you by asking?"

Yvonne did find him too forward. But she was used to it now, "I'm not offended, but I'd rather not share my reasons for writing it. Hope that's okay?"

Evan wasn't flustered by her answer, "that's no problem. The mystique just adds to your words. Anyway, I think it's time to call it a day people. Thank you all for coming and I hope you can make it next week. Stay safe and stay clean", a catchphrase he had come up with since the pandemic started.

The group said their goodbyes and began to get their stuff together to leave.

As Yvonne approached Jack, her mood and expression dampened, "right then. Let's go get this done". She walked on past him.

Jack knew this wasn't gonna be an easy meeting, but it had to be done all the same. He needed answers.

Out on the street, Yvonne kept up a quick pace as she marched down the path, "surprised you even showed up today. Thought you got enough of a scare yesterday"

Jack wasn't the type to take a dig lying down, "I'm surprised to see you doing poetry. How long have you been at that?"

Yvonne stopped in her tracks and turned to face him, "what the fuck does that mean?. Do you think I'm not good enough to do it?"

Jack had forgotten how scary Yvonne could be in her early years. He could still remember a fight in school, when she took down two girls at the same time. As a first year with an ever growing sex drive, Jack had found all the hair pulling and ripped shirts, a turn on. Even now, Yvonne's eyes might be manic, but there was something strangely sexy about them as well. But now wasn't the time to bask in her beauty.

"I'm not saying you're not good enough", Jack replied, "that stuff you read in there was pretty good. It's just that I remember you from back in school and you seemed more interested in fellas and fighting, rather than poetry and churches"

Yvonne stopped again outside a nearby coffee shop, "I've only been properly writing the stuff for the last year or two. And the only reason I was on church grounds, is because it's where they meet up. Wouldn't catch me dead inside that place on any other normal day"

Jack cheekily smiled, "you may not have a choice in the matter when it comes to that decision. My cousin was an atheist and when he died of cancer, his parents did everything that he had asked them not to do. The whole church service and all. He would have been pissed"

Yvonne pointed at the sandwich board menu beside them, "I'm sure you're right. Now, I'm getting a coffee. Would you like one as well, before we find somewhere to chat?"

Jack pulled a twenty euro note from his pocket, "let me get this for you"

Yvonne snatched the money out of his hand and headed inside. It was only then that Jack realised that she hadn't even asked what type of coffee he wanted, but he figured it best not to dwell on it.

A few minutes later, Yvonne was back out with a coffee for each of them. She turned the corner and headed down towards the quays. The two of them found a quiet part and sat down on the edge. Their legs dangling over the still waters below them.

There was an awkward silence at first, but Jack wasn't long filling it, "you said there was only a chance that I could be the father. How many one night stands did you have around that time?"

Yvonne struggled to hide her anger. It wasn't working very well, "what fucking type of girl do you think I am?. I don't just go around fucking random guys all the time. You were just a moment of madness. I'm sure you've been there yourself before"

Jack had many a time, if he was honest, "okay then. I'm sorry for wording it like that. It's just that you showed up that night and suddenly we were having sex in the car park. Then you just walked away after and that was that. It just didn't make any sense"

Yvonne had enjoyed the excitement of that night. The wild carefree sex. Letting go for once in her life. But she wasn't gonna admit that. Especially not to him, "I had my reasons. That's all you have to know"

Jack wasn't letting it go that easily, "you gotta give me more than that"

Chapter Six

The place was a mess. Beer bottles and cans lay strewn around the floor and furniture. Cigarette butts had been stubbed out in the plant pots and slices of pizza had been squished into the couch cushions. Yvonne couldn't believe that someone could do this to her beautiful apartment.

She'd only been gone one night. Thanks to her father once again. A large quantity of money being found during a so called random Garda search, had given the detectives enough reason to drag the whole lot of Yvonne's family in for questioning.

It didn't bother her too much. When you grow up in a family whose main source of income is through selling drugs, you kind of get used to the authorities showing up when you least expect it. The worst time being when she was having sex on the front wall at two in the morning with an ex boyfriend and the guards raided the house. That had been embarrassing.

But last night had been a total pain in the arse. Yvonne had only been in the house for a quick visit, because she wouldn't be around the following night for the usual celebrations. Yvonne's long term boyfriend Stewy, had gotten them two tickets for a New Year's Eve party in the Earth nightclub and was insisting on going.

Yvonne wasn't one for nights out around Christmas time. She found them way too busy for her liking. But she'd agreed just to keep Stewy happy. They hadn't been living together too long and she really wanted to make it work. Just a pity that Stewy didn't seem to be trying as hard as her.

Yvonne had tried to call him the night before, but he hadn't picked up. Now she knew why. The bastard had thrown a party in her absence. All the beautiful fixtures she had bought to make the place a home, had been thrown around or broken. Yvonne kicked numerous cans out of the way, as she marched towards the bedroom. Throwing the door open, Yvonne recoiled in horror as she walked in on an unconscious Stewy, lying naked next to her friend Sarah.

Yvonne had noticed over the last few months, that they had been getting on pretty well, but she had always figured that was a good thing. Not many girls could boast that their boyfriend got on with one of their closest friends. Now she could see why!. The used condom was still hanging off Stewy's flaccid cock. But what killed Yvonne most of all, was that her favourite bed sheets were still on the bed. The black silk ones that she had especially bought to enhance their love making. Looked like Sarah had gotten more use out of them than her. She wanted to scream at the pair of them. Wake the fuckers up from their slumber. But Yvonne was frozen to the spot, unable to react.

Suddenly Sarah's tired eyes opened and when she spotted her friend, they quickly turned to panic, "oh fuck", she shook Stewy frantically.

Yvonne felt her knees begin to buckle. So she sat down in a nearby chair, "how could you do this to me?. I thought we were friends"

Sarah sat up in the bed and pulled the sheets around her naked body, "I'm sorry. I didn't mean for this to happen, you gotta believe me"

Yvonne had a strong suspicion that needed answering, "Tell me the truth. This isn't the first time, is it?"

Sarah glanced over at Stewy for help. But he was still out for the count, "it's not the first time. I didn't mean for this to happen. We just started to feel something for each other. We both tried to fight it. But it just happened. You weren't suppose to find out like this"

Yvonne started to find her strength again, "tell me then. How the fuck was this suppose to go?. How were you two gonna break the news to me?. Can't wait to hear this", she folded her arms tightly in defiance.

Sarah went silent for a moment as she looked down at the dirty sheets she was now wrapped in, "I don't know. I just know it wasn't suppose to be like this"

Suddenly Stewy began to move around the bed, as he searched blindly for the sheets, "stop hogging the bed covers. I'm fucking freezing", he finally grabbed a handful of material and pulled the sheets off Sarah, who was left totally uncovered again. She quickly grabbed a pillow to protect her modesty.

Yvonne was finally starting to find her strength, "morning Stewy. I'd love to hear what you have to say about all this"

Stewy was still struggling to go back asleep, "about what?"

Yvonne struggled to keep her voice steady and calm, "I want to hear your bullshit excuse about why you're fucking Sarah behind my back"

Stewy's eyes suddenly flicked open, "you out already?"

Yvonne stood up and opened the wardrobe, "yes I'm out already. No thanks to fucking you", she pulled out a small suitcase from the bottom and began to pack her clothes. Crumpling and creasing her outfits as she went.

Stewy sat up in the bed and noticed that Sarah was still beside him. He quickly searched for an excuse, "it's not what it looks like. I was on my own in this bed when I went to sleep last night. This one must have just wandered in after"

Sarah wasn't impressed by the double cross, "fuck you asshole. Don't fucking hang me out to dry. Just to save your own ass"

Yvonne stopped packing for a moment and pointed at his cock, "think that used johnny says different"

Stewy looked down and noticed the cum filled condom hanging off his cock. He quickly pulled it off and fired it to one side, "I don't know how that happened. I was fucked out of it last night. This one must have took advantage of me"

Sarah punched him hard in the shoulder, "fuck you asshole. I've told her that this wasn't the first time"

Stewy held his arm in pain, "why the fuck would you do that for?"

Yvonne had heard enough, "look, you two can fucking have each other. I'm finished with you both. If we meet on the street Sarah. Don't even try to talk to me. Just stay the fuck out of my way", she then turned her attentions to her now ex boyfriend, "and as for you. I would recommend staying out of the way of my brother for a while. Because he never even liked your ass in the first place. Always said that with your boney ass and crappy bleach blonde hair that you looked like a poor man's Eminem. He'll be even less impressed when he hears this. Especially with who you were fucking behind my back. So you've been warned", and with that, she shut her suitcase and stormed out of the room.

It was difficult to pass through the apartment one last time. Knowing that with each step, that she was never gonna be back there again. But how could she, after everything that had happened. It was a relief to the system when she finally stepped out onto the busy street and took a much needed lungful of air.

But then it finally hit her. The emotions and pain that she'd been holding back for the last few minutes. Yvonne fell back against the building wall and slid down to the pavement. Pulling her suitcase close to her. She may have been emotional, but not stupid. Some little cunt would have nicked it, if they seen an opportunity. Yvonne pulled a tissue from her pocket and attempt to clear her nose.

An old lady wandering past, stopped and attempted to help, "you okay love?"

Yvonne hadn't been aware that she was bringing so much attention to herself, "I'm sorry. Didn't mean to get like this"

The old woman opened her handbag, pulled out a packet of tissues and handed them to Yvonne, "you've nothing to apologise for, think you need these more than me. Bet it was a man who left you in this state. It's always a feckin man"

Yvonne couldn't believe that someone else could see her pain, "caught my bastard boyfriend in bed with my friend"

The old woman just smiled, "best thing you can do is move on with your life. That will kill them the most.

Don't let them see you're bothered. Be strong dear", and with that, she hobbled off down the street, leaving Yvonne lost to what her next move should be.

There hadn't been many avenues left open to Yvonne except to go home to her parents. This wouldn't have been her first choice. Especially after what happened the previous day. But what choice had she got.

Yvonne's parents lived in a mid terraced property in one of the more dubious estates in the town. Her mother Samantha, or Sammy for short, had come from the countryside. Her parents being settled travellers, who had been persecuted in their first few choices of council properties. But since moving to Drogheda, had found life improving. Yvonne's father Bernard was a troubled soul at best. Fell out with his family at an early age. Distancing himself from even his sisters and followed his dreams of being a hardened criminal.

Unfortunately that hadn't worked out for him. In and out of prison for more petty crimes than you could shake a stick at. An embarrassment to the local criminal community. Always getting caught for any scheme he tried his hand at. So in the end, he agreed just to hold large quantities of money and drugs, when asked upon to do so. It was risky since he was so well known to the guards. But that didn't stop him taking the chance all the same.

As Yvonne approached the front door, she spotted her mother out in the front garden. She was scrubbing down her chairs with the help of a large basin of soapy water and a thick sponge. She spotted her daughter approaching, "you only get out now?"

Yvonne held up her small suitcase, "no, I've been back to my place already. Caught Stewy in bed with Sarah. It's over"

Sammy fired the sponge into the water and got up to hug her daughter tightly, "oh god love you dear. Knew that little creep wasn't good enough for you. And as for that Sarah one. She was always a little sneak. Come on inside and I'll make you a coffee. An Irish one if you're up for it", she led her daughter into the house and shut the front door behind them. Leaving most of the kitchen furniture, out on the front lawn.

Sammy boiled the kettle as Yvonne looked around at the damage the guards had caused to the house the night before. Large holes had been punched into the plasterboard in several areas of the kitchen walls. Even the hallway was in ruins. Yvonne pulled her denim jacket off and placed it over the back of a broken chair. One leg had been ripped off during a scuffle between her brother Dermot and the guards. His mixed martial arts techniques, suddenly coming into play. Not the best type of training for someone who couldn't deal with their own temper.

"Is Dermot still at the station?", Yvonne leaned against the kitchen counter.

Sammy poured a good measure of whiskey into each cup, before topping both off with hot water, "you know him. Couldn't control his temper last night. They'll have him for punching that guard. Pity he didn't hold out for twenty four hours. Then he would've had that prick Stewy to release his anger on. Wait till I fucking see him and that little bitch Sarah. Wouldn't mind giving both of them a good bloody beating"

Last thing Yvonne needed was for her family to do something stupid in her defence. Wouldn't be the first time either. Dermot had battered an ex boyfriend of hers, when he heard that the prick was mouthing off about what his sister was good at in bed. He soon regretted his actions as Dermot punched him black and blue down a nearby alley. No one fucked with his family. Especially not his little sister.

"I've dealt with it. Said my peace to both of them and now I want to move on. That's another thing. Can I move back in for a while?. Till I get another place", Yvonne knew her mother would have no problem with it, but felt only right to at least ask.

Sammy handed her daughter a freshly made Irish coffee, "you know that you don't have to ask. This'll always be your home. Room might need a bit of tidying. Guards pulled it apart last night. Fucking assholes. You'd swear we were murderers or something just as bad. Our family has just become a scapegoat for all those feckin guards looking for an easy conviction. Your poor father can't handle the stress of it anymore"

Yvonne could see her mother's face starting to go a strange shade of dark red. Which concerned her deeply, "and what about you mam. Are you feeling okay these days?. How's your blood pressure?"

Sammy hated to worry her daughter. So played down the constant health problems she was facing, "I'm grand. Doctor gave me stronger tablets last week. Have it under control. So stop your worrying"

Yvonne sensed that her mother was lying. But felt it best to say nothing about it for now, "have you any plans for bringing in the new year tonight?"

Sammy looked around at her damaged home, "we were suppose to have some of the neighbours over. Not too sure about it now. How can I let them see the place like this"

Yvonne was used to seeing her family home like this. Just went with her father's career choices, "I think you should have it anyway. At least they can't leave the house in a worse state"

Sammy couldn't agree more, "fuck it. You're right. I'm gonna have the party. Hopefully your father and brother will be back in time for it. Are you coming?. Or are you still going to Earth tonight?"

Yvonne had forgotten all about those plans. She opened her handbag and pulled out the tickets, "not sure now. I was suppose to go with Stewy. Don't even know who to bring now. Unless I ask Jamie"

Sammy suddenly remembered something, "shit, that stuff you ordered, arrived this morning", she went out to the hall and came back with numerous black packages, "at least you won't be short for something to wear, why don't you try this lot on and see does it fit"

It wasn't long until Yvonne was dressed up in her new clothes and back downstairs. She pulled awkwardly at the hem of the dress, which was worryingly too short, "one good gust of wind and my arse cheeks will be on show"

Sammy stood back and admired her daughter, "you look drop dead gorgeous. I'll do your hair for you tonight and you'll be all set for a good night out. Did you ring Jamie yet?"

Yvonne looked back down at her outfit, "honestly mam, do you not think it's a bit too short for me?"

Sammy flicked through a pile of neatly stacked clothes that sat on the sideboard. She pulled out a pair of her big black knickers and threw them to her daughter, "wear those for the night then. Way better than your crappy dental floss undies. Now go ring Jamie and organise your night out. No way you're wasting those tickets. Sitting in depressed will only mean that little prick Stewy still has a hold over you. Never let a man keep room in your head like that"

Yvonne knew her mother was only trying her best to cheer her up. She walked into the hallway and took another good look at herself in the full length mirror. Yvonne had to admit it. The outfit did look pretty damn hot on her. Maybe going out would be a good idea. Better than being stuck here. Ringing in the new year with their boring neighbours. Yvonne pulled out her phone and made the call. There was no going back now.

Chapter Seven

Hoovering up her fourth line of cocaine for the night, Yvonne threw her head back and enjoyed the sudden surge of adrenaline, that she so needed, "fucking hell that feels good"

Yvonne handed the rolled up note to her friend Jamie, who snorted up a line off the poorly cleaned baby changing table, that was screwed to the wall in the disabled toilets of their favourite pub.

Jamie was the friend Yvonne could rely on for a good night out. You couldn't tell her shit about your personal life, because she had a habit of telling everyone. Especially her bitch of a mother Ellen, who was one of the biggest gossips on the town. Jamie was well known for sleeping around with any fella she took a fancy to. Even Yvonne's brother being one of her many conquests. Her skirt was as short as her friend's. Except Jamie chose to wear a thong. Which meant that anytime she bent over to get anything, her bare cheeks were on show. But she was still a good laugh all the same and that's what Yvonne needed right now.

Jamie stood back against the toilet wall and enjoyed the buzz, "I fucked in here before"

Yvonne laughed as she made up another few lines, "that doesn't fucking surprise me"

Jamie wasn't finished though, "see that baby changing station. Was doing it up on that and the whole thing ripped off the wall. Fell in a heap on the ground. Thank god no one came in to investigate. Then when we were leaving, walked straight into some young fella in a wheelchair. Poor little shit was waiting to use the toilet"

"Oh fuck", Yvonne could only imagine how embarrassing that situation must have been, "what you do?"

Jamie threw her a cheeky smile, "little fella just gave us a big thumbs up. Probably went home wanking over the thought of me"

Yvonne loved her friend's confidence. Nothing ever seemed to get Jamie down. Not even her constant family problems, that were well known around the town, "bet you love the idea of a fella wanking about you?"

Jamie pulled her underwear down and sat on the toilet seat for a much needed piss, "damn straight. The more men wanking over me, the better. I bet there's loads of fellas thinking about me when they're fucking their wives and girlfriends. I love the idea of that. Have you never given the knickers you had on, to a fella you've just fucked. Or even just a fella you really fancy?"

Yvonne shook her head in disbelief, "not a hope in hell would I do that. You give your knickers to fella's you fancy?"

Jamie couldn't see what the big deal was, "best way to tell a guy you like them. Even better when their wife is next to them. I just discreetly push my undies deep into their jeans pocket. Maybe even get a sneaky feel of their bulge as well. Men want me. They're just too afraid to admit it"

Yvonne snorted up another line as she held back from what she honestly thought about her friend's promiscuous ways, "men want you for sex and that's about it. Think you just love the power of that"

Jamie wasn't fazed by her friend's comments, "and that's the way I like it. Why settle down with one man. When you can have loads of fellas you like. I've got an idea", and with that, she took her knickers off all together and swung them around on her little finger, "right then. We're gonna have a little fun with these"

Back out in the bar, the two friends got a couch that was mounted on the wall, that was facing up towards the rest of the pub. Jamie scanned the bar for a good looking target to initiate her plan on, "pickings are slim tonight. It's either a feast or a famine in this place. Can you see any good looking fellas?"

Yvonne didn't much care for any type of fella that night. But the distraction was nice all the same. Then an idea hit her, "why don't you make some ugly fella's day. Push your knickers into someone's pocket that really needs the moral boost"

But Jamie had an even better idea, "wait here", and with that, she got up and marched like a catwalk model, down the centre aisle of the busy pub.

Yvonne watched on with interest as her friend passed by many men. She had no idea where Jamie was going. Suddenly her friend stopped next to a middle aged woman with short hair and glasses. It was common knowledge in the town that the lady was a lesbian. Her lover was nowhere to be seen. Probably in the toilet. Yvonne watched on as Jamie moved in close to her and began to whisper. Pushing her knickers discreetly into the woman's hand. The poor lesbian seemed to be lost in the moment. As if waiting for a kiss that wasn't gonna come.

But then it did. Jamie planted a long lingering kiss on the middle aged woman, before turning and walking back towards the table. A big smile across her face, as if victory was hers.

Yvonne was briefly lost for words, as her friend sat back down beside her, "I can't believe you just did that"

Jamie took a large swig of her double vodka and coke, "I love a challenge. Besides, she looks happy now", she gave a little wave down the pub towards the now delighted looking woman.

Yvonne knew there was more to it than that, "what did you say to her?"

Jamie still kept smiling and glancing down the pub, "told her that I'd love to get her alone later on and that I'll be out in the car park in twenty minutes if she wanted to get a bit more intense"

Yvonne wasn't normally shocked by her friend's behaviour. But this was definitely a new string to her bow, "you really don't care who you flirt with. You even kissed her and all"

Jamie just shrugged her shoulders, "it's no big deal. Great way to get all the fellas attention when you're out. Me and Sarah have done it before", she suddenly noticed her mistake, "sorry for bringing her name up"

Yvonne knew her friend didn't mean it intentionally, "it's okay. Let's forget about that bitch for the night. So tell us. Is it true that you had a threesome with her and some fella?".

That had been a rumour going for the last few years. The two girls had been out one Saturday night and supposedly they met this good looking fella whose family owned a pub. The three of them had gone back there with him after the nightclub. Unfortunately that's were the story went a bit hazy. The fella was saying one thing. While the two girls couldn't agree on what happened either.

Jamie leaned in a little closer for discretion, "it wasn't a full on threesome. We both had sex with him at the same time. But me and Sarah didn't touch each other. We just did a bit of kissing. Just messing like. But nothing else. Unfortunately Sarah was embarrassed by the whole thing. Begged me to stay quiet or she was telling my parents about me and Mr Carroll down the street. I don't mind them knowing a lot of things. But not that. There will be murders if they find out that"

Yvonne had no idea what her friend was on about, "whose Mr Carroll?"

Jamie had honestly thought she'd shared that story in the past, "he was the guy who took my virginity when I was seventeen. I can't talk about it because he's older than my father and still lives down the street. Anyone I told in the past, said that he sounded like a dirty old man. But you should of seen him. He was so fucking handsome. And he was a wonderful lover. Better than the little pricks that came after him. Pity he called off our arrangement after his wife got suspicious. He was definitely a man I would have settled down with. Now, what about you?"

"What you mean?", Yvonne replied.

Jamie elaborated further, "how and who did you lose your virginity to?"

Yvonne hadn't the most spectacular story, "up against a wall out the back of the student disco. Can't even remember the guy's name. He was good looking and I was pissed. Big mistake when I look back on it"

Jamie dismissed her friend's regrets, "we all make mistakes. No big deal. It's when we dwell on them too long, that's when it causes a problem. Look, let's not drag the mood down of this night. It's your turn to dump your knickers on someone. So pick your target and get going"

There was a number of reasons why Yvonne felt she couldn't take part in her friend's weird game. For one thing, she still had her knickers on. Two, she hadn't the confidence to just walk up to a fella and hand them her underwear. And three, it seemed a tad sleazy to her. But maybe that's what she needed. To let go and just act a little wild for once. Throw caution to the wind for once in her life.

"Keep a look out as I slide these off", Yvonne whispered as she arched her back and slid off her knickers, before placing them up on the table.

Jamie picked them up and admired the rather large size of them, "I normally only wear knickers this big when I'm on my period. Are you on the rag?"

Yvonne snatched them out of her friend's hand and put them down on the seat beside her, "I'm not on the bloody rag, as you so elegantly put it. It's just the dress is so bloody short. Didn't want to be showing my bare ass all night like you"

"I've a great little arse, I'll have you know", Jamie was defiant as always, before looking around the pub for a target. Then an idea came to mind. The middle aged lesbian that Jamie had hit on already, had just headed off to the busy toilets and now her long blonde haired partner, was left alone waiting for her return. It was easy to see that she was definitely the feminine one in that relationship.

Jamie nudged her friend, "dare you to hit on my lesbian's girlfriend. Look, she's over there alone and my one has just gone to toilet. You've got loads of time and it'll be a laugh"

Yvonne wasn't too sure, as she scanned the pub for a better target, "I don't feel comfortable hitting on another woman. Is there no decent fellas that I could do instead?"

But Jamie was adamant, "you're not really hitting on them. Think of it as giving hope to those who need it most. That woman over there will be delighted with a young attractive woman like yourself, hitting on her. Just go for it. The longer you think about it. The worse it's gonna be"

Yvonne gripped her knickers tightly in her hand, as she mulled the plan over in her head, "right then. Fuck it", and with that, she slid off the high couch and marched across the pub with a new spring in her step.

As she drew close, Yvonne noticed the target was busy on her phone. This was gonna be more difficult than she thought. Yvonne leaned onto the edge of the cigarette machine beside her and attempted to act sexy, "how are you?"

The middle aged blonde looked up from her phone, "I'm grand thanks. Can I help you with something?"

This wasn't going how Yvonne had planned. But she still soldiered on, "I've been sitting over there all night and I just couldn't keep my eyes off you. So I just wanted to give you something", she pushed her knickers into the woman's open hand. Mission was complete.

The woman glanced down at the used underwear in her hand, "so you seem to think that it's sexy to just walk up to a complete stranger and shove your dirty knickers into their hand. Am I getting that right?", she dropped the soiled panties onto the floor and kicked them away with disgust.

Yvonne froze on the spot, as she felt lost at what to do next, "I was just trying to show you how I felt. That's all"

The woman moved in close. Her menacing eyes focused harshly on Yvonne, "I've been watching you and your friend for the last while. Two sneaky little bitches who are up to no good. This shit just proves it. Think you can take the piss of me. Just because I'm into women. Well I'll tell you one thing you stuck up little slapper. I'm out with my wife tonight and she's the only woman for me. And no skinny little cunt like you would ever tempt me"

Yvonne seen red as she heard this. But wasn't the type to resort to violence straight away. There was always another way, "maybe you should have words with your wife then", she regretted going there, but felt the blonde bitch deserved being brought down a peg or two.

The blonde's face was filled with confusion, "what's that suppose to mean?"

Yvonne felt she'd come too far to turn back now, "she has my friend's knickers in her pocket. Kissed her and all. Has even planned to meet her out back later"

The blonde was far from impressed, "I don't fucking believe you. Now get the fuck out of my face before I do something you regret"

Yvonne couldn't help but get in one final dig, "check her pockets then and see who's fucking lying", and with that, she marched back towards her table, already regretting her actions.

Jamie was still looking on eagerly, as she waited to hear what happened, "she doesn't look too impressed. Take it you didn't pull?", she joked.

Yvonne knocked the last of her drink off the head, "we better get going before those two kick off"

Jamie was confused until she looked over at the lesbian couple, who were now arguing loudly, "what the fuck did you say?"

Yvonne swallowed the contents of her mouth, "told her that her girlfriend had your knickers in her pocket and that she was flirting with you. So grab your jacket. We're out of here before there's any trouble. Had enough hassle for one day already"

Jamie reluctantly grabbed her stuff and got up to leave, "would have been a laugh to see what happened next. Can we not stay and watch?"

Yvonne pulled her jacket on, "one thing watching. Quite another thing if we end up in the middle of it all. Now let's get going. Wanna get into Earth before the crowds start arriving", and with that, the two of them headed out into the cold night air, in search of a good night and a reason to forget in Yvonne's case.

Chapter Eight

The Earth nightclub was packed from wall to wall with
sweaty partygoers of all ages, as they tried to welcome in
the new year. Yvonne was starting to regret going out
that night. Her short dress and lack of underwear had led
to many awkward occurrences, as fella's brushed past
her. In some occasions, a sneaky hand grabbed a quick
feel. Unfortunately in the busy crowd, it was impossible
to see who did it.

Jamie returned from the bar with four more bottles of
Smirnoff Ice and placed them on the small counter in
front of them, "fucking queue for that bar is a joke.
You'd think they'd have more staff on tonight. Place is
jam packed"

Yvonne took a swig from her fresh bottle, "even the
dance floor is crammed. Where the fuck are we suppose
to dance?", as she scanned the busy nightclub, her eyes
stopped on a particular couple.

The place was pretty dark, but it was easy to recognise
Stewy's bleach blonde hair among the crowds of people
and he was kissing the face off Sarah. Looked like
they'd gotten over their little tiff that morning.

Jamie noticed where her friend was looking and seen the
amorous couple as well, "those assholes have some
cheek. How'd he even get tickets at the last minute?"

Yvonne's eyes stay transfixed on the couple. It was difficult for her to see them together. Hugging and kissing like they once had. It was never truly love. Just nice to have someone who was on the same wavelength. But there had always been cracks there. The drink, drugs and sex had just hidden the truth for longer than expected.

Yvonne couldn't deny he was a brilliant lover. Going for hours upon hours when cocaine was involved. His long expert tongue working deep inside her pussy with an expertise that no other ex came near to. He'd introduced her to the joys of anal. Helped her explore a fetish for spanking and bondage. Somehow Yvonne knew, she wasn't gonna meet another fella that even came near. Now Sarah was gonna be enjoying Stewy's bedroom skills from now on. Well, until he traded her in for another one.

Jamie was visibly getting angry, "I'm gonna go over there and tell them what for", she went to leave.

But Yvonne grabbed her arm, "don't even bother. Just let it go. Besides, Sarah is still your friend. You might be pissed at her now. But sooner or later, you'll be talking again"

Jamie forced her drug fuelled body to relax again, "I don't know. I'm fucking super pissed at her as well. Can't believe she fucked you over like that. What if she did that to me. I wouldn't be as fucking calm as you are now. I probably would have battered the pair of them in the bed"

Yvonne tried to force that image to the back of her mind, "fuck it. I need to get out on the floor before my head explodes"

The two friends spent the next three hours, dancing, drinking and snorting more coke in the toilets. All was going well until Yvonne went to the toilet and couldn't find her way back to where Jamie was waiting. As she passed the entrance to the smoking area, she decided to go out in search of a cigarette. It wasn't long until she came face to face with Jack.

Something inside her had yearned for sex as soon as he started to talk to her. Yvonne wanted him there and then. Throwing caution to the wind and letting him sink his surprisingly large cock inside her. Stewy's erection had been narrow and about seven inches long. That had always satisfied her until now. But when Jack slid his thick, ten inch erection, deep inside her, Yvonne couldn't imagine going back to a smaller size. It had been fast and exciting. Everything she wanted at that very moment. The feeling of his big hands, tightening on her skin as he shot his load deep inside her.

But then a strange guilt filled Yvonne's head and all she wanted to do was get away from Jack. Get back inside to Jamie and try to forget her minor moment of madness. Her first and hopefully last one night stand. Yvonne wasn't the type of girl to usually act like that. Which annoyed her since fellas had still called her a slapper in the past. Just because of some of the company she kept over the years. Then you'd just have the assholes who would lie, just so they wouldn't look bad in front of their friends.

Yvonne finally spotted Jamie being chatted up by two older men. One of them had his hand on her side as he moved in closer.

Yvonne figured it might be a good time to save her friend from herself. Moving in alongside her, "looking all over the place for you", she purposely ignored the two older men.

But Jamie was quick to make introductions, "I've been here the whole time. You're gone ages and these nice fellas offered to keep me company until you came back", she went to introduce them both. But quickly realised that she'd forgotten their names.

The older grey haired man did the introductions instead, "the name's Harry and my friend here is David. Just seen your young attractive friend here and thought she'd like a bit of company. Nice to see she has a cute friend as well. And what might your name be?"

Yvonne kept her guard up, "Yvonne. So lads. Where are the wives tonight?. Sitting at home with the kids?"

Harry tried to pretend to look shocked, "why do you think we're married?"

Yvonne grabbed his hand and held it up for Jamie to see, "well, the wedding ring is a bit of a giveaway. Don't you think!"

Harry pulled his hand away, "what the wife doesn't know won't hurt her. How about the four of us go get something to eat after this. Get to know each other better. What do you say love?"

Yvonne totally blanked him and turned to Jamie, "can we just head off now?. Last thing I need is a man tonight. A kebab and a milkshake will do me grand. What do you say?. Can we go?"

Jamie noticed the sad eyes on her friend and nodded, "fuck it. Let's go", she turned to the two men, "right fellas. We're off. Hope you enjoy the rest of your night", and with that, the two of them pushed their way through the sweaty crowd and escaped out into the cold night air.

It wasn't long until they were both sitting on the side of the path outside the takeaway, eating their food. Unfortunately Jamie had accidentally spilt her tub of curry chips onto the ground and was now trying to stab the chips with her plastic fork.

Yvonne took another bite of her messy kebab, "that's absolutely disgusting. Why don't you just go in and buy another one"

Jamie picked up one of the chips with her fork and ate it, "they're okay. The curry is acting like a layer from the path. Not a bother on them"

Yvonne tried not to look at her friend in disgust. But the alternative was even worse. Across the road was Sarah hugging into a drunk Stewy. He was stumbling towards their flat. Probably bringing her back for a quick shag. Before he'd pass out and Sarah would have to finish herself off. Yvonne knew exactly how he was gonna end up that night. Too many weekends experiencing it herself.

Sarah suddenly spotted her friends across the road and quickly hurried Stewy along towards the door to the apartment.

Jamie soon noticed the couple as well and shouted across the street at them, "two sneaky bastards. You have some fucking cheek to be out on the town. Rubbing it in Yvonne's face. Some friend you are"

Stewy looked around when he heard the familiar voice. His eyes soon landing on Yvonne. He smiled with relief and began to stagger across the road towards her.

Suddenly he was thrown into the air, as a taxi hit him hard. Everything seemed to go slowly, as the car screeched to a halt and he fell down hard onto the road. Sarah ran to his aid, while Jamie and Yvonne still sat there, shocked at what just happened. People were shouting and screaming on the street. Camera phones were out and recording everything.

Stewy finally opened his eyes and screamed. Both his legs were now pointing in different directions. Bones jutting out through the skin and blood dripping onto the road, "SOMEBODY GET ME A FUCKING AMBULANCE", he roared.

Sarah held his hand tightly, "don't worry hun. I'm sure somebody has called one. Just relax. Try and breath gently"

Stewy was still frantic, "where's Yvonne?. I want to see her"

Sarah tried to hide her annoyance, but it was clearly visible, "just stay calm. You can't be stressing"

Yvonne pushed through the crowd and kneeled down beside Stewy, "I'm here. Now just stay calm", she held his free hand.

Stewy smiled up at her, "I'm sorry about going off with Sarah. I still love you. She means nothing to me"

Sarah dropped his hand, "fuck you", she got up and pushed her way out of the crowd.

Jamie finally got to the front of the crowd and kneeled down beside them, "fucking fool. What were you

thinking. Running across the road like that. You could
have been killed"

Stewy gripped Yvonne's hand tightly, "I just wanted to
tell you that I fucked up big time. I don't wanna lose
you"

Yvonne rubbed his cheek, "I'm sorry. But it's a bit late
for that"

Suddenly the paramedics arrived and pushed through the
crowd. They straight away got to work. Yvonne and
Jamie stood up and stepped back into the crowd.

Jamie leaned in and whispered, "can't believe you said
that. You could have at least lied"

But Yvonne didn't regret her actions, "last thing he
needs is false hope. But I better go the hospital with him.
Make sure he's okay. That's the least I can do"

Jamie lit up a cigarette and handed it to her friend, "I'm
coming and all. Might meet a cute doctor while I'm up
there"

Yvonne had a bad feeling that it was gonna be a long
night. But there was no way she could walk away at a
time like this. No matter how much of a two timing little
asshole he was. Stewy couldn't be left to deal with this
alone, even if Yvonne had a strong suspicion, that if the
shoe was on the other foot, he'd be gone in a flash.

Chapter Nine

"So I was just rebound sex?", Jack had been there before. But for some reason, this time actually hurt his feelings.

Yvonne lit up a cigarette and handed him the box, "do you want one?"

Jack took one out of the packet and was lighting it up, when the horrible truth dawned on him, "how many of these are you on a day?"

Yvonne blew out a cloud of white smoke, "less than ten now. Was on about twenty, six months ago. But it's tough to give them up altogether", she only then realised where he was going with this, "you better not be about to give me shit over this. It's hard enough trying to get by on my own. Even harder when you can't take drugs. I can't even fucking smoke the way I want to. Even my drinking has been affected. My mother will only keep beer in the house. She's afraid I'll be on the vodka all the time. Maybe she's right. There's days I just wanna go out and get pissed. Suppose this pandemic came at the right time. No pubs or nightclubs to tempt me"

Jack figured it was best to let that subject drop for the moment. There was bigger issues to deal with, "so tell me. Did you end up getting back with this Stewy fella?"

Yvonne took another pull of her cigarette, "not a hope in hell. That doesn't stop him from harassing me all the time. He wants us to get back together. Thinks I'm lying when I told him that the child is not his. Reckons I'm just trying to punish him"

Jack still couldn't keep his eyes off her smoking. It worried him something shocking, "isn't that a bit cruel?. Especially since he might be the father. At least if you just said that it was his child. You might get a lot more support than you would with me"

Yvonne threw him a dirty look, "I'm not looking for any fucking financial support off you. So get that thought out of your head. I wasn't even planning on telling you"

Jack was kind of wishing she hadn't, "so why did you tell me then?"

Yvonne shrugged her shoulders, "it just felt like the right thing to do and as for money, I'll just get more from the social for being a single mother. Get my own house in a few years and all. But there is one thing you can help me with"

Jack wasn't sure where this was going, "go on then"

Yvonne took a deep breath, "my parents are giving me shit about not giving Stewy a second chance. Think they feel sorry for him after he broke his two legs"

Jack quickly stopped her there, "how'd he do that?"

"Hit by a car", Yvonne carried on as if it was no big deal, "they are of the opinion that it would be better for the baby if I stayed with the father. They both think I'm lying about a one night stand as well. So I want you to come to my house this Saturday night and meet my family. Prove to them once and for all, that you're feckin real"

Jack had hoped that he wouldn't have to admit the next bit, but he was left with no choice, "I've got a girlfriend. Soon to be a fiancé if things work out. If she finds out that I got another woman pregnant, she'll end up dumping me. And as for my parents, they'll fucking freak it as well. They're always telling me to be careful and not get…"

Yvonne finished his sentence for him, "some little slapper who works the tills of the local supermarket, pregnant. Was that what you were going to say?. Something along those lines"

Jack rubbed his head nervously, "I know that sounds really bad, but they do want better for me. I'm more worried about Denise finding out. She doesn't deserve this"

Yvonne could see the hurt in his eyes, but somehow she felt no sympathy for him, "I'm not trying to ruin your life. I just want to prove to them that you exist. They'll get off my fucking back about Stewy and we can both get on with our lives. What to you say?"

Jack took a long hard pull from his cigarette, as he weighed up the options open to him, "can I ask you something first?"

Yvonne tried to move around on the spot to ease the pain in her ass, "go on then. May as well get all this out now"

Jack felt his throat dry up, "why didn't you go for an abortion?"

Yvonne threw the butt away from her cigarette and lit up another one, "I couldn't do that to the child. It didn't ask to be conceived and to be honest, I'm actually looking forward to being a mother. But I don't want hassle from my ex all the time. That's why I'm asking if you'd meet my parents. Make them see that you're the better choice of a father than the other fuck up. Then you can walk out of my life for good. I'm not gonna expect any money off you. You don't have to take him at weekends. All you have to worry about is looking after that girlfriend of yours. What was her name again?"

"Denise", Jack pulled his phone out and showed her the screensaver.

Yvonne took the phone and examined the image. The shoulder length, curly haired blonde, smiled happily for the camera as she stood in a well lit room in just a skimpy bikini. She had the body of a model and a sweetness to her smile that sickened Yvonne. A far cry from her own red hair and freckled skin, "she's fucking stunning. Surprised you went slumming it with me. Must have been all the drugs in your system", she handed the phone back.

Jack hated to admit the truth, but he couldn't let her feel like she was just another easy shag, "you were more than that to me. I don't think you remember this, but we were in the same school at one time. Every morning I'd arrive in and you'd be sitting with your mates beside the shop. All of you would be in a row. Your skirts pulled up high over the thighs and legs fairly wide open. That was my favourite part of the day. The other girls would only be wearing plain white or black knickers. But you used to wear these skimpy little thongs. The amount of times I purposely dropped something. Just to stop and gaze up at that beautiful sight, made my day"

Yvonne was hard to embarrass, but Jack was already sending her in that direction, "and when you went home that night. Did you think of me as well?"

Jack hated to admit that he'd wanked off to that image of her poorly concealed fanny many a time, but he couldn't dare say that to her, "I did think about you. Most nights"

Yvonne threw him a cheeky smile, "I bet it was several times at night. Weird to think we ended up together years later. Bet that was one off your bucket list"

Jack was still debating her request. It was a lot to ask of him. Putting all he cared about, at risk. But he couldn't just walk away from Yvonne and expect her to deal with all this on her own. It was a small request in comparison to what she was taking on, "I'll do it"

Yvonne had lost track of their conversation, "do what?"

Jack couldn't believe he had to say it out straight, "I'll go to your house and meet your parents. I just hope you're right about how this will go. I can't see them being impressed with me showing up and claiming to be the father, then I fuck off and not come back again. I just hope I don't bump into them with my parents or girlfriend"

Yvonne still couldn't find sympathy for him. But the memory of those days back in school, came back to the forefront of her mind. Sitting beside the shop. Her friends having a laugh as they smoked their way through a packet of cigarettes. When she searched her mind a little further. The memory of a young student passing by each morning, finally revealed itself to her. She could remember his innocent face, staring up between her legs.

Yvonne and her mates had laughed at the poor kid's embarrassment. They loved to make the young lad feel uncomfortable. Now here he was in front of her. He'd grown into a handsome man. A fella that she would have considered out of her league. But that hadn't stopped them creating a baby. Well, she hoped that was true. The alternative scared her more than anything else in this world.

"It'll be grand", Yvonne glanced at her watch for effect, "I better get going. Give us your phone for a sec?"

Jack handed it over reluctantly, "are you on social media?"

Yvonne typed in her number and saved it onto his phone, before handing it back, "I don't bother with all that. Too many assholes online. I always seem to end up in disagreements with people. I much rather face to face. Now, ring me Saturday morning and I'll tell you where to meet me. And please don't let me down. This is all I need from you. Then I won't bother you again. Have we still a deal?"

Jack went against his usual cautious behaviour and dialled her number. Yvonne's phone rang in her pocket and he hung up straight away, "there you go. You have my number as well. Hope that puts your mind at ease?"

Yvonne was starting to find him strangely charming, "thanks for this. And I promise you. It's not gonna be as bad as you think. My parents are pretty sound. It's just they want me to have a more traditional style family. They still live in the past. My brother has two kids to two different women and he doesn't get as much shit as I do"

"Parents are always harder on the girls", Jack had heard that off many girls in college. Including Denise.

Yvonne struggled up to her feet, "have you a sister yourself?"

Jack followed suit and got up as well. Wiping down his good clothes, "no, I've only got a brother"

"Do youse get on?", Yvonne asked.

Jack didn't want to get into it, "he's dead now. But we never got on when he was alive. We were polar opposites in personalities"

Yvonne wasn't sure how to reply to that, "I'm sorry about that. I better be getting off. Call me Saturday", and with that, she headed off down the street at a fast pace.

Jack watched on as she disappeared into the distance. He was now left with an awful feeling that he'd made a terrible mistake by agreeing to her demands. No way was her parents gonna be impressed about a complete stranger showing up, confessing to getting their daughter pregnant and then fucking off for the rest of their grandchild's life. But he'd agreed to it now and there was no going back. As his father always said, "when faced with a sea full of shit, better to hold your nose and just jump in and swim". That never really made sense to Jack. Until now.

Chapter Ten

It didn't matter how many times Yvonne past the large
boulder that sat at the entrance to her estate, she still
always found the corrupted title amusing. Her home was
in the Rock estate no one had a feckin clue why it was
called that, but someone had drawn the head of Austin
Powers beside it. Blanked out the word estate and had
added to the rest with a few new words. So that it now
read, Rock hard baby. Yvonne hoped no one would ever
remove it.

She past by another burnt out car that had been crashed
into a nearby wall. Bags of household rubbish had been
thrown around it's burnt out shell. The locals trying to
get rid of their rubbish for free again. The fire brigade
probably getting to the fire before the rubbish had a
chance to take light. Now there was probably gonna be a
lot of households getting a litter fine in the letterbox in
the next few weeks. Yvonne just hoped none of that
rubbish came from her house.

Yvonne turned the corner into her street and straight
away spotted the Garda cars parked outside her house.
That was the last thing she needed. Guards would have
wrecked the house again. Which would mean a whole
day of cleaning up after them. There wasn't even any
point in telling her father to quit his illegal profession.
His name had already been blackened by the guards.
They'd still come down on him, no matter how long he
had retired. Yvonne would never admit it, for sounding
bad, but it was a bit of a relief when her father ended up

in prison for a few months. Meant that she didn't have to live in fear of the guards smashing down the front door at any time of the night.

But as she got closer, Yvonne noticed her neighbour, Eddy Simpson, up on the roof of his house. He was totally naked and waving a large sign that read, 5G CAUSES CORONA. Yvonne knew he was a nutter. But this was a new level of madness, even for him.

The neighbours were gathered around in front of Eddy's house. Yvonne spotted her mother among them and nudged her shoulder discreetly, "what the fuck is up with Eddy?"

Her mother Sammy was smoking away on one of her special joints. Just enough grass in it to get a buzz. But not enough to draw attention with the smell. Handy when you're standing around a load of guards, "he just fucking snapped this morning. He was posting conspiracy crap all night on Facebook. Then the guards showed up because he was sending death threats to some local politician, because he thought they were involved with the virus coming into Ireland. And now he's making a statement by getting his lad out for the neighbours. To be honest love, I'm surprised by the size of it. Always thought he'd have a small dick"

Yvonne couldn't help but glance up again for a better look. She'd seen bigger. But it still was a good size. Felt strange to scrutinise the cock of a man who had been her neighbour for nearly the last three decades, "well we now know his wife didn't leave him for having a tiny dick"

Sammy laughed, "no, she left him because he's fucked in the head. That's pretty obvious now"

"Where's dad?", there was no sign of him. That didn't surprise Yvonne. He normally distant himself from any Garda activity in the street. Always complaining that it could just be another set up to drag him into the station as well.

Sammy leaned against a nearby Garda car and folded her arms, "you know him. We won't see him till night time with this lot around. They won't fuck off until they have this nutter in cuffs"

Suddenly the front door of Yvonne's house swung open and out marched her brother Dermot. All he had on was his tight, white underwear. His many tattoos on show over his large muscular body. Finished off with his Conor McGregor style beard. Dermot's hero since he started body building, before moving onto mixed martial arts.

Dermot stared up at Eddy on the roof next door, "will you fucking get down already. Making a fucking show of us with all this shit. At least put some fucking clothes on mate"

One of the guards threw Dermot a dirty look, "why don't you shut the fuck up and get back in the house before I arrest you for public indecency"

Dermot looked down at his sweaty physique, "what's fucking wrong with me?. None of my bits are on show"

One of the elderly neighbours suddenly piped up, "I've no complaints love. Nice little package on you"

Sammy could see the situation was about to turn volatile and pushed her son towards the front door, "come on son. Before you say or do something you regret"

Yvonne followed after them. She could sense the dirty looks being thrown in their direction from the four guards. Some things never changed.

When Yvonne entered the kitchen, Dermot was standing next to the sink, still displaying his bulge proudly. It was bad enough when he only wore his underwear around the house, but since he found a new love of wearing tight white briefs, it was becoming even more uncomfortable, "can you please put that fucking thing away. You're a fucking embarrassment".

Dermot glanced down at himself, "what the fuck is wrong with what I have on?. I'm not fucking naked like Eddy out there"

Sammy couldn't see what the big fuss was all about, "it's only underwear love. Only showing off the body that god gave him"

Dermot shot that statement down, "god gave me a weak body mam. I gave myself this awesome body", he kissed his bicep for effect, "no one helped me look this good. All my own fucking work"

Yvonne loved her brother, but boy was he a fucking handful to deal with. Especially since he found a love of body building. Back when he was into just drugs and drink, he was actually more likeable. Now he had a habit of trying to fuck every one of her friends, Jamie and Sarah included. It wasn't like he wanted any kind of relationship with either of them. He just seen them as conquests, like all women. Annoying to try and have nights out with your friends, when after a few drinks, they would end up discussing how good Yvonne's brother was in bed.

"What if I went out front in just my knickers and started posing for all the elderly men on the street?", Yvonne announced, "bet you two wouldn't be happy about that"

Dermot nodded towards her growing bump, "no one is gonna touch you now with that little package onboard"

Sammy quickly scolded her son, "shut your mouth. There's nothing off putting about a woman being pregnant. The amount of men that tried to get off with me when I was pregnant with you, was unbelievable. I'd be down the pub. Eight months pregnant and many a hand would still grab my ass as I past by. Your sister looks radiant and I better not hear you knock her again or I'll give you a bloody good slap. Have you got that?"

Dermot knew better than to push his mother. Wasn't worth the hassle in the long run, "okay mam. I won't open my mouth again", he turned to his sister, "I'm sorry for being rude to you sis"

Yvonne knew he was being insincere, but she was used to it, "no problem. But forget all that for the moment. I've got something else to tell you both. I've been talking to the guy that supplied me with this little bundle of joy", she rubbed her swollen belly.

"You mean the guy that you said fucked you in the Earth's car park?", Dermot added.

Sammy threw him a dirty look, "I'm fucking warning you", she turned back to her daughter, "go on love"

Yvonne took a deep breath, "I know you still don't believe me. So I asked him to call up to the house on Saturday. Prove to you once and for all that this child has nothing to do with Stewy. And I hope after that, I won't have to hear you lot going on about getting back with him"

Dermot couldn't hold his tongue, "whether the child is Stewy's or not. He's making a shit load of money out of those crappy paintings. He wants to be the child's father.

I say let him and take the prick for every cent you can get out of him", he turned to his mother for moral support, "tell her mam. At least with Stewy, she'll be set for life"

Sammy sat down at the kitchen table and thought about her next words carefully, "if the child's not Stewy's, then it's not right to pin it on him. If Yvonne says this guy is the father, then I'm happy with that. At least we finally get to meet him. Bad enough you got pregnant from a one night stand, but to not even know his name was even worse"

Yvonne couldn't believe what her mother was saying. She pointed at Dermot angrily, "but this prick got two girls pregnant and one of them was a one night stand"

Sammy lit up another one of her special cigarettes, "but at least he knew her name"

Yvonne was fit to be tied, "that's because it was Mrs O'Brien down the road. Mr O'Brien still doesn't even fucking know he's bringing up another man's baby"

Sammy hated to be reminded of that black cloud hanging over their family. Even worse that the child had a big head of ginger hair, "and no one is ever gonna find out about that. Not gonna end up being hated on this street. Already had a few of them trying to get some of the others to sign a petition to get the council to evict us. Feckin bastards. You'd swear their own shite didn't stink"

Dermot still had other things on his mind, "ah fuck them mam. I'm more interested in meeting this fella that shot the golden load"

Sammy threw him yet another dirty look, "don't fucking say it like that"

Dermot just laughed off his mother's annoyance, "conceived in a feckin car park. That's one story she won't be telling her child"

"You can't talk. Me and your father conceived you on the bonnet of your grandfather's car. So shut your mouth", Sammy hadn't shared that story before, but now seemed the right time.

Dermot was about to say something that couldn't be taken back in a hurry, but decided to do the wise thing and stormed out of the room and up the stairs.

Yvonne sighed with relief, "he's gotten more unbearable since he built up the muscles"

Sammy noticed her smoke building up in the kitchen, so opened the sliding door, "it's being cooped up for all these months that is getting to him. Dermot's been training to fight and that's not happening. God only knows when he'll be back in the ring. Only output for him is verbally abusing people or shagging one of those dirty young slappers around the estate. Heard off Mrs

Murphy down the street that he was caught down an alley with that Susan one you used to baby sit for"

This was the first time that Yvonne had heard about it, "that girl is barely twenty. Think Dermot is hitting a midlife crisis and he's only thirty four. Not even my friends are fucking safe around him. He goes around fucking everyone"

Sammy didn't wanna hear this argument again, "it takes two to fucking tango. Don't start putting all the blame on your brother. Jamie and Sarah weren't forced to shag him, so please direct your anger elsewhere. Besides, you don't even like Sarah anymore. Why would you give a fuck if he screwed her or not?"

Yvonne attempted to keep her temper at bay, so lit up another cigarette and prayed the nicotine would help in some way, "but he fucked Sarah after she slept with Stewy. He's not exactly supportive"

Sammy had been holding back something that she was hoping would have died with the delete button, "Dermot didn't tell you this, because I asked him not to. But he only slept with Sarah because he secretly taped her giving him…", she tried to think of a nice way of saying it.

"Blowjob", Yvonne begrudgingly prompted.

Sammy was visibly relieved, "exactly. Said he wanted to get revenge on her for what she did on you. But I told him to delete it. No matter what Sarah did on you. She doesn't deserve that. Shit like that stays online forever. I know your brother doesn't show it. But he does care"

Yvonne struggled to believe that her brother cared so much. He didn't show it at the best of times. But no fella would ever cross her for fear of what he'd do. Stewy had gotten off with a mild beating, thanks to the two broken legs that he had already received from the taxi. Yvonne just hoped that her family wouldn't give Jack a hard time on Saturday. More for her own sake, than his.

Chapter Eleven

Jack arrived home to a quiet house. The taxi hadn't been cheap, but it was better than ringing either of his parents for a lift home. He was still struggling with his decision to help out Yvonne. Part of him kept screaming to back out before it was too late, but he wasn't the type to back out on someone.

Jack poured himself a large vodka and sat down in his father's saloon style bar. He still couldn't believe how tacky the whole place looked. No way would any house he'd own in the future, look like this.

His mother's laptop was sitting on the coffee table in front of him. Jack knew the password and he hadn't spoke to Denise since arriving home. So it seemed only right to turn it on and log into his zoom account. He sent her a message to join a private conversation. It didn't take long for Denise to appear on the screen. She was sitting on a large cream couch, wearing only shorts and a very small T-shirt.

Her face lit up when she saw him, "was waiting for you to get in touch. How you getting on at home?"

Jack wouldn't have considered it long since they last chatted. But figured it best to say nothing, "it's going okay. Mam and dad threw a welcome home party for me last night. Told them not to make a big fuss. But they never listen"

Denise leaned in close to the camera, "I've missed you something shocking here. I'm all alone. Only got my rampant rabbit to keep me satisfied"

An idea began to form in Jack's sex starved mind, "wanna get it now and let me watch you get yourself off?"

Denise didn't need to be asked twice, as she jumped up off the couch and disappeared off screen. She appeared back a few moments later with her favourite sex toy. Jack watched on as she pulled off her shorts and knickers. Before sitting back down on the couch and spreading her legs wide, so that he could clearly see her shaved pussy. Denise pressed the on button and her rampant rabbit began to vibrate. She rubbed it gently off her clit. Moans of ecstasy, emitted from deep inside her body.

Denise smiled at the camera, "I'm not doing this on my own. Get your lad out and get pumping. I wanna see that big thick shaft I love so fucking much. I wish you were inside me right now. And with that, she slid the vibrator deep inside her wet pussy.

Jack got up and opened up his pants, before pulling the lot down to the ground. He sat back down and began to stroke his long, thick erection, "keep going honey. I wanna shoot my load while watching you. I miss that tight little pussy so much"

Denise pulled off her T-shirt with her free hand and began to play with her perky little nipples, "fuck I'm so horny. I'm about to cum already", and with that, she moaned loudly as a gush of vaginal fluid shot out onto the couch in front of her, "that felt fucking awesome", she kept on playing with her clit, as the vibrator did it's job properly.

Jack wanked furiously as he watched on. It wouldn't be long until his own sticky load would make an appearance, "keep going baby. I wanna see more of your sexy love juices"

Denise came again and shot another load of pussy juice out onto the couch in front of her, "oh fuck. I want you so bad"

Jack finally shot his load out onto the laptop in front of him. Spraying the screen with his cum, "fucking hell. That felt good. Can't wait to be balls deep in you again"

Denise came one more time before falling back on the couch defeated and tired, "you fucking wore me out without even being in the room. I miss you so much. Maybe I should come down and stay with you in a few weeks"

Jack was still looking around for some tissue to clean the laptop. But was quickly distracted by her offer. There was no way she could visit. Not now, not ever, "there's no point in you calling down. You wouldn't like it here. I don't even like it here. Hopefully I can get back sooner rather than later. My life is with you in Cork, not stuck here in the past. You're my future"

Denise held her hands to her bare breasts, "oh my god. That's so sweet. I miss you too. It's not been the same since you left"

Suddenly the front door opened and Jack could hear his mother's high heels, clacking off the wooden floor as she marched down the hallway, "oh fuck", he quickly stood up and pulled up his pants before she entered the room. He sat back down to hide the fact that his pants weren't buttoned up, "hey mam. Where were you?"

Denise pulled a blanket around her naked body, "hi Mrs O'Dwyer. Nice to finally meet you"

Ellen sat down next to her son, "nice to meet you love. My son tells me fuck all, so it's nice to finally talk to you. How are things down in Cork?"

Denise pulled the blanket a little tighter around herself, "it's okay. A bit lonely since your son went home. My parents are in their villa in Spain. So there's no point in going home to an empty house"

Ellen's face lit up when she heard the word villa. A home in Spain meant money. Money normally meant power, and Ellen liked to be close to anyone in a high position, "I'd love to meet them some time, hopefully before you get engaged"

Denise went red in the cheeks, "we haven't discussed that yet"

Ellen noticed the white stains on the screen. At first she thought it was Denise's camera. But she soon came to realise that the problem was on her side, "did you get yoghurt on the laptop?"

Jack tried his best to wipe the screen clean with the sleeve of his light jumper, "sorry mam. I'll have to be more careful when I'm eating"

It was only then, that Ellen noticed her son's open pants and she put two and two together, "I think I walked in on a private moment here. I better leave you two to it", she turned back to Denise on the laptop screen, "You're more than welcome to come stay with us some time. And another word of advice, when you're on a webcam dear, make sure your sex toys aren't in the shot"

It was only then that Denise noticed the rampant rabbit lying on the couch beside her. She went even redder in the cheeks, "thanks for the advice Mrs O'Dwyer. I'll be more careful next time"

Ellen got up to leave, "and please clean that laptop when you're finished", and with that, she walked off out of the room to wash her hands.

The young couple looked at each other awkwardly and laughed. Jack took a much needed swig of his drink, "won't hear the end of that for awhile. Bet she'll tell my dad and all"

Denise opened up her blanket to show off her naked body, "well here's a little mental image for you later on. I better go have a shower. I'm all sticky and wet, the way you like me. Love you honey"

Jack rubbed the screen and wished he could touch her naked body, "love you too. I'll call again soon".

Jack shut the computer off and rested his head back onto the couch. He was digging himself a deep hole and he hadn't a clue on how to get back out of it.

Chapter Twelve

After carefully cleaning the laptop, Jack figured it was in his best interest to disappear out of the house for a few hours. Thankfully he'd remembered Paul's offer of calling around to his place. It wouldn't have been his first choice, but it was still better than staying in his house. There was always a strange vibe at home, that had only dulled over the years, but never left. No matter how much his parents tried to pretend it had. As his grandad used to say, you can gift wrap a lump of shit, but it's still shit.

Paul's house was just as fancy as his own. A two storey building which had been recently renovated to add on a gym area for his mother. It included a small swimming pool, sauna and jacuzzi. Jack's mother had been persecuting his father to get something similar, but he just said it was a waste of money. Especially since she had an exclusive gym membership, which offered complimentary spa treatments and relaxation classes. Ellen had begrudgingly agreed with her husband. Jack just hoped the rumours weren't true about his mother screwing several gym users in the changing rooms, while his father watched on. But somehow Jack had a sneaky suspicion that it was fact.

Jack banged hard on the large front door. For such a big house, they still hadn't bothered getting a new doorbell. Jack was about to give up when he could hear the latches opening on the inside and Mr Foley poked his head around the edge of the small gap, his eyes struggling to see the young man in the dark, "is that you Jack?"

Jack felt a little awkward since he hadn't darkened this old man's door in years, "yeah, I was just calling around to see Paul. Is he here?"

Mr Foley pointed towards the side of the house, "he's out back in the new sheds, go ahead round. Told me he was expecting you", and with that, he just shut the door tightly without saying goodbye.

Jack didn't question it. Paul's father had always been a bit weird. For such a high flying businessman. He had pretty shit people skills.

Jack wandered around the back of the house. It was getting difficult to see as the sun got low in the sky. The place could have really done with some sensor lights. Not a load of feckin solar lights, that illuminated fuck all and pretty much led to Jack falling over a flower bed. That had been surprisingly painful.

He spotted the large shed in front of him. It was timber built with numerous windows along the front. The lights were on inside and Paul was clearly visible. Working away at a bench, while bits and pieces of electrical equipment lay around him. Paul had always been a bit weird. Preferring his own company at the best of times. He'd always had a thing about taking things apart and putting them back together. Or trying to make them even better. But that rarely worked out.

Like the time they'd gotten pissed off trying to mow his large garden. So Paul had thought up the idea of opening up the engine and removing the inhibitor. Then jacking up the speed of the motor to as high as possible. Each of them stood at either ends of the long front garden. Paul had strapped the handles down with rope and set it off across the garden. It took off at high speed. It had started off pretty well. Then smoke began to pour out of the engine. That soon turned to flames and by the time it was drawing close to Jack. He knew it wasn't in his best interest to try and stop it. So decided to jump clear and let it run into the hedge behind him.

Unfortunately it was the middle of summer and the hedge was extremely dry. So it went up like a petrol soaked bonfire. By the time Paul's mother came out to see what the burning smell was, most of the hedge was already destroyed. Surprisingly she wasn't angry, just glad that neither child was injured by the incident. Jack had been surprised at her attitude, but as he grew older, he'd heard more stories from his parents about his old friend's mental health problems. Jack kind of felt bad for never realising the obvious. He'd been too busy dealing with his own brother to notice his best friend's behaviour at the time. But all that was in the past now.

Jack tapped the glass panel on the door and waited for a reply. Paul looked around and seemed delighted to see him. Opening the door wide, "come on in. I was just setting up something to film"

Jack entered the surprisingly warm cabin. It's interior covered with classic movie posters and semi naked women. All of them framed neatly and properly hung. Probably costing a good bit of money to do so, "this is a nice place you have here. Better than the old garage. Did your dad finally throw you out of it?"

Paul went back to fiddling with some light metal wire, that he was bending into a circle, "he got pissed after the last fire I started in there. So he bought this place for me. Whole thing was put up in one day. It's actually a lot warmer than the garage. And there's more room in it to work"

Jack could see a major flaw in Paul's father's plan. Well, he hoped it was a flaw, "so you're saying. He moved you into a completely wooden building, because he considered you a fire hazard"

Paul carried on with his work, "he was afraid of me wrecking the Bentley. Suppose he has a point. Nearly blew up the garage when I tried to test a theory that you could build a flamethrower out of a gas canister and a nail"

Jack hated to think what his friend did, but still couldn't help but ask, "what did you do?"

Paul looked far from bothered, "hammered the nail through the side of it and lit the escaping gas. Was getting great footage for my YouTube channel. But it looked like it was about to explode. So I did a runner.

After that, my dad banned me from doing experiments near the house"

Jack had heard about his friend's YouTube channel. He'd even checked it out once. All that was on it, was Paul doing weird experiments, that were either extremely dangerous or just plain stupid. He still got a lot of views for each one. Especially a video were he detonated an oil canister under pressure and let the contents fire up the side of his parent's garage wall. Leaving the gable end of the house looking like it had a massive Guinness induced shit streak.

Jack glanced at the weird items on the workbench, "what are you making now?"

Paul held up the circular piece of metal with a cross in the centre, "remember we used to make the Chinese lanterns before it was fashionable?. I've come a long way since then. Don't launch them at night anymore. I attach a GoPro to the bottom and it sails through the sky for miles and miles. Then I chase it down till it crashes and recover the footage"

Jack spotted a major flaw in his friend's plan, "could you not just buy a drone?. Would be a lot easier to launch and recover the footage. And you can steer it as well"

Paul dismissed his friend's idea with a wave of his hand, "don't be silly. Where's the fun in something working so clinically perfect. Anyone can operate a drone and post the footage online. This is a unique experience that takes the control out of my hands. Besides, people love to watch them crash. You don't get that so much with a drone. Too expensive"

Jack had fond memories of those times they'd spent together. Anything to get him out of the house and away from his own family problems. The best of those times being when they were both around ten years of age. The peak of their adventures. Building dams in a stream in the local fields. Constructing treehouses and of course, launching homemade Chinese lanterns at dusk. Then they'd follow them for miles on their pushbikes. One time it landed next to a barn full of hay. That had been a close call. Another time it landed in a small car park nearby. It adjoined onto a park that was popular with people from the town.

Unfortunately at night, it attracted a different crowd of people. The two curious ten year olds arrived to find a car with numerous men standing around it. Inside was a couple making out. They couldn't figure out what was happening at the time. But as years brought maturity, they'd both come to the conclusion that they'd walked in on a dogging site. That was one story that they hadn't shared with their parents as years went by. But for totally different reasons.

Jack noticed two large syringes on the table. They were way bigger than anything he'd seen being used by a doctor, "what have you got them for?"

Paul put down what he was working on and picked up the syringes. A large smile spreading across his face, "this is one thing you can help me with", he picked up a large canister of petrol and headed outside into the darkness.

Jack followed after him, fearing what was gonna come next.

Paul sucked up petrol into each syringe, "these are for cattle. That's why they're so big. It's for dosing them. Robbed them out of an old farmyard down the road", he lit a small fire on a nearby wall with a small drop of petrol and a match, "now, we're ready to rock and roll", he handed his friend his mobile phone, "I want you to film this. Stand back a bit, so that you get a good wide shot of the whole thing"

Jack reluctantly took the phone and did what he was told.

Paul got down on one knee and aimed the syringe at the flame, "are you filming?"

Jack double checked the screen, "yeah, go on"

Paul punched the plunger on the syringe, which forced the petrol out at high speed. The flammable liquid hit the flame and projected on past as a massive fireball. Before disappearing as quickly. Leaving a few burning embers on the long grass.

Paul stood up and looked across the wall to see was there any damage, "that went better than expected. How far do you think that went?"

Jack wasn't great with guessing measurements. But still gave it a try, "I'd say about ten feet. What were you hoping for?"

Paul took the phone off his friend and replayed the footage, "thought it might go about twenty", he then had an idea, "how about you do the second one?. You always had stronger arms than me. You might be able to send it even further"

It wasn't long until Jack was on one knee, waiting patiently for his friend to call action. He felt a bit stupid, but decided to keep his feelings to himself. It was only then that he realised his friend's mistake. Paul had hit the flame at an ascending arc. Which meant the flame had to climb before it had an opportunity to fall. Jack reckoned the best option was to raise his body a little higher, so that the syringe was equal to the flame on the wall. Paul called action and Jack gave the plunger a whack with as much force as possible. The petrol launched out at a surprisingly fast speed and hit the flame. Sending the burning stream far out into the field on the other side of the wall. It disappeared quickly amongst the long grass.

A big smile came to Paul's face, "that was fucking awesome. I'm definitely posting that one up. You must have cleared fifteen feet with that shot"

Jack put the syringe down and wiped the access petrol from his hands, "do you even make any money for all these videos?"

Paul shook his head while putting the phone away, "couldn't be arsed trying to make money out of it. Then I'd have to fill the page full of adverts and click bait. Fuck that shit. I want people to click on my videos and enjoy them. Why ruin that"

Jack didn't see any point in questioning his old friend's dreams. There was something else that was interesting him a lot more, "you said that you were growing your own grass. Can I see it?"

Paul led his friend to a large greenhouse that hadn't been there when they were younger. It was bigger than some people's houses. Jack couldn't see the point of it, "did your parents take up gardening?"

Paul flicked on a number of switches and the energy saving lights, slowly illuminated the room, "they built it for me because I told them that I had an interest in trying to grow crops on a small scale"

The strong smell suddenly caught Jack's nose. The distinctive odour of grass. His eyes then landed on the numerous plants on either side of him. All easily recognisable as marijuana. Some of them stretching up to eight feet tall, "oh my fucking god. How the fuck do you keep this lot hidden from your parents?"

Paul led the way towards a number of work counters that were covered with gardening tools and fertiliser, "I told them that they're all just tomato plants. They just accepted it and haven't bothered me since"

Jack could see a major flaw in his friend's plan, "but don't they expect to see the fruits of your labour?. A few tomatoes for all this effort"

Paul lifted the lid of a nearby bin to reveal a load of empty punnets from a local supermarket, "I just buy them and pass them off as my own. I don't think they even fully believe me, but they don't say nothing. So everyone is happy. Think they're just glad that I haven't tried to top myself or something", he joked. But then he realised his mistake and went somber, "I'm sorry about that. Didn't mean to joke about it"

Jack dismissed his friend's worries with a wave of his hand, "that's all in the past. I've gotten over that a long time ago"

Paul picked up a pre made joint and handed it to his friend, "do you still think about it?. Mam said it was you that found him"

Jack took the joint and lit it up. He didn't like to talk about that dark time in his past. Something he preferred to forget about and leave up to his parents to commemorate each year, "Oliver had his problems. Didn't matter how many years he went to a psychiatrist, or how many fucking antidepressants he took each day to ease his pain. You know how much he used to mentally torture me"

Paul sat up onto the counter and lit up another joint, "remember when he tricked you into destroying all your matchbox cars?. There was only halves of them all left. We even tried sticking them back together. Think we melted the plastic in the centre a bit and hoped the whole thing would gel in some way. But it just wasn't working"

Jack hated to be reminded of that day. All his favourite cars destroyed in one giant swoop. Only seven at the time and Oliver was eleven. They used to play in the old dog run that never got used, because the dog always got out of it somehow. The entrance to the adjoining kennel had a steel plate that no one seemed to know why it was there. It just appeared and no one questioned it.

Oliver had suggested that they get all their little toy cars and put them one by one under the thick metal sheet. His brother would then drop it down and pretty much slice the car in two. They were supposedly having great fun for a good while. That was until Jack realised that the large pile of broken cars seemed to be mostly made up of his toys. But on closer inspection it turned out it was all his feckin toys. Jack then noticed his brother's jacket lying on the ground beside him and the penny dropped. He pulled it away to reveal his brother's whole matchbox car collection, all safe and in one piece. That memory never left him. No matter how much he tried to bury it. Along with all the other tormenting moments that his brother put him through over the years.

A good while later, the two friends were sitting outside in the dark again, smoking away at the picnic table outside the greenhouse. They'd talked about many aspects from their childhood and after. How their lives had separated in so many ways.

Jack wasn't even sure if his legs would work any more, "fuck this is pretty strong. It's better than any stuff I ever smoked in college"

Paul wasn't doing much better, "it's the same stuff that most big drug dealers grow. It's just that I give it the time to mature. That lot just rush the process through, just to keep the money flowing faster"

No matter how far Jack's mind was out of it, he still couldn't stop thinking about the upcoming meeting on Saturday, "remember I was telling you about that Yvonne one?"

Paul's eyes suddenly widened once more, "yeah, I didn't know whether to mention it again. Did you sort all that out?"

Jack wasn't sure how to word it. It still felt surreal to him, "she's asked me to meet her parents this weekend"

Paul sat up straight when he heard this, "fucking hell. That sounds a bit formal. Thought you already had a girlfriend?"

That was another thing that Jack didn't need reminding of at the moment, "I know. This isn't looking good. But Yvonne wants to prove to her parents that the child is not her ex boyfriend's"

"Even though it might be?", Paul asked.

That was something else that Jack didn't need to hear right now, "there's a stronger chance that it's his. But she doesn't want anything to do with him. All she wants is for me to just show up at her house. Let the parents scrutinise me for a while and that's that. I'll fuck off back down to Cork and that's the end of it. It's that simple"

Paul looked even more confused, "that sounds like a total mess. This isn't gonna end well. Maybe you should ring her and back out before it's too late"

Jack was kind of wishing that option was still open to him, "it's too late to back out now. I've agreed to it and I'm gonna go through with it. I just hope it doesn't come back to haunt me in the future"

Paul threw his friend a stern look, "it's a child. That sort of thing haunts you for the rest of your life. Maybe you should bite the bullet and tell your girlfriend, because these things have a habit of coming out in the end. Look at my parents. My mother was having an affair with some fella for years and it only came out last year because she brought home a sexually transmitted disease. They've gotten even more distant since then. Don't know why they don't just break up and move on"

Jack felt that now wasn't the best time to mention his parent's threesomes with Paul's mother. That probably wouldn't have ended well, "at least they're not like my lot. Fucking riding around the house all the time. Last thing you need to see when you come home from a surprise visit from college, is to find your parents trying anal on the couch in the sitting room, while one of your father's mates watches on from a nearby chair. Still can't get that disturbing image out of my head", not the worst image he'd ever come across at home. But that conversation wasn't for now.

"Some people are together so long, it just seems like too much fucking hassle to break up", was the kindest way Jack could put it.

Paul lit up another joint, "your parents have lasted the test of time. Even after everything with your brother"

Jack wasn't even sure if that was always a good thing, "sometimes I think they've just tried to bury their problems and move on. They don't talk about him anymore and I don't bring it up. Works for us all in some fucked up way", it felt nice to vent with someone who knew his past. There was so much that he had wanted to talk about for such a long time now. But he was always around people who didn't know about his brother and what happened, "I'm glad I bumped into you the other night. It's nice being around someone who understands my family history"

Paul looked up from buzzing off the glowing red tip of his joint, "same here. Never really got close to anyone since primary. Think everyone thought I was a weirdo"

Jack felt bad for thinking the same thing about his friend, as the teen years arrived, "you're not a weirdo and I hope we can keep hanging out for the next few weeks while I'm home"

Paul's face lit up with delight, I'd be happy to. Nice to have a bit of company for a while. Especially with the way my parents are acting these days"

Jack felt there was finally a bit of light at the end of this god awful tunnel that was his life. A valve to take the pressure off, from his hell of a visit home. The sooner he got back to Cork. The better.

Chapter Thirteen

The day had finally arrived. Penney's had reopened its doors and what seemed like the entire female population of the town was now queuing from outside the front door, around the corner and down to the bottom of the alley, where Sammy and Yvonne waited patiently for their turn to get in the door and find some much needed bargains.

Sammy lit up another one of her special cigarettes and glanced up the queue to see how long they'd be, "this is a fucking joke. They should just let us all in the feckin door and let the strongest survive. I'd batter any little clown faced teenager who gets in my fucking way of a bargain"

Yvonne lifted her short T-shirt to reveal her little bump, "don't think I'm in any state for a punch up mam. Those days are gone for a while"

This dragged Sammy's mind back to what was happening the following day, "so are you gonna get any nice clothes for this fella coming to the house tomorrow?. Maybe a nice little set of undies to tempt him"

Yvonne was sick of hearing all these hints from her parents. Probably wasn't the best idea to tell them about Jack's well off parents, "I don't wanna be with him. I'm just doing this so that you and dad will finally believe me that it's not Stewy's baby. That's all I want from him and then we can both go back to living our separate lives. I've got no problems about being a single mother. So the less I hear about needing a man off you and dad, the better"

Sammy spotted that the elderly woman in front of them was ease dropping on the conversation and had thrown a dirty look their way. Sammy was having none of it, "excuse me love. Have you got a bleedin problem about my daughter here being knocked up?. Or is it the fact she's being an independent woman and going it alone?. I can't wait to hear which, because you've been listening in long enough"

The old lady turned away and pretended not to care about the verbal abuse she'd just received. Yvonne was now mortified, "please mam. I just want a quiet day. I'm nervous enough about tomorrow. I can see dad or Dermot getting pissed and ruining the whole bloody thing"

Sammy thought she had a better idea, "fuck those two then. Me and you could meet him somewhere besides home and I'll do the reporting back. Give them my honest opinion on him"

But Yvonne had her reasons to do the meeting at home, "that won't do. I need dad and Dermot to meet him. Both of them still think I'm lying. Even you have your doubts. If they had it their way. Dad would have me marry Stewy, and Dermot would get me to demand a high level of child support. Just because Stewy's making a few quid off his paintings now, doesn't mean he'll still be doing well in a few years. Think most of the attention he gets is down to his injuries and less about his shitty paintings. I've seen four year olds that can paint better"

Sammy moved forward with the queue, "ain't that the truth. But you know these rich snobby types. They see something in his shite that we don't. And they're willing to pay for it. He should be giving you a cut of the profits. If it wasn't for you, he wouldn't be the success he is now"

Yvonne had already heard this same bullshit off her father. But that had been even worse, because he was quoting from an article in the local paper. They'd interviewed Stewy about his sudden fame during the pandemic crisis and how his paintings were selling for thousands at a time. In the interview they asked him what had brought his mind and body to a place were he felt his only root of expression, was art?.

The little wanker had poured his heart out about the love he felt for Yvonne and how his heart was so lonely without her. He then felt it acceptable to tell the reporter than his injuries were received while trying to cross the road to get to the woman who broke his heart. No fucking bloody mention about all the two timing he was at with one of her friends. No, he was the victim and the local women lapped it up. Now, even on two crutches, Stewy was still pulling women. But now they were better looking and more intellectual than the usual type he went for. The little prick had landed on his feet once again.

It was then that Yvonne spotted her friend Jamie coming down the street. But she wasn't alone. Sarah walked alongside her and the two of them were laughing and joking as they approached. Jamie had been trying to stay on the good side of them both, hoping that the long term friends would finally bury the hatchet and talk again.

Jamie spotted her friend in the queue and stopped to say hello, while Sarah moved away to a safe distance. Most likely still afraid of the threats that Sammy threw her way over the last few months.

Yvonne just ignored her and smiled at Jamie politely, "you joining the queue for Penney's as well?"

Jamie noticed the amount of people behind her friend in the queue, "we were thinking about it. But I'm not sure if it's worth the hassle"

Sammy was listening into the two girls talking and had an idea, "just join us here. No point in you going all the way to the end"

But Jamie knew there was one big flaw with that plan. She leaned in a little closer to speak, "but what about Sarah?. I can't leave her out of this. We've been planning this since they announced the reopening"

Yvonne looked past Jamie and noticed the awkward stance of Sarah, who kept trying not to make eye contact. She didn't wanna keep hating her friend anymore and held out a metaphorical olive branch, "wanna join us in the queue Sarah?"

Sarah was surprised to hear her friend's kind offer, "you sure about this?"

Yvonne wearily nodded, "I don't wanna keep fighting with you Sarah. We were good friend's for too long. So do you wanna join the queue with us?"

Sarah didn't need to be asked twice, as she jumped in beside her old friend, "I'm really sorry about what happened with Stewy. I never meant to hurt you. I hope you know that"

Jamie was relieved as well, "at least I don't have to keep going between the pair of you. Too much fucking hassle"

Sammy had her own opinion on it and she wasn't one to keep it to herself, "friends shouldn't be fighting and falling out over men. There's plenty more cock in the sea girls. Why fight over one in particular"

"That's fucking queue jumping", shouted a middle aged woman from behind them.

The four women turned around to face her. But all of them knew that the only person they needed to speak for them, was Sammy. She held up her fist to drive her point home, "and this is a fucking fist. You'll be meeting it if you keep mouthing out of you. Have you got that?"

The middle aged woman backed down and fumed silently, while the four women went back to men hating and the usual, they're only all bastards, conversations. It was like old times again. A relief for Yvonne, if she was brutally honest.

Three quarters of an hour later, the four of them finally got through the door and swarmed out quickly in the hope of finding a bargain. On the plus side, the clothes shop wasn't as busy as the old days. This two metre distance rule, had its perks at times. Yvonne was drawn to the baby clothes. There was some selection on show. But unfortunately she had held off from knowing the sex of the baby. It seemed like a good idea to leave a little surprise at the end. But there was still no harm in stocking up on the white baby vests and socks. You couldn't go wrong with them. No matter what sex the child was.

Yvonne moved onto the underwear sets and felt strangely tempted to buy something special for the following day. She knew it was a stupid idea. But still she picked up a skimpy underwear set and placed it in her basket.

Suddenly her mother appeared from around the corner of the clothes rail, "I knew you'd buy sexy underwear for tomorrow. You do have a thing for this fella"

Yvonne tried to hide her embarrassment and annoyance at her mother, "I'm buying the fucking things for me, and definitely not for any fucking man"

Jamie and Sarah appeared around the other side of the clothes rail. Jamie had a big smile on her face, "did someone mention something about fucking men?"

Yvonne threw her eyes up and took a deep breath, "I'm bringing the father of my baby up to the house tomorrow and mam thinks I'm trying to buy sexy underwear for him. Can you please tell her different?"

Jamie had heard about the quick shag her friend had at the back of the nightclub, but one particular detail still stood out, "is this the guy with the porn star sized cock?"

Yvonne was hoping this detail wouldn't come up, but unfortunately it had and her mother picked straight up on it, "porn star sized cock. What size are we talking here?.

Yvonne's cheeks went red, "it doesn't fucking matter. It was just sex like any other time"

But Jamie remembered the details. Even showing the length with her hands and then the girth, "he's suppose to be about ten inches and as thick as the handle of a baseball bat. Wouldn't mind that inside me for one night. Wouldn't matter if he couldn't operate it properly. I'd just do all the work. I'm used to that with the men I end up with"

Sarah picked up a little pink slip and knickers set, "think you'd look great it that one instead"

Yvonne couldn't agree more as she wearily took it out of Sarah's hand. She missed having her sound advice when it came to buying clothes, "thanks. You always had a good eye for fashion"

Jamie was glad to see her friends talking, but couldn't help getting in a sneaky dig, "pity both of you hadn't as good of taste in men"

Sammy nodded in agreement, "ain't that the fucking truth"

Chapter Fourteen

The Rock estate didn't have the best reputation. It was well known for having a high level of crime and anti social behaviour. The type of place that most people would warn others about not entering under any circumstances. Jack couldn't boast about never being there before. A rather drunken night out in his youth had led him to going home with an older woman of near fifty. Quite difficult to have a decent shag, when her teenage kids kept coming into the room moaning about their own personal problems. Even worse when she started to answer them. Even though she was semi naked on top of his wanting erection. Thankfully he had shot his load and got out of there pretty quick.

But a few years later he'd fallen into the same trap again, being dragged back to the Rock estate. It was in a caravan that sat on the front driveway of one of the houses. This time the sex had been drug fuelled. He could still remember the caravan rocking and creaking as he fucked the ass off the fine little thing he'd pulled that night. Then they'd both fallen asleep and the next morning Jack had woken up with a clear head. He figured it would be best for him and his one night stand, if he just snuck out of the caravan and made his way home. All was going well until he stepped out the door and met the girl's mother on the front driveway. The same woman he had screwed a few years earlier. Ended up having to enjoy an uncomfortable breakfast with both women that morning. Thankfully that was the last time he'd seen either of them again.

Jack was patiently waiting at the entrance to the estate for Yvonne to make an appearance. He drew some funny looks from the locals as they past him by. He'd given up trying to be polite with the odd greeting. The elderly being just as rude as the younger people. The only thing that brought a smile to his face was the large boulder next to him and the graffiti that covered it. He'd always been a fan of Austin Powers. Nice to see that he wasn't the only one.

Yvonne appeared around the corner of a nearby street. Jack couldn't help but admire her beauty as she approached. Short denim skirt and white blouse. Her long red hair bouncing as she walked. He could feel a tingling downstairs, "whoa, you look absolutely stunning today"

Yvonne didn't break a smile, "are you trying to say that I normally look a wreck?"

Jack struggled to backtrack quickly, "no, I didn't mean that, I was just saying you look more stunning than usual"

Yvonne eyed him suspiciously, "okay then. I'm not doing this just for you today. I normally dress like this anyway. So get that thought out of your head"

Jack felt it best not to say too much, "never crossed my mind"

Yvonne seemed happy with his answer and led the way back to her home.

As they walked through the estate, Jack couldn't help but notice the amount of broken glass that was scattered around the ground in different areas. There was also piles of half burnt rubbish, that was packed up against alley walls. But that was the least of his worries as he spotted the stares from a gang of young teenagers. They didn't look like they took too kindly to outsiders.

"Working on your next child already?", roared one of the group.

Yvonne just stuck her middle finger up at them, "at least I can keep my legs shut. Unlike your mam whose fucked most of the fellas in this estate. I'm gonna buy her knee pads this Christmas, so that she won't cut her knees again while sucking fellas off out the back of the pub", she had her say and walked on with a confident stride to her step.

Jack rushed along beside her, for fear he'd get separated from his guide if he wasn't careful.

The two of them turned onto Yvonne's street and as usual the guards were breaking up a domestic disturbance between an elderly couple who lived at the start of the dead end street. The extremely old man was being put into cuffs, as he roared abuse at the officers, "fuck the lot of you. Wasting fucking time on stuff like this, when you could be out catching real criminals"

His elderly wife stumbled out the front door with blood gushing from a wound to her head. She held up a poker and started to beat her restrained husband over the head, "let's see how you fucking like it", she roared, while raining down blows on mostly her husband. But the two guards took some of her aggression as well.

Yvonne just ignored them and walked on, "fucking embarrassing to see people carrying on like that. Drags the whole look of the street down.

Jack had to admit that the street was in better shape than most of the estate. Most of the houses had been renovated from the original structure and now had a unique look to the front. Some had bay windows, while others had splashed out to get the original red brick work pebble dashed. Which made the houses stand out from the original council style.

"This is my place", Yvonne walked up the driveway of her home, past a white Ford Mustang car that was parked in front.

Jack stopped to admire the vehicle. He'd never seen one outside of a car show, "does this belong to your dad?"

Yvonne opened the front door, "it belongs to my brother. He won it in a fight"

Jack was surprised at how well kept it was, "is your brother a boxer?"

Yvonne hated when people took an interest in her brother's career. But she answered anyway, "he does mixed martial arts. Fought some fella who couldn't pay up after losing. So they agreed on the car instead. Won't let anyone else fucking drive it. Not even my father. Now come on inside and I'll introduce you"

The interior of the house was well kept and clean. Ornaments and paintings, lined the walls or sat on pieces of old furniture, that would have looked better suited in an antique shop. Yvonne led him into the kitchen. Jack noticed how the room looked like it had only be renovated recently. The fixtures seemed to be fairly new.

A weird noise of something rubbing against glass, distracted him. He looked up to see an older blonde woman, scrubbing away at the glass with a bucket of soapy water. Her large cleavage moving vigorously, as she scrubbed the window roughly.

Yvonne tapped the glass to get her attention, "hey mam. He's here"

Sammy stared in the window at Jack and smiled, "heya love. I'll be in, in a minute. Just let me finish off this", and with that, she went back to scrubbing.

Yvonne opened the fridge and took out two bottles of supermarket branded beer. She twisted them open and handed Jack one, "you'll probably need this before you meet my lot"

Jack couldn't see what she was worried about, "your mother seems nice though"

Yvonne took a much needed seat at the kitchen table, "it's not my mother that I'm worried about"

Sammy came in the backdoor, pulling off her big yellow latex gloves, "glad that's done. They've been bothering me all morning. You can never do enough cleaning on a home"

Yvonne had been hearing her mother say that for many years and honestly it was getting pretty irritating, "yes you can. It's just you don't know when to stop"

Sammy would hear none of it and turned to Jack for some moral support, "you look like you're from a well kept household. How often does your mother clean the house?"

Jack was embarrassed to admit the truth, but blurted it out anyway, "my mother has a cleaner in three times a week"

"A cleaner", Sammy was visibly surprised by his answer, "I'd love one of them here. Maybe then I wouldn't be so fucking knackered tired. You wouldn't believe how wrecked I do be some days. Your parents must be well off?"

Jack hated to talk too much about his family's wealth. He felt it always brought out a negative reaction from most people, "my father has his own building company, so he's done pretty well for himself over the years. You've got a beautiful home yourself", he felt it best to throw the attention back off himself.

Sammy was delighted with the compliment, "thanks very much. Just wish my lot were as appreciative as you are"

Yvonne wasn't in the humour for her mother to start making everything about her again, "I do appreciate what you do mam. Please don't start"

"I'm not starting", Sammy took a beer from the fridge and sat down next to Jack at the table, "So, what about all this baby stuff?. How you feeling about becoming a daddy?"

Jack felt like a rabbit in headlights, "not really sure if I'm honest. Had never any plans about becoming a father, up until now. It's come as a pretty big shock"

Suddenly the backdoor opened and in came Yvonne's father Bernard, struggling with a rather heavy gym bag, "fuck this thing weighs a lot", he dropped it on the floor with a large bang. He looked up to see a strange young man sitting at his kitchen table, "whose this young fella?"

Yvonne threw her eyes up in disbelief, "I told you the other day dad. It's the father of my baby. His name is Jack"

Bernard wiped his hands on his pants before putting his hand out to greet the young man, "Nice to meet you son. Take it you're the fella that's hung like a donkey?"

Yvonne threw her mother a dirty look. She'd only discussed that with her the night before and already it seemed to be up for open discussion.

Sammy just shrugged her shoulders, "you shouldn't be embarrassed love. I wouldn't if your father was hung like that"

Yvonne covered her ears in the slim hope that it would block out her mother's words, "please god don't talk anymore. I don't need to hear about dad's bits"

But Sammy wasn't bothered as she turned to the young man with a big smile on her face, "so are you really hung like a donkey?"

Jack was strangely finding himself at ease around Yvonne's parents, "I've been told that in the past"

Sammy went a little red in the cheeks, "take that as a yes then", she turned to her daughter, "you see. He's not embarrassed to talk about it"

Bernard gave up on his bag and sat down at the table. Lighting up a cigarette and blowing the smoke into the air above them, "so enough about the size of this fella's dick. I'd like to know what's gonna happen from here on in", he turned to Jack, "how are you planning on doing right by my daughter?"

Yvonne quickly cut in before Jack had a chance to answer, "I've already told you dad. I'm doing all this alone. Jack is just here to prove to you two that the baby has nothing to do with that wanker Stewy. I've got no problem with going ahead as a single mother. Jack here has a bright career in front of him, so he hasn't time to start a young family. All I'm asking is for you two and Dermot to support me in my decision. That's all"

Bernard seemed to deal with his daughter's words like water off a duck's back, "okay then. It's your decision at the end of the day", he turned back to Jack, "hope you're gonna stick around for a while and have a few beers with me?"

Jack couldn't see any harm, "okay then", they all seemed like nice people. A far cry from the image that had been long seared into his mind over the years.

Bernard got up from the table and started to struggle with the heavy gym bag again, until finally a better idea came to mind. He turned to Jack, "any chance you can help me with this thing?. Need to get it upstairs to the hot press"

Jack jumped up from his seat and lifted the bag with ease off the floor and threw it over his shoulder, "you lead the way and I'll get it there for you"

Bernard opened the door into the hallway, "thanks for this. My back isn't able for all this heavy lifting anymore"

Jack was just happy to help. Anything to get him away from the flirty looking mother in the kitchen. He had a sixth sense for knowing when women wanted to fuck him and that vibe was radiating off Sammy something shocking. Normally it wouldn't bother him to shag an older woman like her. But he felt it wouldn't help the already awkward situation in any way.

When Yvonne was sure the two men were out of ear shot. She leaned across the table so that she could speak more discreetly, "what's in that fucking bag?"

Sammy lit up one of her special cigarettes, "think he was collecting a few parcels of cocaine today. He's only holding onto it for a few days"

Yvonne's jaw dropped, "for fuck sake mam. Last thing I need is for Jack to find out about what dad does for a living. Why did he have to collect it today of all days?. He knew this was happening", still didn't surprise her that he put his own needs before her's once again.

Sammy didn't even look fazed, "money is money love. Can't stop working, just because we have visitors. Don't be worrying. It'll be out of sight and out of mind, soon enough"

Somehow Yvonne didn't share her mother's views on all of this, but said nothing further for a quiet life.

Upstairs, Jack watched on as Yvonne's father moved floorboards from inside the bottom of the hot press. He knew there was something dodgy about all this, but he chose to say nothing and just watched on.

Finally Bernard had cleared enough room for the bag and stood up out of the way, "right. That's ready now. So if you can just lower the bag into this space and that'll be great"

Jack did as he was told and stood back and watched as Bernard covered the opening in the floor back up with the lumps of floorboards, until finally you wouldn't even know the bag was there.

Bernard got up and stood back to look at his handy work, "that's that done. Think we deserve a good drink after that. Come on downstairs and you can tell me more about yourself", he started off down the staircase as if what they had just done was just another normal daily task.

Jack looked back once more at the hot press. He couldn't help but wonder what he had just helped hide under it. Even more worrying. The gym bag was now covered in his finger prints. He tried to push these fears to the back of his mind and followed Bernard downstairs, whilst making a mental note to ask Yvonne about the suspicious bag, when he got the first chance.

Chapter Fifteen

The afternoon had been long and the conversation was getting repetitive. Bernard constantly complained about the black lives matter protests around the world. Calling them a bloody disgrace when it came to showing respect for the elderly and the social distancing rules. Jack had been tempted to admit that some of his best friends in college were black, but he felt it wouldn't help the already awkward situation.

Sammy could see their guest was uncomfortable and tried to steer the conversation back on track, "it's a shame you two aren't willing to give it a go. You'd make a cute couple"

That was the last thing Yvonne needed right now. Her mother trying to do a spot of match making, "for god sake mam. Please don't start. I'm happy being on my own and Jack has a girlfriend already", the words were only out and she already regretted them.

Bernard looked like he'd had a heart attack and his head was only beginning to realise it, "fucking hell love. You never said you were the other woman"

Yvonne tried to hold her temper in, "I didn't know he was with someone. So don't start. These things happen and that's that"

Sammy dragged on her special cigarette, "these things do happen. At least you're both being adults about it.

That's ten times better than the way Dermot carries on with his kids. He never bloody sees them"

Bernard had heard enough and got up from his chair, "I'm just going in the den for a bit"

Sammy suddenly had a bright idea, "you into boxing Jack?"

Bernard wasn't happy where this was going, but said nothing.

"I use to box in college", Jack replied, "won a few awards and all"

Sammy pointed at her husband, "well this is the Louth championship winner. Three years in a row. You should have seen him with his fists back then. I'd get fanny flutters from just watching him in the ring", her mind was wandering to those wonderful sex filled days.

Yvonne hated it when her parents talked about sex. Especially when they had company over, "please mam. Jack doesn't need to hear about your wild sex days"

Sammy got back on track with her train of thought, "anyway. Bernard has heaps of boxing trophies that he won over the years, you should see his collection", she looked up at her husband, "bring him in and show him all your stuff. You love showing them off"

Bernard finally gave into his wife's demands, "okay then", he turned to their guest, "would you like to see my collection?"

"Sure", Jack got up off the couch and followed him into the other room, leaving the mother and daughter alone to talk.

Sammy wasn't one to hold back, "you like him more than you're letting on"

But Yvonne wasn't giving in that easily, "cop on. I just brought him here to keep you and dad happy. Besides, you heard it for yourself, he's got a girlfriend already. No need for another one like me in his life. I'm happy to go it alone. So please let it go mam"

Suddenly Dermot marched in the door, like a man on a mission, "let what go sis?. And where's this fella of yours. Wanted to see him for myself"

Sammy handed her son the last of her special cigarette. Only way to calm him down at night, "your father is in the den with him. Showing him all the trophies he won over the years. The fella used to box himself"

Dermot fixed the belt on his low hanging jeans, "better go get a look at this fella", and with that he disappeared out into the hallway after the other two.

Yvonne lay back into the couch and wondered if this day could get any worse.

The den was a raging fire's wet dream. Wall to wall wooden panels and heavy wooden cabinets that would keep a good bonfire going for hours. Inside each glass panelled shelf where various trophies or framed photos that commemorated Bernard's achievements over his early years.

Jack was impressed. He'd never received one trophy for all his years as a boxer, "what age were you, when you retired?"

Bernard sat down in a heavy wooden office chair with large squeaky wheels on the base, "I think I was about twenty nine. That probably sounds young, but when you feel the muscles going, you're better off giving up before the comedown arrives. I'd seen too many of my friends have very high profile defeats. I didn't want to be like one of them. Better to get out while you're still at your peak. Did you have many professional fights yourself?"

Jack was starting to feel like his sporting career wasn't much in comparison to Bernard's. Unfortunately there was no way of making his own fighting past sound any better, "I just fought people in the college. I was never good enough to be put on any of the teams. Probably for the best. Would have just embarrassed myself even further. Lost more fights than I won"

Bernard tapped the side of his head, "it's all up here. The body is only a small part of winning. But if you're in the right frame of mind against an opponent, you can fucking take down anyone. Trust me. I've gone up against many a tougher opponent. But I took them down each time. You know why?"

Jack wasn't in the humour for such bullshit boasting. But played along anyway, "why?"

Bernard tapped the side of his nose, "I'll have to get you in the ring and show you"

Dermot barged in the door like a bull in a china shop, nearly knocking over a trophy cabinet, "heard you two where in here", he looked Jack up and down, "so this is the fella who got my little sister knocked up. Shot the golden load, as they say. How's it going?", he put out his hand to greet Jack.

Jack was good at reading people's body language and this new fella was screaming male dominance. He was gonna do everything to make him feel small. Jack figured it best to play along for the moment, "it's going great. Your father is just showing me his trophy collection. Quite impressive. Hear you're into the professional fighting as well"

Dermot did a bit of mock fighting footwork, "mixed martial arts all the way baby. Gonna be the next Conor McGregor someday. You mark my words. But I used to box before that"

Bernard's mood dampened upon hearing his son's boasts, "you could've of gone far in the boxing ring, if you hadn't of let your temper get in the way" he turned to Jack, "he ended up getting a five year ban from the sport. Tried to do a Mike Tyson on some poor fella's ear"

Dermot didn't even look bothered that an old allegation was being thrown his way again, "his ear just fell into my mouth. That's all. Didn't even know it was there until I bit down"

Jack noticed a flaw in Dermot's excuse, "what about your gum shield?"

But Bernard had heard this story many times before, "that mysteriously fell out of his mouth as well"

It was at that moment that Bernard had, what he thought, was a brilliant idea, "how about we set up the ring and have a quick boxing match?"

Jack glanced at his watch for effect, "I have to head off soon. Haven't time to be going anywhere else"

But that didn't deter Dermot, "we don't have to go anywhere else"

Jack was totally confused. They were in a mid terraced house with little room to possibly house a full size boxing ring. But for fear his bluff was about to be called, he tried to think of another excuse, "I haven't the right equipment"

Now it was Bernard's turn to help, "I've got loads of spare stuff in the shed from all the coaching I do. Should be something in there that fits you"

Dermot's smile went a tad sinister, "you see. Nothing to stop us now"

Surprisingly it wasn't long until Jack found himself out in the garden, dressed in somebody else's sweaty shorts and with two fairly battered boxing gloves on either hand. Turns out the boxing ring was made up of long elasticated cords that ran from the fence on either side of the garden. While the other two sides were made up by the heavy wooden fencing that looked like there wasn't much give in them, if he was thrown roughly in there direction. It definitely wasn't a regulation ring. But he felt it best not to point out that detail.

Sammy and Yvonne, sat on the bonnet of a broken down car, that was parked in the unusually long back garden. They seemed even more eager for this fight to happen.

Sammy's eyes were staring down at Jack's crotch area, "better be careful you don't fall out the leg of them love"

Jack suddenly felt a little self conscious and discreetly checked if his dick was on show. Thankfully it wasn't. But now he was way too aware of it falling out from here on in.

Suddenly, blaring music started to come from the garden shed. It was an old 2unlimited song that used to be used by sports teams around the world. Dermot marched out of the shed. He was wearing uncomfortable looking tight shorts that showed off his package. He banged his gloves together as he readied himself for the fight ahead, "I'm ready to take you down"

Jack wasn't even sure what the fuck was going on anymore. But he hadn't time to think as Bernard climbed into the ring and pretended to be the referee. He waited until the two young men were beside him and went through the rules. Finishing off with, "right fellas. I want a fair game and both of you fight to win", he quickly made his escape to a safe distance.

Sammy held up her phone and played an automated dinging bell noise, "go for it lads"

Jack felt this was some kind of weird masculine test. All he had to do was prove he wasn't a totally useless fighter and go home with a bit of self respect. That was easier said than done when it came to the opponent he was facing down. Dermot looked like a man who had put people in hospital in the past. Jack didn't want to add to that list. Only thing for it was to go in with the first punch, which he totally missed, as Dermot side stepped his assault and nudged him into the wooden fencing. The pain soared through Jack's shoulder from the impact.

Dermot banged his gloves together as he waited for his opponent to recover, "you okay?. Or do you need a little break after that minor injury?", his mocking tone was clearly evident to everyone watching.

Yvonne was getting sick of her brother's asshole behaviour, "cop the fuck on and fight fair. Or I'll jump in there myself and take the fucking head off you"

Dermot laughed at his little sister, "you'll probably give me a better fight than your boyfriend here"

Yvonne wasn't sure what annoyed her more, "he's not my fucking boyfriend"

Jack had heard enough and went in for an unexpected dig. But Dermot spun on his heels and thumped him hard in the forehead, sending Jack falling to the ground in a heap. Made even more painfully since the ground was made up of loose gravel and broken glass from a busted windscreen.

Dermot stood over him in a taunting stance, "think you've had enough mate. Maybe you should quit while you're ahead"

But Jack wasn't going out that easily as he stumbled back to his feet, "I'm only getting started mate"

Dermot seemed delighted with the reply, "okay then. Think it's time to move my game up a bit. Not go so easy on you from here on in"

Jack knew he was gonna regret what he was about to say next. But the words had to be said. If only to save his ever dwindling male ego, "I wouldn't have it any other way"

Dermot jumped around the ring like a highly allergic man with a bee up his arse, "come on then. Try and hit me. I'm gonna give you a shot. All you gotta do now is take it. One good hit and I'll go down like a ton of bricks. Seen it done before. Anyone can get the golden shot. Just like you did with my sister. Now prove to me that you're the right man to be the father to my nephew"

Jack reckoned there was more to this so called male bonding session. There was only one thing for it. He had to get at least one good right hook on this asshole. No matter what the comeback was for his actions. So he lunged at his opponent with his right fist raised. Dermot didn't move and took it hard on the chin.

But as Jack stood back to see how well his attack had worked, it became pretty obvious that it had no affect on Dermot, who just smiled and said, "my turn", before following through with a major blow, aimed towards Jack's head.

All Jack could do was shut his eyes and lean into it. A poor attempt to take the full force on his forehead. Rather than an eye socket. Last thing he wanted was to have to explain a black eye to his parents. Then everything went dark.

There was a lot of screaming and crying. People's panicked voices filled the air, but strangely Jack wasn't too bothered. It was actually nice down there on the ground. No one hitting him or talking shit to his face. His eyebrow felt pretty sore, but he was sure that was where he'd just been punched.

But as his head began to get clearer. Jack slowly realised that the person screaming, was actually Dermot. But why would he be screaming?. He opened his eyes to see Dermot on his knees beside him. He was clutching his hand tightly, while Bernard unwrapped the tape that kept the gloves on. He then pulled it off his son's hand, to reveal a wrist that was pointing at an unnatural angle.

Bernard was quite calm about it all, "think you've fucked up your hand son. Told you about hitting people so hard, but you never fucking listen"

Dermot squeezed his forearm in a poor attempt of stifling the pain, "it can't be fucking broken. That wasn't even a hard punch. It's probably only sprained"

Bernard looked his son dead in the eyes, "it's fucked son. We need to get you to the hospital and get you sorted out", he helped Dermot up off the floor, before noticing the cut across Jack's eye, "that's a nasty gash. You'd better get Yvonne to sort that out". He turned around to his daughter, "you deal with your fella and I'll get your crying baby of a brother to hospital"

Sammy came out of the kitchen with a tea towel filled with ice, "this should keep down the swelling a bit", she stuck it onto her son's hand without any warning, which made him roar out in pain, "don't be such a baby", she scolded.

Yvonne helped Jack to his feet and walked him over to lean against the car, "you okay?", she stared into his pupils to see were they responsive.

All Jack could see was Yvonne's beautiful face. He so wanted to kiss her there and then, but resisted temptation. Old feelings were starting to come to the surface once more, and part of him didn't want to fight it.

Chapter Sixteen

Thankfully Yvonne's parents had both decided to bring their son to casualty. It was a journey that suited them both since a friend of theirs was having a house party and they'd been invited along. It worked in their favour that no one was allowed to stay with Dermot in the hospital.

This left Yvonne and Jack to have some alone time, as she tended to his badly cut eyebrow. Most people would have gone to hospital with such an injury, but Yvonne's family was used to dealing with them, so normally did the bandaging themselves. The two of them sat at the kitchen table. Both drinking beer and picking at a bag of bacon flavoured crisps.

Jack was struggling to not look deep into Yvonne's eyes, as she dabbed his eyebrow with disinfectant, "wasn't expecting today to end up like this"

Yvonne tried not to smile, but it still crept up onto her face, "I figured they were gonna do something embarrassing, but not fucking this. I was meaning to ask you, how come you're only finishing college now?. Thought most people normally started into third education, straight after secondary"

Jack hated being asked this, but for some reason he wanted to share with her, "when I was finishing up in secondary school, there was a lot going on at home with my brother Oliver. He was causing a lot of trouble for my parents at the time. Constantly vandalising stuff around the house and threatening to kill himself any time they went away for a few nights. I used to lock my bedroom door at night. That's how afraid I was of him. He was totally unpredictable"

Yvonne was visibly shocked by these new revelations, "Jesus Christ. He sounded like a fucking nightmare. Did your parents never get onto him?"

Jack took a swig of his beer for some alcohol induced courage, "They didn't like to push him too much. He'd been abused at an early age by a local priest. Used to give him lifts home from secondary school and touch him up in the car. Oliver was only thirteen at the time. Fucked him totally up. We didn't find out about what happened until he was nineteen. Still didn't make him any less of a nightmare"

Yvonne couldn't believe what she was hearing, "hope you got that bastard of a priest arrested?. Sick fucks like that shouldn't get away with abusing kids", her blood was boiling already.

Jack couldn't agree more, but that wasn't the difficult part of the story he was trying to get across, "the priest was a few years dead when we found out about it. I don't think my brother wanted to drag up the past again. But when it all came out, it just made Oliver even more unbearable to live with. My parents had already been turning a blind eye to his temper and violent outbursts, which were taken out on different items around the house. But after the abuse came out, he just seemed to get worse. One time he even threw darts into my leg and said it was an accident. Something I definitely don't believe to this day. He was aiming for my leg all along"

Yvonne could see Jack was hurting and prompted him to move on, "what happened in the end?", she began to carefully place butterfly stitches over his cut.

Jack was struggling to hide the pain, "Anytime my parents went away, it wouldn't matter if it was a foreign holiday or just in Ireland, he'd be on the phone, threatening to kill himself. He'd even widened the doorway into the attic when they were away one time. He said it was to make it easier to get in and out of it. I reckon it was because he wanted a clear drop when the time came. And that day did come. Parents were away in Spain. I had gone to stay in a friend's house. Came home to find him hanging out of the attic door. A leather belt around his neck. It broke his neck instantly. He didn't feel a thing. Imagine putting that much effort into your own suicide. Who really does that?. It just made no sense to me. Still doesn't. Sometimes I wonder was it all just an excuse to torment my parents even further. People keep telling me it's terrible that he died. I just can't feel it. No one seems to be aware of the mental torture that he put my mother and father through. It wasn't good for their health. I reckon the stress brought on my dad's heart attack. It was either them or my brother who was gonna end up dying. And I'm probably gonna sound bad for saying it, but I'm glad it was him. All that pain, suffering and anger, ended right there. We finally had our life back", his eyes began to water slightly as he spoke. Things he had suppressed a long time ago, had bubbled to the surface.

Yvonne rubbed Jack's cheek gently and kissed him on the forehead, "I'm sorry to hear about your brother. But how did that lead to you going to college late?"

Jack tried to force a smile, "my parents felt it was all too much on me. Finding him and all. Thought that starting college would be a lot on me. So they sent me off to Australia for a few years. Living in a house on the beach. Working in an Irish pub. It was a great laugh. Think I really needed that time away. Get my head together"

When Yvonne thought of Australia. There was one thing that came to mind, "bet you ended up with your fair share of good looking, tanned, bikini wearing women"

Jack felt it best not to admit the full extent of his shagging about abroad, "I had my share", he rubbed Yvonne's face gently, "but none came close to you", he leaned in and kissed her gently on the wanting lips.

Yvonne responded positively, as she put her hand around the back of his head and pulled his lips closer. Tongues met as hands began to open each other's clothes.

Yvonne pulled Jack's boxer shorts down at the front and his erect cock shot out, "fucking hell. That stood to attention fast", she began to wank it gently, before sliding forward on the chair, to get down on her knees.

But Jack stopped her before she got a chance, "you shouldn't be on your knees in your condition. I'll stand up for you instead", he stood up and let his boxers fall to the floor.

Yvonne smiled up at him, "always the perfect gentleman, but I'm far from a lady", and with that, she began to kiss and lick the shaft of his cock. Working her way down the side towards his large hairy balls.

Jack looked down at Yvonne at work and hoped she wasn't one of those girls who do nothing else but kiss and lick. That would be a negative tick against her. But that wasn't a worry anymore as she deep throated his erection with an expert skill, bringing her lips down his ten inch shaft and back up again.

Yvonne came up for air, "fuck. Been a while since I had a length like this in my mouth", she went back in for another go at it. Sucking hard on his cock with the skill of a woman who was far from innocent.

Jack's knees began to buckle with her efforts. He held onto the edge of the table as he felt his load about to fire already, "oh fuck. I'm about to cum", and with that, he shot his load straight to the back of her wanting throat.

He fell back onto the chair exhausted, "my god you're good. Now it's your turn", he lifted her by the ass up onto the table and pulled her knickers off to reveal a neatly shaved pussy. Two beautiful pink lips stood between him and her pleasure palace. He separated them gently with his two fingers and leaned forward, sinking the tip of his tongue deep inside her. Felt strange to have her belly sitting on the top of his head. But the pleasure had overridden the situation. He could feel her body tighten as Yvonne reached her first orgasm. That just drove him on to keep the pleasure going. Making her cum, three to four more times until her pussy was soaking wet.

Jack stood up between her legs and showed off his fresh erection, "I'm ready to go again"

Yvonne turned her whole body around on the table. So that her ass was now next to the tip of his cock, "I want it from behind"

Jack wanted to be sure before he stuck it in. He'd made that mistake in the past before and it had ruined the night, "your sure you wanna try anal?"

Yvonne never looked around. Just nodded her approval as she waited for the pain, "just go for it. Get something to lube my ass up with"

Jack couldn't spot anything off hand. But the fridge seemed the best place to look. He opened the door and spotted the butter straight away. He pulled the tub out and began to liberally cover her tight hole in Kerry Gold. Putting his fingers back in for another good handful. Which he worked deep inside her carefully. Soon it felt loose enough for him to enter.

Each inch went in slowly, until his whole length was buried deep inside her tight ass. He began to pump away, being careful not to put too much pressure on her swollen stomach. Yvonne moaned with delight with each thrust deep inside her. She began to play with her clit. Soon another orgasm made an appearance. Followed by another and another. It wasn't long until they were both exhausted. But each wanted more. It didn't take long for Yvonne to suggest they retire to her bedroom. The night was only getting started.

Chapter Seventeen

Casualty was surprisingly quiet that night. People seemed to be still avoiding hospitals and doctors for fear their waiting areas were filled with Corona germs, that had a good chance of killing them. Dermot wasn't complaining. Made his unwanted visit pass a lot quicker than expected.

He was used to being in hospital. Normally with a friend who'd been injured on a night out. Very rarely was he injured himself. Except for that time when someone tried to cave in his head with a baseball bat. Mistaken identity in the end, but that didn't make the thirty stitches required, hurt any less.

So far tonight, Dermot had gotten an X-ray for his wrist and now he was just waiting on the doctor to tell him how fucked it was. This was the last thing he needed. Out of action for a couple of months at the least. No way could he chance going into a fight against an opponent without being a hundred percent. He cursed the air as his mind wandered back to that brutal punch that should have done more damage to Jack, rather than himself. He couldn't help but wonder if this was a sign that he was past his prime. Mixed martial arts was a young man's game and he was on the wrong side of thirty. He'd no qualifications and had put all his time and energy into training. But it would all be for nothing. All he was good for now was doing the door of some shitty old men's pub off West Street. Dermot was washed up and he knew it.

Suddenly the curtain opened and in walked a young black nurse. Her short black hair, made her stand out to Dermot. He had always found that short fuzzy look quiet appealing. Even though he'd never admit to it.

The nurse put down the tray of equipment she was carrying and put on a pair of disposable gloves and a face mask. Dermot was just waiting for her to start speaking with some terrible broken English. He hated when he had to deal with someone like that. There should have been a law that if you had to work with the public, then you should be able to speak properly. But there was no way that was ever gonna happen with all the equal rights shite nowadays. Dermot reckoned his father was right when he said that Ireland wasn't for the Irish anymore. That its cultures was dying along with the elderly and what was left of old Ireland would be sold off to the American tourists. It was only a matter of time.

But it didn't take Dermot's eyes long to find something to focus on. The nurse had a beautiful big arse that he couldn't keep his eyes off. Strange since he was never into large bottomed women in his younger days. Especially not black ones either. But there was something about this one that caught his eye.

Dermot finally looked up and came face to face with the smiling nurse. He'd been busted, "sorry about that. Just thought I seen something on the floor beside your foot"

The nurse just laughed, "take it that it was somewhere around my general ass area"

Dermot couldn't help but notice that she had a thick north side Dublin accent, that seemed out of place with her skin tone. He couldn't help but ask, "are you originally from Dublin?"

The nurse opened up a few pieces of necessary packaging before turning to look at his wrist, "I am. Why do you ask?"

Dermot felt a little bit put on the spot. He didn't know whether to admit to his reason for asking, "it's just your accent is pretty distinct"

The nurse held his wrist tightly, "this is gonna hurt for a brief moment. You ready?". But before he had a chance to answer, she positioned his broken wrist into the right place with a large cracking noise.

"FUCK", Dermot roared loudly as the pain shot up through his body and ran around his head like a little angry Olympic runner.

The nurse just carried on with her work. Bandaging his wrist carefully with some heavy material that would hold it in place, "my parents moved over from Nigeria before I was born. My father's a doctor in the Maher in Dublin. Think he hoped I'd be a doctor as well. But I'm happier with the nursing profession. You get to work with the public more"

Dermot was still trying to pretend he couldn't feel anymore pain. Even though he was pretty sure he ruined that illusion with the initial roar he let out. But he still tried to carry on with the act, "how are you finding it working here now since all this virus shit started?"

The nurse attached a few clips to keep the bandage in place, "the virus shit, as you so elegantly put it, has been a major pain in the ass since it started. Have to wear these face masks all the time. Which isn't the easiest for me with my asthma. But it looks like it's the new norm"

Dermot reckoned he hadn't long until their little private moment would come to an end. This meant less time for him to turn on the charm. Black girls were never his first choice for dating. Then again, when he thought about it, the only black girl he'd been with before was a one night stand on a trip to London. But actually dating one was a whole other kettle of fish. He knew his parents would give him shit, but that still didn't put him off.

"What's your name?", Dermot nervously asked. Totally unlike his usual confident attitude.

The nurse smiled awkwardly at the attention being bestowed on her, "why do you wanna know my name?"

Dermot hadn't been expecting that answer, "it's just that I'd like to know who my own little Florence nightingale is"

The nurse grabbed his sling and began to attach it carefully, "my name is Julia. Not exactly an elegant name like Florence nightingale"

"Julia", Dermot ran the word over his lips, "beautiful name for a beautiful lady. Just wish I could see that beautiful smile to go with it. Any chance I could bring you out on a date?"

Julia fixed her face mask carefully for fear it was about to fall off, "I'm not getting much time off these days. When you don't have any kids or dependents. The powers that be, will keep asking you to come in all the time. I don't mind. Better to be kept busy when the whole world is going to shite around you"

Dermot was surprised by her brutally honest attitude, "bet the terminally ill patients love your bedside manner"

Julia laughed loudly, "sorry. Sometimes I just can't help myself. I can have a bit of a morbid outlook on life. Not great in my profession", she fixed his sling to the right height and stood back to admire her handiwork, "that's you all sorted now. I'll get one of my coworkers to sign you out of hospital and then you can get home.

But Dermot wasn't letting this moment go so easily, "when do you get a break tonight?. I don't mind waiting around if it means getting to talk to you a little more"

Julia tidied up her equipment and placed it back in the plastic tray, "why are you so obsessed with asking me out?. I'm sure there's plenty of women throwing themselves at you"

Dermot moved his new sling around and tried to get it in a comfortable position, "I'm not gonna lie to you. I do get my fair share of young ones throwing themselves at me, but they couldn't even hold a candle to a beautiful woman as yourself"

Julia mulled his offer over for a moment, "what does, hold a candle to, mean?. I've heard people saying it before, but I just don't get it"

Dermot had never thought about it himself either, "not really sure. It's just something that people say. So are you interested?", he wasn't letting the conversation move off topic.

Julia looked around at her coworkers mulling around in a hurry as they tried to keep up with the steady flow of patients, "okay then. You seem like a nice fella. I'm getting a break in about forty minutes. Wait outside the casualty entrance and I'll come out to you. Now I better get off. Work never stops these days"

Dermot smiled widely as he couldn't hide his delight, "I'll be there"

Julia grabbed the tray and headed out of the cubicle, before turning to smile at Dermot once more. She then closed the curtain and left him alone to enjoy his little achievement. He'd pulled many women in his years on this earth. But for some reason, this felt different. Dermot liked Julia in a way that he hadn't felt with women in the past. He just hoped he wouldn't fuck up this opportunity with his mouth. Slow and steady the whole way was all he kept telling himself. It was time to rethink his pulling and flirting technique before they met for coffee. That was gonna be a major task within itself. But it was a task worth taking on.

Chapter Eighteen

Warm, muscular, hairy arms. That was all Yvonne could feel wrapped around her naked body, as she woke up in her own single bed. It was only then that she was reminded of one of the few things she missed from her relationship with Stewy. The sex had been great. Some of the nights out could be fun and a good laugh. But everything else in that relationship was mostly shit. But those morning hugs were the one thing she truly missed.

Now Yvonne was in the strong arms of Jack. She looked up at him still sleeping. Drool running out of the corner of his mouth as he gently snored. The poor guy was worn out from the rampant sex session they had taken part in the night before. It was easy to tell that there had been no condoms involved, as the dried cum on her body had hardened and tightened the skin in that area. A shower was definitely needed. Yvonne slowly edged her way out of the bed, threw on a dressing gown and escaped to the bathroom.

The warm water felt nice as it ran over her naked body. Yvonne rubbed her baby bump gently and prayed that the child belonged to Jack. It didn't matter if they weren't gonna be together. He would still be a better name to give the child when they finally came asking. Part of Yvonne wondered if sleeping with Jack again, had been a terrible mistake. Last thing she wanted was for him to think that there was a chance of things moving on from there. Only time would tell.

Back in the bedroom, Jack awoke to see a number of semi naked male pop stars on the bedroom walls around him. For a brief second he had a worrying feeling that he'd slept with a teenager the night before. But it wasn't long until the truth hit Jack and a strange relief washed over him.

Yvonne came back into the room. She was drying her long red hair with a towel, "see you're finally awake. That was some night we had"

Jack lifted the blanket to show off his already growing erection, "we could have another go this morning if you like"

Yvonne was tempted. But her fanny was still sore from the night before, "think we should leave last night were it is. It was fun. But today's a new day and we have to move on. You can go back to that girlfriend of yours"

Jack hadn't been expecting such a reaction and sat up in the bed, resting both his feet on the floor and pulling her body towards him. He gently opened her light gown and caressed her naked body, "it doesn't have to be the end. We could carry on seeing each other. See where things go"

Yvonne was enjoying the feeling of his strong hands on her body. She wanted him so badly. But years were passing her by and one thing couldn't happen again, "I'm not gonna be the other woman. I've done it before and it ended in tears. You've got a bright future in front of you. Please go back to Cork and live your life. Let this finish on a high this morning. You came through for me when I asked for help. I never even thought you would do that. So please just go live your life and forget about me"

Just as Jack was about to protest Yvonne's decision, the bedroom door was flung open and Sammy stuck her head in, "anyone for breakfast?", it was then that she noticed his throbbing erection, "fuck, that's some size"

Jack quickly covered his crotch with the duvet, "sorry about that"

Sammy was busy making a mental note of that image, "don't apologise love, I can see now what all that squeaking was about all night"

Yvonne's cheeks went red, "fuck sake mam. I didn't know you could hear us"

Sammy started to back out the door again, "heard you!. Your dad wanted to come in and oil the bed, during the night", she shut the door tightly behind her.

Yvonne sat down on the bed and tried to decide whether her mother was taking the piss or not, "were we really that noisy?"

Jack put his arm around Yvonne's side and kissed her on the cheek, "maybe we just got lost in the moment"

Yvonne looked him dead in the eyes, "and that's all this is ever gonna be. One beautiful moment that'll never be repeated again. Now let's go down and have some breakfast and then you'll have to get going"

Jack reluctantly nodded in agreement, "okay then", he began to pull on his clothes while secretly seething inside. He didn't want it to end like this.

Downstairs, Sammy was frying a pan filled with sausages and bacon. The toaster popped up once more. She loved to make sure that her family was well fed each day. Bernard sat at the table, reading through his Sunday tabloid. He wasn't one for reading many words. The briefer the article, the better. Only highlight of the first few pages was the variety of photos of what skimpy outfits Maura Higgins had on that week. She was one fine young lass with her fanny flutters and potty mouth. If he had of been twenty years younger, he'd be definitely tapping that fine little arse.

"Will you stop drooling over that fucking Maura one again", Sammy past by the back of him as she placed the plate full of toast in the middle of the kitchen table.

Bernard quickly turned the page, "I wasn't fucking drooling over her. I was reading the bloody article next to her"

Sammy went back to the cooker and carried on with her frying, "didn't look to be much of an article next to her.

Or are you struggling over three or four sentences these days?"

Bernard was getting sick of his wife's smart attitude. Just because her sex drive was drying up didn't mean that his was as well, "what's wrong if I was taking a look?. I'm a man and a man likes to look at young, good looking women"

Sammy didn't turn her back and just kept on cooking, "answer me this then. How would you like it if old fellas were ogling over photos of Yvonne like the way you are now?. Knowing that there's probably guys wanking over her sexy photos. You'd fucking crack up and don't even deny it"

Dermot shut the paper altogether and fired it onto a nearby sideboard, "you just can't help but ruin everything for me. Why do you have to say stuff like that?"

Sammy smiled to herself. Knowing that her husband couldn't see it from where he was sitting, "just like to keep you on your toes love"

Yvonne came in, followed by a nervous Jack, who wasn't too sure how her father was gonna take the fact that he stayed over and may have even heard their entire sex session, "good morning", he nervously smiled.

Bernard looked Dermot up and down, "definitely a good morning for you. Judging by the noise of that bed last night. I would of asked if you used a condom, but there's no point now since the damage was done months ago"

Yvonne threw her dad a dirty look as she sat down at the table, "don't start. Had to listen to you and mam at it for years. Not easy to forget all those nights"

Sammy tipped the contents of the frying pan, out onto a large plate and placed it in the centre of the table, "dig in you lot", she sat down herself and opened the tub of butter, before spreading a thick layer of the creamy stuff out onto her slice of toast.

It was only then that Jack remembered what he had used the same tub for, the night before. Last thing he needed was for one of Yvonne's parents to find his pubes on their toast. There was only one thing for it.

Jack picked up two slices of toast and began to cover them in an uncomfortable amount of butter. He could see the strange looks from everyone else at the table. He felt a reason might be necessary around now, "I just really like my butter"

Bernard picked a few sausages off the plate for himself, "that you do. Can't be good for your cholesterol, but each to there own"

It was only then that Yvonne copped on what Jack was up to. She nudged his side discreetly and whispered in his ear, "think you were enjoying filling me up with that stuff, rather than yourself"

Jack took a large bite of his extremely buttery toast, "not as much fun this morning, as it was last night"

Suddenly the back door opened and in strolled a tracksuit wearing Jamie. Her hair and makeup was perfect as always. She hated to be seen out without her face on, "morning all. Hope you don't mind me calling around so early. Over to see how Yvonne got on", it was only then that she noticed Jack sitting at the kitchen table, "looks like it went a lot better than expected"

Sammy didn't even look up from her breakfast, "you should have heard the bed going last night Jamie"

Yvonne threw her mother a dirty look, "don't start mam"

It was only then that Jamie recognised Jack, "you're the guy who slept with my mother and sister"

Sammy suddenly looked up from her breakfast, "fucking hell. Looks like Jack has ridden his way around this estate already"

Jack felt he should say something in his defence, "that wasn't planned. It was only after I slept with your sister, that I knew they were related"

Bernard took a slice of toast and began to butter it, "Jesus Christ Jack. You're definitely a ladies man. How the fuck did you end up with Yvonne here?"

Yvonne was now struggling to keep her temper in check.

Jamie grabbed a slice of toast and went to take the butter. But Yvonne discreetly shook her head. Jamie nodded in Jack's direction. Yvonne gave a little nod. Jamie put the butter back and grabbed the marmalade instead, while mouthing the word, "again?"

Yvonne wearily nodded.

Jack had seen this secret conversation as well and leaned in close to Yvonne, "again!. How many times have you been lubed up with the family butter?"

Yvonne didn't want to get into it, "not as many times as you think"

Thankfully Dermot marched in the door and grabbed the toast out of his father's hand and began to munch away happily, "good morning everybody"

Jamie noticed Dermot's injured wrist, "fucking hell. What happened to you?"

Dermot nodded over at Jack, "broke my fucking wrist off his hard head. But the lord works in mysterious ways. I've met a woman"

Sammy threw her eyes up, "please god don't tell me that you picked up another drugged up slapper in the casualty waiting area again"

But Dermot had been working up to this big announcement, all the way home, "she's a nurse mam and her father is a respected doctor up in Dublin. We're going on a date later in the week. I definitely think this is the one"

Yvonne's brother pissed her off something shocking at the best of times, but it was nice to see him happy all the same, "well I hope it works out for you", and she meant it.

Not long after, breakfast was over and it was time for Jack to say his goodbyes. Yvonne walked him out to the edge of the estate and they both stood awkwardly for a moment until Jack felt he had to say something before it was too late, "is there any chance I could see you again?"

Yvonne crossed her arms tightly, "you'll probably see me the next time you're out grocery shopping with your mam"

Jack wasn't sure if Yvonne was taking the piss of him, "not like that. I'd love to spend more time with you. I love being around you"

Yvonne looked down at the discarded chewing gum covered pavement below them, "it wouldn't work out. I'm not even sure if this child is yours. You've got a girlfriend and we both have totally different lives and plans for the future. You're better off going back to Denise in Cork and getting your life back on track.

Maybe I'll see you around in a few years. You can tell me how things are going for you and vice versa. Thanks again for yesterday. Hopefully that's the end of my parents giving me shit over Stewy"

Jack thought of one more last ditch effort to win Yvonne over, "what if I wasn't with Denise. Would you go out with me then?"

Yvonne leaned in and kissed him on the cheek, "but you are with Denise and I'm not gonna be the woman who breaks the two of you up. I'm not in the humour for more hassle in my life. Besides, from the way your mother looked at me in the supermarket. I could tell that I would never live up to her high standards. So let's draw a line under this and move on. See you around sometime", and with that, she walked off back towards her house.

Jack watched on until Yvonne disappeared around the corner. Part of him wanted to go after her. But instead, he turned and started the long walk back into the centre of the town. He needed some time to think and also quench a strong urge for a barista made coffee.

Chapter Nineteen

Many people had said over the years that falling into old
habits was bad for your health. Mentally, physically or
both. But Jack couldn't give a shit about all that. The last
few weeks at home, had been a total pain in the arse. The
only outlet he had was online sex with Denise and
hanging out with Paul most nights. As for his home life,
it had been fairly minimal. For people suppose to be
under a lockdown. His parents still had a pretty good
social life. Throwing parties at least once a week in the
family home. Going to other people's houses, to do god
knows what. Jack preferred not to know too much about
their private life.

Tonight was gonna be another one of their weird parties
and Jack had already planned to spend most of the night
over in Paul's house. Yes, he probably could get a quick
shag off another one of his parent's frustrated friends.
But he couldn't be arsed with all that anymore. Even
wanking off to a naked Denise, was losing its appeal.
Only one woman kept running through his thoughts and
she had shut down any chance of them going any further.
And it wasn't for the want of trying. He'd tried to call
numerous times. But Yvonne had just diverted it to
message minder. Texts had gone unanswered. Jack had
been tempted to visit her in work. But felt he might be
crossing a line that would just push her away further.
Maybe Yvonne was right. That it was a wonderful night
of sex and that it should be just left there. But Jack didn't
want to. There had to be a way to show Yvonne how he
felt. But what?.

Jack found himself roaming around his house aimlessly. He passed the door with the pink unicorn on it. His parents had said that it was just for storage. Cagey as always about its contents. He just left his curiosity there and moved on. But as he passed by his brother's old room, Jack could hear his mother crying from inside the closed door. Part of Jack wanted to move on, but against his better judgment, he pushed it open and stepped inside.

Jack found his mother sitting on the edge of his brother's single bed. The sheets still the same as the day he died. Ellen suddenly noticed her son's appearance and wiped the tears from her eyes, "I'm sorry. Your father keeps telling me not to come in here so much. Says it only upsets me. He's right you know, but I just can't help it. I like to feel close to Oliver. This is the only way I can achieve it", she glanced around the sparsely furnished room.

There was some specialist books on a shelf. A laptop and some runners stacked in a corner. Oliver had never been one for belongings. The walls were painted yellow with no framed pictures or mirrors on any of them. It was always strange to sit in there for any length of time. It was out of place to the rest of the house. Jack found it hard to be in there. Especially since his brother used to tell him to get out of his room all the time. It just didn't feel right to be sitting in there, "I know you like feeling close to him mam, but is it helping you?. These last few years have been tough enough on you, and sitting in here is just opening up old wounds"

Ellen ran her fingers over the worn duvet cover, that was once jet black, "I've just been thinking about him a lot lately. He's stuck in my thoughts so much these days. I keep wondering how he would have dealt with this pandemic. Then again, he left the house so rarely, that he probably wouldn't have even noticed"

Jack smiled to himself, "he would have been in his element with all this", he pulled a book off a nearby shelf and held it up for his mother to see.

Ellen read the title, "a survival guide to the apocalypse. Jesus, he really thought ahead. Oliver would have loved all this then"

Jack put the book back up on the shelf, "maybe you and dad should get away for a few days. The hotels are back open and I really think it would do the two of you good"

Ellen thought about it for a moment, "but all the leisure facilities will be shut in them. Even the spa treatments and nail bars. Be no point in getting away with all those things shut"

But Jack wasn't giving up that easy, "mam, you always look amazing", he lied. No point in bringing up the over use of her plastic surgeon at this time, "you don't need to worry about all that. Just go and enjoy yourself for a few days. I'll hold up the fort here"

Ellen got up off the bed and fixed her short dress back down, "might say it to your father when he gets home. Go stay somewhere with a nice area to go walking in. The Bloomfield in Mullingar would be nice at this time of the year. Just have to get through this party later. Suppose I can't change your mind about staying tonight?"

Jack was definitely not putting himself in a position to be hit on again that night, "I'm sorted thanks. Paul's expecting me and we've got plans"

Ellen headed out into the hallway with her son following at a distance behind her, "can't believe you two are getting on so well again. Thought when you hit secondary school. That it was definitely the end to your friendship. Paul was always just too quiet for you. Not being rude. But I reckon he would have held you back if you had of gone to the same secondary school. Thank god for small miracles"

Jack found his mother's words highly insulting to his friend. But somehow he knew she was right. But there was no way he was gonna admit that, "he's not that bad. Think you just have too much of a high standard when it comes to your friends, as well as the rest of the family", he'd never said that openly before and now he wasn't too sure if this was the right time to bring it up.

Ellen marched down the stairs and into the lounge to check on the cleaner, who was dusting down all the bottles behind the bar, "how are you getting on Maria?. Hope all is nearly finished for tonight?"

Maria was an elderly woman who looked like her brightest years were long behind her, "nearly all done. Only the kitchen left and I'm finished"

Ellen nodded her approval and turned back to finally address her son's accusation, "I only ever wanted the best for me and my family. I'm not gonna apologise for that. I've always encouraged you and Oliver to better yourselves. That's just being a good parent and I'm never gonna feel guilty for that. Now I need to go get ready for tonight", she marched off once more in the direction of her giant walk in wardrobe.

Jack had thought he was finally getting somewhere with his mother again. But she'd dashed those chances against the jagged rocks that protected her emotions from the rest of the world. There was no getting through to her. She'd built up a lifestyle and false personality, that was never gonna be torn down with anything less than a wrecking ball.

Chapter Twenty

Work was surprisingly busy that Thursday. The queue
stretched across the front of the shop and the check out
was constantly filled up with lonely old pensioners who
just seemed to want a quick chat with anyone who was
willing to listen. Yvonne was always popular with the
older community. She was happy to listen to their
problems and complaints about the changing world
around them. This didn't sit well with her manager, who
constantly got onto her about holding up the queue. But
Yvonne would just ignore their moaning and carried on
with the way she normally did things.

Being nearly six months pregnant, had meant that the
bosses had moved her onto the tills for ten items or less.
Yes, this sounded a lot easier. But the reality was much
different. The queue of customers was always longer.
Mostly pensioners who came into the shop everyday, in
the hope of some much needed human interaction. The
virus hasn't put them off from what their mind needed
most of all.

An old regular was filling Yvonne in on his latest health
scare. Mr Gibson was a constant worrier about his health
and had a habit of regularly darkening his local doctor's
waiting area. Now that he couldn't visit it as often as he
wished, he was finding it difficult to fill the gaps in his
week that those long visits to the doctors took up, "if you
seen my legs. They're swollen to some size these days.
You wouldn't believe the bloody size of them. Rang the
doctor and he wouldn't even see me. Made me go

through all my ailments over the phone. Then had the cheek to send my prescription by bloody email to the pharmacy. Who does that?. You can't diagnose someone without seeing them. That's like asking you to have your baby while the doctor talks you through the process on the phone. It's just not right"

Yvonne glanced down at her ever growing belly. She hadn't expected it to get so big by six months. But more and more people were pointing it out to her and it was really starting to piss her right off, "think child birth and your leg problems are two totally different things. Your doctor is only worried for your safety", she noticed her disgruntled manager, pointing at her watch. Yvonne knew it was in her best interest to move the old man along, "right Mr Gibson. That's you sorted. Hope you have a nice day"

Mr Gibson grabbed his two small shopping bags and lifted them off the counter, "thanks for listening. I'll see you tomorrow. Look after yourself", he shuffled off into the busy crowds of people that bustled around the street outside.

Yvonne couldn't help but feel sorry for Mr Gibson. The world just wasn't made anymore for people of his vintage. The times of respecting the elderly, had long since died out. It just didn't seem fair. Those that helped build this world were now cast aside to make way for the next generation. Their achievements and hard work never recognised. Just seen as a burden and a drain of the much needed resources in these modern times.

Even the virus only seemed to attack pensioners. Which left the millennials caring even less about their elderly relatives well being. Yvonne's own grandparents had long since died. A victim to their own addictions. Two of them dying from the effects of smoking. Another one was an alcoholic. While her grandfather Ben had been badly beaten up over a gambling debt. He ended up dying from his injuries a few weeks later. No one had been arrested for the crime. The guards reckoned it was hired help brought in from Dundalk and there was nothing they could do to the men he had owed money to. It was bullshit when people said that everyone would be punished for their sins in the end. There was nothing fair about this world. The sooner people recognised that truth about life. The sooner they could start looking out for number one.

Yvonne sprayed her till and counter with disinfectant, before wiping the whole lot down with some heavy blue tissue. If it was up to her, she would have only cleaned the bloody thing, once an hour. But the other staff were watching and she had no choice but abide by the rules.

Yvonne was still busy cleaning when somebody hobbled up to the counter and placed a bottle of vodka down in front of her. It was her favourite brand and all, Smirnoff. It had been a long time since her last shot of that. And it was gonna be a long time more.

Yvonne looked up and came face to face with a sad looking Stewy. No way was he there for any other reason, than just to talk to her, "what the fuck do you want?"

Stewy fixed his crutches in a position that made it a little more comfortable for him to stand on the spot, "I just want to talk to you. That's all. I fucked up with Sarah. If you can forgive her. Why can't you forgive me as well?"

Yvonne scanned the bottle through, "because she's easily led. I know what you're like when you turn on the charm. Sarah always thought you were a catch. How far from the truth was she. Don't even know what I ever seen in you"

Stewy placed his card on the chip and pin device, "can we at least talk?. I just want to get a few things off my chest and hopefully you can do the same thing. What do you say?"

Yvonne noticed her manager throwing dirty looks her way and pointing at her watch. She had to get rid of the annoying little prick before she got in trouble again, "we've nothing to talk about. You made your choice when you stuck that hairy sausage of yours in Sarah's fanny. And god only knows who else you fucked behind my back. Now get the fuck out of here before I get in trouble"

But Stewy wasn't one to back down in a hurry. Especially when he had his heart set on something, "I'm not going fucking anywhere until you talk to me"

Yvonne had no other choice but give into his demands, "I can't talk here. But I'll be off for a break in fifteen minutes. Meet me in the back alley and we'll talk"

Stewy's smile grew bigger with delight, "just like the old day. Meeting you out back for a quickie and a fag"

Yvonne threw him a dirty look, "you'll be getting neither off me. Now get the fuck out of here, before I get in trouble"

Stewy looked over at Yvonne's manager and roared, "THIS IS THE BEST FUCKING WORKER IN THE SHOP. YOU'VE GOT A GOOD ONE HERE", he then turned back to his ex, "always like to put a good word in for you. Talk to you soon", and with that, he hobbled off on his two crutches. His bottle of vodka, stashed neatly into his jacket pocket.

Under different circumstances, Yvonne would have punched the head off him. Unfortunately now was not the time for that.

Twenty minutes later, Yvonne was beating Stewy around the head with her fist, "you stupid little bastard. Fucking making a show of me as always. You can't fucking help yourself", it felt strangely good.

Stewy dropped his crutches as he tried to shield himself from the blows, "for fuck sake Vonny. Calm the fuck down. I just wanted to chat"

Yvonne punched him in the stomach, "this is the only talking I want to do", she grabbed the bottle of vodka out of his jacket pocket and took a large mouthful. The burning sensation was strangely calming, "that tasted fucking lovely", she continued to drink the bottle until there was only three quarters left of the litre bottle.

Stewy grabbed the bottle out of her hand, "you can't be fucking drinking that much. It's not good for the baby", he then continued to drink a large amount of it himself.

Yvonne opened up her cigarette box and took out one of her mother's special cigarettes. She lit it up and enjoyed the feeling of the smoke filling her lungs, "that feels fucking good"

Stewy sat down on a nearby window ledge and tried to ease the pain in his damaged legs, "is that a joint?"

Yvonne blew the smoke into his face, "don't start. I'm trying my best to cut back. It's not fucking easy. Besides, what do you care?. It's not your fucking child anyway"

Stewy lit up a cigarette and tried to accept her cruel words, "I still love you. That hasn't changed. Please take me back. I don't care if the child belongs to another fella. I just want to be with you. And I'm not a waster anymore. I'm making loads of money with my paintings. If things keep going up. I'll be able to buy us a nice house in five years. And on the plus side. I can't fuck around because I can't move that fast on these legs. I'm like your man in misery. So what do you say. Will you give me a second chance?"

Yvonne was tempted. Yes she wanted to go it alone. But the offer of security and money, was tempting. Stewy hung around her circles, so life would pretty much be the same. But that image of him lying next to Sarah was running through Yvonne's mind. She couldn't go back to that life again. Fearful of coming home each day and hoping he wouldn't be balls deep in another one of her friends.

"I'm gonna do this alone", Yvonne replied, "I've no need for a man anymore in my life. Especially not one that's gonna be fucking around on me all the time. I'm too old for all that shit. Just go find someone else. With all that feckin money, I'd say you have all the women in the estate after you"

Stewy reached out and held her hand, "I only want you. Please give me another chance?. If I fuck up again. I won't even stop you leaving. Please Vonny"

Yvonne hate to be called that. It was a stupid nickname, that he thought up during sex, "please don't call me that", she knocked his hand away.

Stewy knew he was losing Yvonne and tried one last ditch effort to win her back, "who are you gonna get to do all that kinky stuff you like?. Not all fellas like the spanking, anal and domination sessions. I get you. I know what you like and vice versa. That's hard to find these days. We're kindred spirits. You can't deny that"

Yvonne flicked away the last of her fag and took the vodka from him, "yes we had something good. But good times have to come to an end sometime. We're both about to hit thirty. It's time to move on. You'll find someone else and hopefully I will someday. But for the moment, all I'm worried about is this baby inside me. And until the day this child is grown up and gone out into the world on their own. Only then will I start worrying about my own needs again", she took another slug from the vodka bottle and handed it back to him, "I better get back inside before I get in more shite. Please don't make a show of me again"

Stewy struggled up onto his crutches, "why are you doing this?. We're meant to be together. Can't you feel that?"

Yvonne opened the fire exit door and stepped inside. She glanced back briefly at her ex, "that feeling is long gone Stewy. See you around sometime", and with that, she shut the door tightly behind her, before taking a deep breath.

Had she done the right thing?. There was a nagging doubt there, that just wouldn't shift. The closer to the birth of her baby, the more Yvonne doubted her abilities to raise a child on her own. Only time would tell.

Chapter Twenty One

The night in Paul's had started off pretty slow to begin with. But it didn't take long for the two of them to come up with a great idea to put an ounce of grass into a brownie mix, that they had found at the back of the press in the kitchen. An hour later, they had eaten their brownies with a nice cup of coffee.

All had started off so well. But Paul had decided not to mention that the grass they had used, was a super strong strain, that he'd illegally imported from the Netherlands. They were now that fucked out of it, that the only place they could think of to ride out the buzz. Was on the sloped roof of the house. Their heads lying uncomfortably on the dirty slates, as the feel of gravity pulling against the lower part of their bodies. Seemed to feed the buzz even further.

"Remember when we used to jump off the ladder?", Paul's mind has been wandering back to the past. Memories slipping in and out of his thoughts.

Jack was still staring up at the stars above them, "was a good laugh until you broke your arm. Your parents weren't too impressed either. Wouldn't let us hang around together for weeks after that"

Paul didn't like to come down too quickly off his buzz, so lit up another well packed joint, "my parents were just over protective. Thought you were a bad influence on me"

Jack lifted the joint out of his friend's hand and took a long drag, "would of helped if you had of bloody told them, that it was your feckin idea to jump off the ladder in the first place"

Paul laughed to himself as he remembered that minor detail, "oh yeah, I probably should have told them that. Think I was just afraid of getting in trouble"

Jack handed Paul back the joint, "don't know why you were afraid of them. Your parents were always sound. The angriest I ever seen your dad was when we smashed the windscreen of his car. Even then he just went a little red in the face and went off and drank a couple of whiskies"

Paul was more interested in talking about something else, "I think my parents are both having an affair. Or maybe they both know that the other one is seeing someone else and they're just choosing to ignore it"

Jack didn't want to give away how much he knew about his friend's mother. He figured it would be better to play dumb, "why do you think that?"

Paul just stared up to the clear sky, "found all this stuff on my father's computer. He's been meeting young male escorts. Looks like he's been doing it for years now. And it's not even fucking cheap. He's spending about two hundred euros at a time. And by the looks of it. He's paying for the service about two or three times a week.

You should see the photos they send him. All twenty something year olds with muscular bodies and covered in baby oil. I never once thought he was gay until I found that stuff"

Jack was lost for words. He had been worried that Paul was gonna find out about his mother's swinging behaviour. But this new revelation had just blown that out of the water, "I wouldn't have thought it either. Are you gonna confront him about it?"

"What's the point. Would just make their shitty marriage more visible. My mother is no better. I don't want to sound like I'm starting. But I think your parents are covering for her. All these parties she goes to in your house. I reckon it's just a cover for her to carry on with some fella. Or a woman. I don't even fucking know them anymore. Maybe I never did. Hard to tell these days", Paul held up the joint, "sometimes I think this shit is making me paranoid. But then I always remember those lyrics by Kurt Cobain"

Jack wasn't sure what Paul was on about, "what lyrics were they?"

Paul took another pull of his joint, "just because your paranoid. Don't mean they're not after you. No truer words were ever spoken. Pity he blew his fucking brains out. He probably had a lot more to say. All those words of wisdom that were still rolling around in his head. All ended by a shotgun blast to the head. Amazing how the force of a load of little metal pellets. Can end your life in one quick motion. Nearly did it myself one time"

Jack sat up and stared at his friend in disbelief, "fuck off. You're taking the piss"

Paul didn't look his friend's way, "had the gun in my mouth. Safety was off and all I kept thinking about. The one thing that held me back from pulling that trigger. Was the sneering I imagined myself getting from the bullies that tormented me and the girls that mocked me behind my back. Something inside my head kept saying, don't give the fuckers more ammo. Prove them all wrong"

Jack folded his feet in under himself, "what do you mean by prove them wrong?"

Paul finally sat up and faced his friend. His eyes lacking any emotion, "I once went into the toilets in school and found this chart on the wall. It counted down the five students in the school that were most likely to kill themselves before they'd finished. I was number one. Hurt like fuck to read it. But I reckon it made me stronger. Made me fight back against the assholes of the school. Not physically. But I found other ways to piss them all off. Might have gotten beaten up for it. But I still felt better in the end. That was the main thing"

Jack was glad that his friend had found the strength to fight back against the bullies. Made him feel even more guilty about deserting him at an early age. At a time when his friend probably needed him most. But there was one part of Paul's story that didn't make any sense, "I don't remember your dad ever owning a gun"

A pang of guilt was visible on Paul's face, "remember when we were young. You showed me were your dad kept his shotgun. I snuck into your garage. I remembered where the key was hidden. That was another reason why I was glad that I didn't do it. Wouldn't have been fair on your parents to find another suicide on their property. I'm really sorry for doing that"

Jack had never seen this side of his friend. He wanted to get angry. But somehow he couldn't, "I'm glad you didn't. Just please don't ever tell my parents that story. I don't think they'll be as understanding. Even though they didn't find Oliver. He was already taken down by the time they got home. Sometimes I wonder if he purposely did it on that specific day. Because he knew I'd be the one to find him. One last fuck you after death. I wouldn't have put it past him. Something he'd do. Just to fuck with my head"

Paul had heard a lot of details about Oliver's death. Mostly filtered down from his mother, "he didn't even leave a note"

Jack had normally been able to let such things wash over him. But not this time. His eyes watering, "there was a note. But I destroyed it"

Now it was Paul who was speechless, "what the fuck. Why would you do that?"

There was no way of making the truth sound any better. You can't polish a turd, "it was full of his toxic ramblings. Blaming my parents for everything and anything that went wrong with his life. Calling them terrible things. Accusing them of being compliant in his sexual abuse. Said they could have done more to stop it from ever happening. He laid into me as well. Telling them they'd have to put all their eggs in one basket with me. As if I was gonna be this major disappointment when I was older. You wouldn't believe how much I wanted to prove him wrong. Thought I was getting there and all. But now I'm stuck in this mess with Denise and Yvonne. Bet that fucker is looking down right now. Laughing his fucking head off at me. He always was one sadistic prick"

Paul got up and sat on the arc of the roof instead, "fucking hell. I didn't know that. He really had a lot of hate built up inside him. How are things going with Yvonne. Did she answer any of your calls yet?"

Jack moved up beside his friend. Pretending not to find his new seat as uncomfortable as it actually was, "she's cut off all contact. Don't know what to do next", he couldn't help but feel this whole night was turning into one big depression fest, "fuck this. Is there something else we can do to lighten this night up?. We've turned down a bad road and we need to steer out of it"

Paul thought for a moment, "there is one thing we could do"

Fifteen minutes later, the two friends were huddled around a large upturned plastic shopping bag, as Paul tried to light the alcohol soaked cotton wool that was attached with metal wire underneath, "keep the bag held out wide. We need it to fill fully with smoke for this to work"

Jack found the whole process overly complicated, "why don't you just buy those Chinese lanterns they sell in shops?. Be a lot easier than all this feckin hassle"

Paul blew the flame gently, in an attempt to get it to take hold, "where's the fun in that. Besides, they aren't as well made as the ones I build", he checked the cords that held on the GoPro underneath. Switching it on before letting it hang below the growing flame.

Jack watched on as the bag ballooned out with the heat and smoke from the flame. Suddenly he could feel it rising between his fingers, "think this is trying to take off"

Paul carefully took the bag off his friend and raised it a little higher in his hands, "just need to hold onto it for a bit longer. You want these things to fly up fairly fast. I know it's not that windy. But even a mild breeze can blow these things arse ways and they end up catching fire", he gave it a few more seconds before letting it go, "that should do it"

They watched on as it raised up into the air at a surprisingly fast speed. It didn't take long until the wind caught it and sent it gliding in the direction of town.

Jack wasn't sure what their next move was, "how do we get the camera back?"

It was only then that the horrible truth dawned on Paul. He put his hand in his jeans pocket and pulled out a small plastic box, "I forgot to put the bloody tracker on it. Looks like we'll have to do this the old fashioned way", he ran towards the garage and threw open the door. He flicked on the lights and disappeared inside.

Jack watched on as their homemade lantern drifted away, "won't be long till it's out of sight. If you've got a plan. You better get it into action soon"

Paul came back out with two dusty old push bikes. One was bright pink and had a basket on the front. The other was an old yellow racer. He handed the pink one to Jack, "up for a cycle?"

Jack got on the small bike, "I'm just glad it's dark. State of this bloody thing"

The two of them cycled off after the lantern. Their legs already struggling with the poorly oiled chains.

Three quarters of an hour later. They were still chasing the lantern. Which was now drifting over Drogheda. Jack had already gotten a volley of verbal abuse from a nearby gang, who took offence to his choice of bike. He couldn't give a fuck. Ten years ago, those words would have got in on him. But age had made Jack stronger and more comfortable about his sexuality. No need to prove anything to anybody. Even his current underwear was pink. But that was just for him to know at the moment. And the openly gay shop assistant, who sold him them. Throwing Jack a cheeky little wink at the tills. That had been an awkward moment.

Thankfully the lantern started to lose height. The lower it came back to the ground. The more people that seemed to notice it. The two friends passed a couple of fellas who looked out of their heads on drugs. They were staring up at the strange object that passed over their heads.

Jack felt he should put their minds at ease, "don't worry lads. We can see it too"

One of the fellas gave them a thumbs up as they past by. His eyes still locked on the lantern as it quickly lost height with every second.

Thankfully it was over an industrial estate when it crashed down onto the ground. But that was another problem. Unfortunately the private land were it touched down, was belonging to a fertiliser company. A place with a large amount of security. High fences and cameras lined every side. There didn't seem to be a way in.

Paul fired his bike to the ground in anger, "fuck sake. Not another fucking camera lost. Those bastards aren't cheap"

Jack leaned on the fence and studied the area inside. Suddenly a spot light came on and illuminated the pair, "must be a sensor"

But that meant something worse to Paul, "that means they've probably been alerted in the security office. Better get out of here before they show up"

But Jack had an idea, "help me get over this fence. No way we're coming this far and not getting the camera back. Cup you hands and lift me up"

Paul did what he was told and bent his knees a little. Jack grabbed the fence and put his right foot into his friend's hands and pulled himself up and over the fence. He landed neatly on the other side and ran towards the fallen lantern, ripping the camera free and running back towards the fence.

It was only then that Jack realised that he couldn't get back over the fence from the inside, "probably should have thought this through a little better"

Paul spotted a brick shed, further down the compound, "see can you climb up on that. I'll bring the bikes down there to meet you"

For lack of a better plan, Jack ran towards the shed. He studied its features as he drew closer. Thankfully there was rungs up one side. Suddenly lights appeared in the distance. They were moving fast in his direction. Most likely a vehicle of some description. He wasn't waiting around to find out.

Jack jumped up as high as he could onto the rungs, in the hope of skipping the first few. Unfortunately it wasn't as high as he expected. But there wasn't time to scrutinise his own failings as an athlete, as he clambered up the building and rolled onto the metal roof. The lights were now only twenty feet away. There was no time to think about his next move, as he jumped across the fence and landed with a hard roll along the rough path outside the compound.

Paul had been watching on, "fucking hell. That was definitely some Jason Statham shite right there"

Jack jumped on his bike and turned it around to make their escape, "no time for that now. Let's get the fuck out of here before we get caught", he began peddling away.

Paul quickly followed after him, "thanks for getting the camera back"

Jack was still breathing heavily, "just hope the footage was worth all this hassle", but deep down, he was secretly loving the excitement of it all. Something he missed dearly from his younger years. If only he could get those good times back again.

Chapter Twenty Two

Since the lockdown had come into place. Yvonne's family had struggled to find new ways to keep themselves occupied. Sometimes the whole street had bingo. Other times they dragged a fold out pool table out of one of the neighbour's houses and played in the middle of the street. Every neighbour taking a turn at hitting the ball. Losing a life each time you failed to pot one.

Unfortunately tonight there was no group activities. So the family had decided to play cards. Just a pity that no one could agree on what was the best hand. Searching the internet just led to more hassle. Thankfully the hash smoke hanging in the air was keeping everyone mellow and calm. Jamie had even called over for a break from her own family problems. Ones that she preferred not to share. Not even with her close friends.

Jamie picked up three cards from the stack and discreetly checked them, "where's Dermot tonight ?. Is he still dating that nurse one?"

Yvonne threw her eyes up, "fucking hell. He's obsessed with her. You should smell the bathroom when he's getting ready for a date. There's that much aftershave splashed around in there. That if you lit a match. The whole bloody place would blow up"

Sammy was smoking another one of her special cigarettes, "you should be happy for your brother. When does he go all goofy for a woman. I think it's nice. Can't wait to meet her"

Jamie wasn't great at hiding her disappointment. She'd always had a thing for Dermot. Even sleeping with him when a little attention was thrown her way. Unfortunately she'd been knocked back as quickly. To most she was strong and confident. But Jamie was just like anyone else. It was just that she was good at hiding her true feelings. Too many years being hurt by loved ones, can lead to that.

Jamie tried to act happy for Dermot, "that's good news. What's she look like?"

In Jamie's head, all she could imagine was some supermodel who looked great in bikinis and fucked like Pamela Anderson on her honeymoon.

The other three looked at each other, as if waiting for someone else to answer. Finally Yvonne took the lead, "no one actually knows. He won't say much about her. Which is fucking weird for him"

Bernard picked three cards up and examined his poker hand, "how come Sarah is not with you two tonight?. Thought you were all friends again"

Yvonne couldn't help but feel a little bit jealous of Sarah, "she's seeing a new fella. He's suppose to own a pub downtown"

That could only mean one thing in Sammy's mind, "he must be a lot older if he owns a pub"

Jamie butted in with her own opinion on her friend's love life, "he's fifty eight. But he's really fit for his age. Now, I wouldn't go near him. But I wouldn't knock Sarah for going there"

Bernard mulled over that for a moment, "fucking hell. He's older than me. Bet his kids are older than Sarah. That won't go down too well at the next family get together"

Sammy swapped three of her cards without even looking at her hand properly. She was too stoned to care anymore. But was great at hiding it, "let's be honest here. She wouldn't be with him if he wasn't well off. I'm not knocking her. At least she's thinking of her future. Mark my words girls. Pick a fella that's gonna be able to treat you like a queen for life. Not just a princess for a weekend. See your father here. You should have seen him at the start. All charm and loving moments. That fairly feckin dried up when he got me pregnant with Dermot"

Bernard was highly insulted by this accusation, "excuse me. Who remembers your birthday every year?. And don't I always get you flowers?"

Sammy looked him dead in the eyes, "you only remember it because it's your mother's birthday, two days before. So you get a deal on buying two bouquets of flowers. And don't fucking deny it. One year you left my flowers in the shed and the heat in there dried them out. So don't make out you're all great to these two"

Yvonne could sense that her parents were about to have one of their massive arguments, "please you two. Can't we just not have one night without fighting. Jamie didn't come over to see this"

Jamie wasn't even fazed, "don't worry about it. My lot are ten times worse"

Bernard got up from the table and drank the last of his vodka off the head, "I'm too tired for all this. I'm fucking knackered"

Sammy was visibly annoyed, "what about the game?"

Bernard turned his cards over to reveal a shitty hand, "I hadn't a hope anyway. You lot carry on. See you all in the morning", and with that, he left the kitchen and shut the door tightly behind him.

Sammy just carried on playing the game as if nothing was wrong. But Yvonne couldn't let it go, "what's wrong with you two these days?"

Sammy lit up another special cigarette and took a large drag on it before answering, "it's just this fucking lockdown. We're stuck around each other all the time. The sooner the better this virus shite is over and your father can start spending more time in the pub again.

Don't get me wrong. I love him and all. But as they say, distance makes the heart grow fonder. I'm in much need of a bit of that distance right now"

Yvonne was used to her parents having little disagreements over the years. But never enough to be a concern, "it can't be that bad?"

Sammy looked her daughter dead in the eyes, "I caught him wanking off in the bathroom to a picture of that slapper Maura from love island. Now you tell me how I should take that"

Yvonne was thinking damage control as she pointed at Jamie, "not a fucking word of this is to leave this house", she turned back to her mother, "did you really have to tell us that?. Not exactly the mental image I need"

"But we all pleasure ourselves at some point", Jamie wasn't one to back down from a conversation about sex, "I fingered myself last week. Was thinking about that Leo fella who runs the country"

Yvonne gave her friend a stern look, "you do know he's gay?"

Jamie smiled from ear to ear, "not in my feckin dreams he's not. He's like a wild stallion who knows his way round a woman. But enough about my awesome fantasies. What about you two?. I'm sure you've both fiddled yourselves in the last month at the least", she nudged Yvonne in the shoulder, "I know you have for a fact. Because you only got that rampant rabbit in the mail two weeks ago"

Sammy's eyes widened, "thought you said it was a pair of curling tongs?"

The kitchen door swung open and in marched Dermot with an over confident strut, "how are things ladies?. What we all talking about tonight?"

Jamie began to play with her hair as she smiled up at him, "hi Dermot. We were just talking about pleasuring ourselves"

Dermot nudged his mother's shoulder, "take it you were telling these two about dad. I told you before mam. A man has needs. At least he's not out sowing his wild oats elsewhere. Only thing that's receiving his happy juice is the tissue in the bathroom"

Yvonne and Sammy covered their ears.

"We don't wanna hear this shit", Sammy moaned loudly.

Jamie still wanted to know more about Dermot's personal sexual pleasuring, "doubt you need to worry about wanking yourself off with all the girls after you"

A cheeky smile sprang to Dermot's face, "there's always a lady willing to offer their services. But I think those days are gone. I reckon Julia is the one"

This was news to Jamie's ears, "who's this Julia one?. Is she from the estate?"

Sammy looked the proud mother, as she answered for her son, "she's a nurse in the Lourdes hospital", she turned to Dermot, "when the fuck are we gonna meet her?. You've been seeing her a while now. Hope you're not embarrassed of us?. She might be well educated. Still doesn't make her any better than us"

Thankfully Dermot's mobile rang in his pocket. He took it out and smiled when he seen Julia's name flash up on the screen, "this is her now"

Before he had a chance to complain, Sammy snatched the mobile out of his hand and answered the call, "oh hello love. This is Dermot's mother. I'm just telling him right now, that I'm dying to meet you. Never seen my son so happy. You've really turned his head"

Dermot tried to grab the phone out of his hand. But his mother just slapped his bad wrist and got up from the table, "hold on a sec love", she put her hand over the phone, so that she could speak to her family, "be back in a minute. Gonna get to know this nice girl a little better", and with that, she headed out into the hallway and shut the door behind her.

Yvonne noticed her brother seemed to be a little on edge, "why are you so worried about mam and dad meeting this Julia one?"

Jamie couldn't help but add to that question, "are you embarrassed of her?. Bet she's ugly. That has to be it"

Dermot was quick to shoot that accusation down, "she's not fucking ugly"

"Then what's wrong?", Yvonne pushed.

Dermot took a special cigarette from his mother's box and lit it up, "it's because she's black. And you know what mam and dad get like when they're talking about them. How many times did they warn you not to get pregnant by a black man. Just because they don't want half cast grandkids. I just don't know how to deal with it. Mam might not be too bad. But you know the way dad gets. I just haven't the head for his shit"

Yvonne normally found her brother to be an irritating cunt. But her heart went out to him this time, "you shouldn't let their attitudes get in the way of your love life. I can't wait to meet her", she nudged Jamie for some moral support, "you don't think it's a big deal"

Jamie tried to hide her emotional hurt, "it's only a big deal if you make it one. If you like her. Just go for it. Your parents will get over it sooner or later"

Yvonne was surprised by her friend's well thought out words. But said nothing. Instead she continued to try and help her brother, "I'm on your side. So I'll stand up for you if either of them start. I just wouldn't break the news tonight, because they've been bickering already"

Dermot was used to hearing that, "what about now?"

"Usual shite", Yvonne replied.

Sammy came back in the door with a big smile on her face. She handed the phone back to her son and sat back down at the table, "she seems like a lovely girl. She told me to tell you that she'd ring you tomorrow. Don't know why you haven't brought her up to the house yet. But none of that matters now. Because I've done the inviting for you. Julia said she'll call up for a few drinks some night. So I'll leave that planning up to you son"

Dermot's mouth was open as he stared down at his phone. He was lost for words.

Yvonne leaned across the table with a big smile on her face, "I'll definitely be here that night"

"Me to", Jamie added, "dying to see this one as well". She wanted to size up the competition.

Dermot put his phone away and wondered how the fuck he was gonna get out of this mess. But there was one thing he was sure of. He wasn't giving up on Julia that easily.

Chapter Twenty Three

It was three in the morning when Jack arrived home from his night in Paul's house. He was hoping that his parent's party would be over for the night. But there was still laughing and the sound of glasses clinking, coming from the lounge. He carefully ran past that doorway and up the stairs towards his bedroom.

It was a great relief when he shut the door behind him and locked it tightly. Jack just wanted to be alone. He switched on the bedroom light and jumped back with fright. Someone was in his bed. She turned and rubbed her eyes. It was Becky.

Becky finally recognised him through tired eyes and smiled, "I've been waiting for you to come home", she lifted the duvet to one side, to reveal her naked body.

Jack sat down in the chair opposite the bed, "does my parents know you're in here?"

Becky posed sexily for the young man. Placing one hand behind her head, "they think I'm in the guest room. Told them I had too much to drink. But secretly I wanted to be with you again"

Jack could feel his cock growing. It was like his body was working against his brain, "I'm really tired. I've been out all day"

Becky leaned forward and began to rub his ever growing crotch, "you're a young man. I'm sure you have reserves, for such an occasion as this"

Not long after, Jack was pounding Becky's ass from behind. She was up on all fours, moaning loudly with each thrust. There was times he was struggling to keep the enthusiasm going throughout their sex session. Becky's body just wasn't doing it for him. There was only one girl on his mind.

Jack shut his eyes and began to imagine that it was Yvonne who was on all fours in front of him. Her beautiful little freckled ass bouncing off his cock. Her long red hair swishing to each side as she moaned loudly with delight. Every so often she'd look back at him. Telling him how much she loved him. Dermot moaned as he came close to shooting his load, "I love you to Yvonne"

"Who's Yvonne?", Becky looked back at him, bemused by his outburst.

Jack stopped thrusting his hips, "I'm sorry. I didn't mean to shout that"

Becky turned around in the bed and spread her legs wide in front of him, "I don't mind if you think about other women while you fuck me. Now get back inside me and finish the job. I want you to fuck me like you wanna fuck this Yvonne one"

Jack climbed on top of Becky and thrust his cock deep inside her and began pumping. She held on tightly as he pummelled her pussy with a new found interest. It wasn't long until Becky orgasmed. Several times.

When the both of them were finally worn out, Jack had rolled them up a joint each and both were now sitting up on the bed.

Becky wanted to know more about this Yvonne one, "do you really love her?"

Jack was still struggling with his feelings, "I barely know her. But she's been drawing my attention since I was only thirteen. Now she's slipped through my fingers again. She won't even answer my calls or just text me back. I know I could go to her house or the place she works. But that just feels like I'd be putting her under pressure to talk. I don't wanna do that to her. Could totally backfire on me"

Becky lay back on the bed and thought about his predicament, "has she any interests or hobbies?"

Jack could only think of one thing, "she's into writing poetry and she regularly meets with this poetry group downtown"

Becky took a long hard drag on her joint. Blowing the smoke up towards the ceiling, "well then that's the way to her heart. Write your feelings down about her. Try and make them rhyme a bit and then read them out at her group. She can't avoid you then. And if that works out. Your parents were only telling me tonight that they've booked three nights in a hotel down in mullingar. You should use that time to your advantage. Bring her out here and treat her like a princess. Girls love that"

Jack thought about Becky's plan for a moment. But it just wasn't gelling with him, "I can't write poetry. I've never been the creative type"

Becky wasn't put off, "what hair colour is she?"

"Red"

"And her eyes?"

"Blue"

"And tell me at least one physical feature that catches your attention all the time?"

Jack thought for a moment, "her freckles. I don't know why they keep drawing my attention. I use to be put off by them. Wouldn't have dreamed of dating a girl who was covered in them. Now I can't stop thinking about her naked body"

Becky looked down at her own body, "even when there's a naked woman right here in front of you?"

Jack noticed his mistake, "I'm sorry. That sounds terrible to say. Don't get me wrong. You're absolutely stunning", he lied, "it's just that Yvonne is stuck in my head. Can I tell you something?. But I need you to promise me that you won't tell my parents"

Becky was intrigued. She sat up next to him and leaned on Jack's shoulder, "I'm not gonna say anything. I feel like me and you have an understanding. You get me and I think I get you. Now spill"

Jack looked her in the eyes, "she might be pregnant with my baby"

"Might be?"

Jack explained about New Year's Eve and about Yvonne's ex boyfriend, "so you can see. It's not straight forward. And I still have a girlfriend as well. I have to figure out a way of breaking up with Denise. The webcam chats are becoming more awkward. It's not fair on her. It's not fair on Yvonne. It's not even fair on you. I feel like I'm even using you in a way"

Becky's heart went out to him. Jack looked like a lost little puppy who needed a home. She ran her fingers through his hair, "don't be worrying about me. I'm old enough to know better and I'm still fucking around with younger men. But you do need to sort out your love life. Firstly you need to break up with Denise. That's the first way of showing Yvonne that you are serious about her. Then come up with some kind of poetry for next group. You need to tell her how you feel. But the great thing about a public place is that she can't stop you"

Jack was still stressed, "what the fuck am I gonna write?. I wouldn't know were to start"

Becky held his chest tightly, "it has to come from the heart. That's all that matters", she lay back on the bed once more and spread her legs wide, "now, how about you fuck me again. Like I was Yvonne. I wanna feel that passion inside me"

Jack crawled on top of Becky. Letting his long, thick cock slide deep inside her, "thanks for listening"

"No problem", Becky moaned, "now fuck me"

Jack wearily complied. His body may have been Becky's that night. But his heart and head were far away with Yvonne.

Chapter Twenty Four

The town was extremely busy for a Saturday. As lockdown restrictions eased more and more. The public had come out in hordes. The queues for Penney's was still an absolute joke. But none of that mattered as Yvonne made her way to her weekly poetry group. It was her only way of getting away from everything. And right now she needed it more than ever.

Unfortunately Yvonne was running a bit later than normal. A sudden need for the toilet had led to her delay. As she turned the corner, Yvonne could see the usual group listening to a new voice reading out their work. This wasn't unusual. They normally had different people joining the group. Not all stuck with it. The public speaking putting off most.

The poetry from the stranger was nothing to write home about. But the voice sure sounded familiar. It was only when she turned the corner, that it all made sense. There was Jack, standing at the front of the group. Reading out some terrible poem about an exercise bike. Yvonne froze on the spot.

Evan spotted Yvonne and beckoned her over, "come on in dear. There's a seat over this side", he pointed to the bench next to him.

Yvonne rushed over, trying not to look at Jack as she passed him by. Taking her seat on the opposite side of the garden.

Margaret was the first to question Jack on his work, "you don't look like a man who uses an exercise bike. You're very well built. I reckon you're into sport"

Bethany threw Margaret a dirty look, "you can't say stuff like that. He may well use an exercise bike as part of his workout", she turned to Jack, "don't mind that one. I thought it was a lovely poem"

But Margaret wasn't backing down, "I'm not knocking his poem. I was just making an observation. So mind your own business"

Evan could see the debate was getting out of hand and tried to calm the situation, "that's enough ladies. Think poor Jack here has heard enough of your bickering. Now, Yvonne is next to read", he turned to the young woman, "you can stay seated if you like. Especially in your condition", he glanced down at her bump.

But Yvonne wasn't one to let her pregnancy get in the way of normal life. So even though she would have preferred to stay seated. Yvonne still struggled back up to her feet, "okay then. This one is called the rhythm of life", she took a deep breath and readied herself for that terrible silence as the small group listened to her words.

"Heaving bodies, sweaty thighs,
Wanting hearts, love filled minds,
Two parts, one purpose,
A life being formed,

The seed has been launched,
But their bodies still yearn out for more"

Yvonne sat down quickly and waited for the comments
to flow in. That was the part of the process that she
hated. She hadn't been expecting for Jack to be there.
The poetry group was a safe place. Somewhere to vent
her problems and feelings with the world. Now Jack had
heard her words. Yvonne couldn't help but wonder if
he'd use them against her. She prayed to god that he
wouldn't.

Bethany shifted uncomfortably on the hard wooden
bench, "I take it that's about the creation of your baby.
It's always nice to know when there's love involved with
the process. Are you still with the father?"

Margaret was having none of it, "you can't bloody ask
her that"

But Bethany wasn't backing down, "we're all here to
discuss our poetry and the process behind it. I'm just
asking about the process side of it. And a major part of
that is were the emotions came from"

Yvonne hated to see the two old women fighting and
tried to calm the situation, "I'm not with the father
anymore", she discreetly glanced in Jack's direction,
"but I don't regret this for a minute. I'm glad that I'm
pregnant. I really want this baby more than anything.
And if my child ever asks me about the father. I'll

explain what happened in detail. No point in confusing them. Better to be honest from the start"

Evan got up and took control of the meeting, "right then folks. Time to move on"

The group went around a second time. Each of the members taking another turn at reading out their current work. Then it arrived back on Jack again. It was now his time to shine. Try and get across how he felt about the beautiful, flame haired woman in front of him, "this is called love", he tried his best not to stare too much in Yvonne's direction. But his eyes kept darting that way,

"Watching and waiting,
For that little spark,
A connection with someone,
More than jokes and a laugh.

Common interests,
shared views,
Touching your soul,
In ways that they should.

As life goes by,
It becomes more than just sex,
A deeper connection,
Emotional and respect.

A strong long bond,
That touches you both,
Mostly never acted on,

Another of life's lost hopes"

He quickly sat back down and took a much needed breath. Jack was pretty sure that be babbled through the whole thing a little too quickly. But he forced those worries to the back of his mind.

Yvonne had been listening carefully and straight away wanted to tear into his words, "you sound like a man whose never known real love before. Would I be right in saying that?"

Jack looked her in the eyes. Just in case his words weren't enough, "I've only realised recently that I've never known true love. I thought I had in the past. But so many times I've mistaken wild rampant sex for love. I think that's most young men's problem. They can't tell the two apart at the best of times. Now I want it more than anything. But the path there is blocked off to me. And all I want is for her to open the gates and give me a chance to prove how serious I am"

"I'd happily open my gates", Bethany was lost in his words.

Margaret threw Bethany a dirty look, "you'd open your gates for the milkman if he gave you an extra pint"

Evan could see another argument brewing, "now ladies. Let's not go down that road again", he turned to Jack, "they were nice words. Hope you find what you're looking for. But now it's nearly time to finish up and we still have to hear Yvonne", he turned to her and smiled, "the floor is all yours"

Yvonne stood up and cleared her throat with a mild cough. Only then did she realise that it wasn't the done thing to do around a load of pensioners, during a deadly pandemic. She tried to ignore her worries, "this one is about the media circus going on around the virus and the black lives matters protests around the world. There's so much contradicting information on all these topics, that I haven't a clue what to believe anymore. It's called, future", she cleared her throat once again. Just this time, a little quieter,

"Are my eyes wide open?,
Or has this fake news just corrupt ?,
Lost in the internet,
The truth hidden from all of us.

Photos selected for a purpose,
Videos edited to a fault,
Making the most of the evidence,
That the whole world has mostly sought.

Sometimes ignorance is truly bliss,
Took me years to see that now,
The ugliness of life before us,
Laid out for the first world to see.

I fear my children's future,
And their kids after that,
It's only downhill from tomorrow,

And the following day after that"

She sat back down and waited for the comments.

Evan applauded Yvonne's efforts, "I really enjoyed that. Very current with life at the moment"

The other members of the group nodded in agreement. Yvonne felt on cloud nine. Even though you wouldn't know it by her blank expression. She hated to give too much away.

The meeting finally came to and end and everyone said their goodbyes. The older ladies were more interested in getting to know Jack a little better. Yvonne watched on as the temptation to walk away, was starting to grow inside her. But Jack had made a weirdly large effort to be in her company and she was now dying to hear what he had to say. Yvonne just hoped it wasn't the usual bullshit. She'd had enough of that from Stewy over the years.

Jack finally broke away from the old ladies clutches and approached Yvonne with a nervous smile on his face. He still wasn't sure what way she was gonna take his intrusion, "I hope I didn't make a show of you today?. I just wanted to talk to you again"

Yvonne picked up her bag and slung it over her shoulder in one swift motion, "you only embarrassed yourself. No skin off my nose. And as for wanting to talk to me. I thought you would have got the hint by now, that I'm trying to avoid you. We've said all that had to be said. Dragging it out like this, is only gonna make things worse. So please just let us leave it here and move on. I'll get on with my life and you can go back to Cork and be with Denise", she turned and walked away.

"I broke up with Denise. Told her I had feelings for someone else", Jack still felt bad for dumping her over the webcam. Especially when Denise was only wearing sexy new underwear, that she'd bought just for him, while waving her vibrator suggestively at the screen. It had been a disaster. But it was a disaster that had to be faced.

Yvonne stopped in her tracks and turned back to face him. Her shocked face said it all, "why the fuck would you do that?. Me and you aren't gonna go anywhere. I can't even tell you for sure if this child is yours. You don't want that hanging over your head and neither do I"

Jack was starting to worry for Yvonne's health and since they where standing around a load of free benches, "look, can we sit down and talk for a few minutes. I just don't want you to put your back under strain", he sat down and patted the space beside him.

Yvonne gave into his request and sat down next to him.

Jack finally continued, "you seem to be under the delusion that I'm only trying to get with you, because I think you're having my baby. It's not just about that", he took a breath, "i like you. In a way that I never felt about any other woman in my life. The baby may have brought us back into each other's lives. But when I'm around you. I don't wanna be with anyone else. You fill my thoughts all the time. So can you look into your heart and find the want to give me a chance to show you how I feel?"

Yvonne rubbed her baby bump gently as she thought about his words, "we're just too different. Your family aren't gonna like me. I seen your mother's condescending face in the store that day. Last thing she'd want is me showing up at your front door. And what if it turned out that this wasn't your baby?. She'd definitely freak it then. There's no way of getting over that"

Jack placed his hand gently on hers, "who I want to be with, is not my mother's business and I'm happy to carry on saying that the child is mine. No one has to know any different", he leaned in and kissed her gently on the lips.

Yvonne didn't fight it. Letting his tongue roam around inside her mouth. Both lost in the moment.

Yvonne finally came up for air and rested her forehead on his, "why are you saying these things?. I'm not right for you. My life is a total disaster and my family is even worse"

Jack rubbed Yvonne's cheek. Letting the tips of his fingers, run cross her damp skin, as a few tears ran down from her eyes, "you're perfect. Please never knock yourself again"

Yvonne's mental barriers came tumbling down as she threw her arms around Jack's neck and kissed him passionately. Giving into her own wants for once. Neither coming up for air, for a very long time.

Chapter Twenty Five

A few days had past since Jack had opened up his heart to Yvonne. Things had been going from strength to strength since then. Unfortunately most of those meetings were in the park or just walking around town. Yvonne hadn't wanted him back up near her house. Things had been going from bad to worse with her parents. The fighting had escalated between them.

Jack understood Yvonne's concerns and hasn't pushed her on the subject. Especially since he felt that he couldn't bring her near his house either. No matter how much he wanted to be with Yvonne. Jack knew his mother wasn't gonna welcome her into the family with open arms. She would have seen Yvonne as the type of woman that her son should just use and discard as quickly. His mother would be even more pissed, when she found out he dumped Denise. That had been another thing he'd been avoiding.

But today wasn't the day for this, as Jack's parents were leaving for a three night stay in a five star hotel. His mother in much need of a spa treatment and fine food. While his dad just wanted a few properly poured pints of Guinness. Yes he had his own bar. But Michael could never pour them right. Always leaving the pints over frothy.

Ellen packed the last of her things into a hand luggage bag, "I'm not even sure if I have everything", she marched around the large pink bedroom as she looked for more hair care products.

Jack sat on her small stool, that she used for applying makeup. He couldn't wait till they left. Then his long weekend plans with Yvonne, could come into action, "say you're looking forward to getting away mam?"

Ellen threw her hairdryer into the bag. She hated to use the shitty hotel ones, "pity Denise doesn't live nearer. You could of had her stay over for a few days"

Jack hadn't been planning to get into that topic. But decided to hit it head on, "I broke up with her"

Ellen dropped all that she was doing and sat down on the edge of the bed, "why would you do that?. That girl was perfect. I was even looking up her parents online. They're pretty well connected down in Cork"

Jack had a strong feeling that her mother would check up on his love life. She had a habit of involving herself in other people's business. Especially her own relatives and friends. Didn't come as a surprise to find out she was checking up on his girlfriend, "we weren't working out. It was just a bit of fun mam. I've met someone else. And she makes me feel something that I never once felt with Denise"

Ellen was visibly upset as she got back up from the bed and began to pack her bag again, "can't believe you threw an opportunity like that away. I never met the girl and already I could tell she was the one for you. You would have went places with that family. You'd probably would have walked into a high ranking position if the father took to you. How can you fuck all that up for another woman?"

Jack couldn't believe what his mother was saying. He was used to her forward behaviour. Brutally honest at times, "I think I love this other woman mam. I never had those kind of feelings with Denise"

Ellen threw her eyes up when she heard her son using the word love, "you shouldn't be letting your feelings get in the way of advancing yourself in this world. Do you think I loved your father when I first met him?. No. But I knew he was the right man for me. I grew to love him over time. I kind of agree with those religions that arrange the marriages for their kids. They don't just give them away to just anyone. If their potential partner is not rich or got a good job. You can just say fuck off and go elsewhere looking for a viable partner. If you let love rule your head. You're just gonna end up fucking up your life. Please don't do that. Ring Denise and tell her that you made a mistake"

Jack was getting annoyed at her mother's attitude. But he didn't show it at anytime. Bottling the rage that was growing inside him. There was only one thing for it. He needed to put some distance between himself and his mother. He got up and stormed out of the room. Ellen just kept on packing. Never once trying to call him back. She'd said her peace and that was all that mattered.

Jack stormed into the lounge in much need of a drink. His father was already behind the bar, pouring himself another god awful Guinness. He smiled up at his son, "fancy a pint?"

Jack noticed the badly poured pint in his father's hand, "no thanks. Can I have a beer instead?"

Michael opened a fridge beside the bar and opened up the bottle before handing it to his son, "you look pretty stressed. Did you have words with your mother again?"

Jack took a deep breath, "I was telling her that I broke up with Denise and she's not impressed. Said I should have just stayed with her. Because it would be good for my career options down the line. But I didn't love her dad. I've met someone else and she makes me feel things that I never once felt with Denise. Mam doesn't seem to understand that"

Michael was used to his wife and her attitude towards relationships. Especially when it came to her two sons, "your mother has always been a go getter. Even when she met me. First thing she wanted to know was whether I was financially secure. That would have put most fellas off. But I know a lot more about her childhood that you and your brother was shielded from. Your mother didn't grow up with a silver spoon in her mouth. You probably don't remember where her parents lived, because they died when you were very young. But it wasn't a great part of Dublin. Pretty shitty if I'm honest. Think she's just trying to run from it ever since. So don't be too hard on her. Better to live your life and say as little you can about it", he let those words hang for a moment, before continuing on, "so what's this new girl like?"

Jack's mind was filled with all things Yvonne related, "she's everything I want dad. She's beautiful, funny and doesn't take any shit. When I'm not with her. I can't stop thinking about her. And when I'm in her company, I never want it to end. I think she's the one"

Michael came out from behind the bar and sat up on one of the uncomfortable bar stools, "then follow your dreams son. Don't let your mother get in the way. Hope you've invited her over one of the next few nights. You've got the whole house to yourself. May as well make the most of it"

Jack nervously nodded in agreement, "I've already asked her dad. She's staying over tonight. I'm collecting her later on. I'm gonna try and make the next few days as special as possible"

Michael patted his son's back, "hope it works out for you. Now, I better make a move. Wanna get to the hotel early. Make the most of my break away", he got up off the stool and stretched his tired back, "gonna be a long drive. I'm just glad your mother is doing the driving"

Jack's ears suddenly perked up, "you're not driving?"

Michael stopped briefly, "I'm not complaining. At least I can have a few pints on the day we're coming back"

This only meant one thing. Jack would have to collect Yvonne in his father's car.

Chapter Twenty Six

"The amount of crap she collects", joked Jamie as she lay across Yvonne's bed, searching the bottom drawer of her friend's locker for a set of earphones. She suddenly stopped and threw something across the room at Sarah, who was quietly sitting under the window, reading an old celebrity gossip magazine, "bet they haven't been used in awhile"

Sarah felt the small cardboard box hit off her forehead, before she seen what it was. It was a half used packet of condoms. Sarah smiled when she noticed they were flavoured, "what's the point in having them if you're not gonna use them"

Jamie started back her search of the drawer, "I don't use them all the time. Sometimes things happen and you just go with the moment. Have you never done the same?"

Sarah put the magazine back on the windowsill, "not a hope in hell. I'm not getting pregnant yet. Might never at this rate. Last thing I want is to be a single mother and hitting forty. I'll end up hanging around the bar in my local. Trying to pick up men for one night stands. Fuck that"

Jamie pulled a load of old thongs and threw them aside, "you mean you don't wanna end up like your mother?"

Sarah threw her friend a dirty look, "fuck off. I'll never be that bad"

Jamie's hand grabbed something familiar and she laughed, "looks like somebody isn't going lonely at night". She pulled out Yvonne's large pink dildo and waved it around for her friend to see. It swung around wildly. Bending at the centre with ease. She fired it back into the drawer, "speaking of not going lonely. How's things going with that olde fella you're shagging?. Hope he hasn't had a heart attack yet"

Sarah's mood dampened, "I thought it was going great. But he's starting to ask me to do stuff that's a bit freaky. I've tried out a few things for him. But he keeps pushing and pushing for more. I'm not sure if I should say no and hope for the best that he respects my decision and all will be okay between us. But what if I'm wrong. What if he does break up with me. I don't know what to do"

Suddenly the bathroom door opened and out came a damp Yvonne. A large towel wrapped around her body and another one tied around her hair tightly, "nice to see you both made yourselves at home"

Jamie was still picking through the drawer, "just looking for earphones. My ones broke"

Yvonne looked over the edge of the bed to see the mess that Jamie had created, "you can fucking tidy up that lot for starters. The earphones are in the top drawer"

Jamie pulled the top drawer out and was delighted to see that her friend was right, "grand. Sarah was just about to tell me about the freaky shit her new fella is into to"

Yvonne glanced at a nearby clock. It was already coming up to three and she wasn't even close to being ready for her few nights away. She'd even lied to work about feeling unwell. Just to get a few days off, "can you blow dry my hair Sarah?. I'm running short of time to get ready"

Sarah jumped up and grabbed a nearby brush and the hairdryer, while Yvonne sat on a small stool in front of her bedroom mirror.

Jamie was still waiting to hear Sarah's story, "So what kind of freaky shit is this old fella into?"

Sarah was glad she didn't have to look her friends directly in the eyes as she spoke, "he's started to ask me to dress up for him"

Yvonne couldn't see anything wrong with that. But Sarah wasn't that outgoing of a person, "dress up as what?"

"As a schoolgirl", Sarah replied.

Jamie fired everything back into the bottom drawer, "nothing wrong with that. I've dressed up as the sexy schoolgirl loads of times. Even did it for Halloween. You're just a bit of a prude. That's all"

Yvonne sensed there was more to Sarah's story, "don't mind that one. Tell us the rest of your story"

"They aren't the sexy type of school uniform. They look and feel real. He's got a whole wardrobe full of them. Makes me wear big white panties with them. I don't even own that type of underwear. He actually has a drawer full of them. Then he got me to bend over his knees and he smacked my bottom"

Jamie suddenly sat up with interest, "kinky old git. You wouldn't think it to look at him"

But Sarah wasn't finished, "that's not even the worst part. When he's spanking my bottom raw. He keeps shouting, who's your daddy. I'm not being funny. That's a bit freaky, right?. He has daughters older than me. What would they think if they knew about their father's freaky fetishes"

Yvonne wasn't sure how to answer that head on. So went a different route, "how does he treat you in general?. You know, like bringing you out on dates and stuff"

Sarah wearily smiled, "he's great in every other way. He's caring and thoughtful to my every need. He buys me loads of nice things. He makes sure I'm fully satisfied during normal sex. It's just his fetish that's freaking me out. It's not normal, is it?"

Jamie was quick to share her own views on the subject, "I'd stay with him. Most men have freaky fetishes. Some are worst than others. Yours doesn't sound too bad. I had one fella who wanted me to fuck him up the arse with a strap on"

Yvonne tried to hide her disgust, "please don't tell this story again"

But Jamie was on a roll, "it was all going well until I pulled it out and the whole rubber shaft was covered with his dirty shit. Thought I was gonna vomit right there and then"

Even Sarah's face contorted upon hearing her friend's story, "oh please. I can feel my lunch coming back up"

But Jamie wasn't one to let a topic go so easily, "that only leaves you Yvonne. What was your worst sex moment?"

Yvonne used to be embarrassed about it. But time was a great healer, "suppose it doesn't matter now. But probably the time me and Stewy were having drug fuelled sex all night. We past out from exhaustion. But for some strange reason. We both woke up an hour or two later and went for it again. Unfortunately he'd forgotten to remove the used condom from his dick. Thrusting it away inside me like a demented madman. But it had tightened around his shaft somehow. Which in turn put his cock under more stress than normal. Poor fucker partially ripped his banjo string. He was like a geyser all over the bedroom. You'd swear someone got murdered in our flat"

Sarah covered her mouth in shock, "oh my fucking god. That's terrible. Did he go to hospital with it?"

Yvonne found it weird that she could laugh about it now, "you know him. Was too embarrassed to go. So he just took some painkillers. We couldn't have sex for nearly two weeks. I had great fun taking the piss of him over that time. I'd purposely wear the skimpiest of underwear around the flat. Just to put him on the horn. He'd be in a heap with the pain. Funny as fuck to watch"

It wasn't long until Yvonne's hair was done. Her makeup was in place and the final perfect touch was needed. The right outfit. Unfortunately her two friends opinion on that, totally differed from each other. Jamie wanted Yvonne to go with a short loose dress that barely covered her ass cheeks. Mostly thanks to her bump lifting it higher at the front. While Sarah was steering towards a pink tracksuit.

In the end, Yvonne decided on a short skirt, knee high boots and a loose black top with a low front, that showed off her cleavage perfectly, "how do I look?"

Sarah praised Yvonne's choice in fashion.

But Jamie was more distracted by something outside, "is Jack picking you up in his car?"

Yvonne applied another layer of lipstick, "said he has the use of his mother's car for the next few days. Why?"

Sarah glanced out the window and her eyes widened, "you have to see this"

Yvonne walked over to the bedroom window and looked out to see a large pink BMW pulling up in front of her house, "what the fuck is that?"

Jamie wasn't one to hold back, "it's as fucking pink as my piss flaps. Jesus Christ. He wouldn't wanna park that there too long, or it'll be wrecked"

As he climbed out of the driver's seat, Jack tried to ignore all the dirty looks he was getting off a nearby teenage gang, who had been watching his every move since entering the street. The car was a total eyesore. He'd been hoping to pick Yvonne up in his mother's red Porsche. But that plan had gone right out the window that morning. Thanks to his father. He just prayed nothing would happen to the car. That would lead to an explanation being needed and he wasn't ready for that just yet.

Jamie rushed out the door of the house with a spring in her step, "let's have a look inside the pussy wagon", she opened the passenger door and jumped inside, admiring the smooth leather seats, "nice car. Pity about the colour"

Jack couldn't agree more, "my father just really loves pink. Don't know why. Got the car spray painted after he bought it"

Jamie glanced in at the rather large backseat. It had been a few years since she'd gotten off with some fella in a similar vehicle, "it's your father's car!. I thought it was your mother's"

Wasn't the first time Jack had heard that before, "no, she drives a Porsche"

Jamie's eyes lit up, "I'd love to see that car. Can you bring that around the next time you're calling?"

Jack glanced over in the direction of the dodgy looking gang, "we'll see. Is Yvonne still getting ready?"

Jamie got back out of the car and shut the door tightly behind her, "she's just having another piss. You know with the pregnancy and all. Keeps putting pressure on her bladder"

"This your new fella Jamie?", one of the gang members shouted over.

Jamie put her arm around Jack's shoulder, "and what if he was. Would you be jealous?"

The young fella glanced at the pink car, "not if he's driving round in an eyesore like that"

Dermot was coming around the corner and heard the young fella giving them shit. He slapped him around the back of the head with his good hand, "you shut your fucking mouth", he then spotted the car, "fuck, that's an eyesore", he turned to Jack, "did you lose a bet?"

Thankfully Yvonne came out of the house, followed closely behind by Sarah and her mother.

Sammy has heard about the car and couldn't help but come out for a look, "Jesus Christ. Did you lose a bet?"

Jack was quickly growing tired of the comments. But he didn't show it, "it's my dad's car. He loves the colour pink", he figured it best to answer the second most asked question about the car. Just to save time.

Yvonne was sensing Jack's embarrassment and decided a hasty exit was needed, "right then. Let's get off", she opened the passenger door, while addressing her friends and family, "I'll be back in a few days"

Dermot slapped Jack on the back, "was about to warn you about keeping my sister out of trouble", he glanced over at Yvonne's belly, "but that ship has long sailed"

The group said their goodbyes and the couple finally drove slowly out of the street.

Yvonne had only one thing to say about Jack's father's car, "if you're ever picking me up in this car again. I'll meet you at the entrance to the estate in future"

Jack couldn't agree more.

Chapter Twenty Seven

It only took the sight of the entrance to Jack's family home, for Yvonne to know that this place was not gonna be your average house. The large metal gates automatically opened and the car made its way slowly up the hill towards the peak. Jack parked out front and waited for her first opinion on the place.

Yvonne was still in awe at the size, "fuck me, this house is massive. It's like a hotel", she got out of the car and noticed the view out over the countryside, "can see why your parents chose here to build it. Bet it's great waking up to this every morning"

"You get used to it. But it's not worth the isolation. I'd much rather live in the town. Always dreamed of getting my own apartment in Dublin or Cork. Be on the edge of everything for once. You only realise how far out in the middle of nowhere you are, when you've no money left after a night out and you have to walk home"

Yvonne couldn't keep her eyes off the landscape that was laid out in front of her, "it's beautiful. I've always dreamed of living out in the countryside. You wouldn't believe the amount of times I've been woken up at night because of people shouting in the street or sirens passing nearby", or right to her door if they were looking for her father. She sat up on the edge of the bonnet. Resting her tired back.

Jack took the opportunity to stand between Yvonne's bare thighs and wrapped his arms around her waist. He leaned in for a kiss. Which soon turned to something more passionate. His hands reaching up under her skirt and pulling at her damp panties, "I want you right now"

Yvonne unbuckled his jeans and pulled out his hard cock, "then fuck me like you mean it"

Jack sunk the tip deep inside her. It wasn't long until neither cared who could be watching. They both had needs to be fulfilled.

The couple finally got in the front door and Yvonne was once again speechless as she struggled to get over the size of the hallway. Framed paintings lined the walls. Mostly of landmarks from in and around Drogheda. Including the viaduct. She stopped to study it a bit closer, "this is beautiful. Say it ain't cheap?"

It was just another painting to Jack. Been on the wall for years and it had just become something you'd walk by without giving a second thought to its beauty. But it was nice to see Yvonne taking an interest. Made him study it a little more carefully for once after all these years, "not sure what my parents paid for it. But I know these things aren't cheap"

Yvonne ran her fingers over the long dried out water colours, "they always feel great to the touch"

Jack kissed her forehead, "a bit like you then. Would you fancy a drink?", he headed towards the lounge.

Yvonne followed after him. Still glancing at each painting as she past by, "definitely". This house wasn't at all what she was expecting.

"Fuck me", was all Yvonne could say as she stepped in through the saloon style doors and took in the full splendour of the old western themed room, "this is some place"

Jack went behind the bar and opened a bottle of beer for himself, "what would you like to drink?"

Yvonne had been trying to be good. But the temptation of alcohol filled bottles, was driving her towards an old favourite. One wouldn't hurt, "can I get a double vodka and coke please?"

Jack attempted to act like a veteran barman, as he struggled to make her drink in one fluid motion. Ending with him dropping the glass. Which smashed on the ground next to him, "that could have went better"

Yvonne tried not to laugh at his mistake, "it's okay. Maybe try that again without all the unnecessary hand actions"

Thankfully he got it right the second time. So as Yvonne enjoyed her vodka, he took the time to clean up the broken glass and drop it in the small bin nearby.

Yvonne was still amazed at the work that had gone into the house. Definitely not the type of property that an owner would like to keep to themselves, "bet your parents throw a lot of big parties in this place?"

Jack couldn't help think of the last such party. He'd ended up shagging Becky in his bed. But the less said about that, the better, "they love company. And because they live out here in the arse end of nowhere. They like to bring the parties to them. Unfortunately some of them don't seem to end until the next morning"

Yvonne couldn't see anything wrong with that. She'd been to many parties that hadn't ended until long into the following day. Drugs were normally involved, "sounds like my kind of parties"

Jack went a little sheepish, "not the parties that my parents are into"

"What sort of parties are they into?"

"The kind of parties were they don't go to bed alone"

Yvonne was lost for words.

That was the usual reaction when Jack revealed such details. So it didn't come as much of a surprise anymore, "as you can see. That's why I started spending less and less time here. I know it's suppose to keep their marriage fresh and they seem happy with the way their relationship had progressed over the years. But it's not easy to wake up in your own bed, to find your childhood friend's mother, sucking you off like your life depended on it"

Yvonne's mouth dropped open, "fucking hell. What age were you?"

Jack hadn't told anyone this story before. But Yvonne wasn't just anyone. She was someone who he wanted to be fully open with. Share every detail of his life with. He just hoped she felt the same way, "seventeen. I wasn't a virgin anymore. Had slept with a few women before that. But they were all my own age. But to have an older woman getting off with you, was an unbelievable experience. She took control and all I had to do was lie there and take it. Wasn't long till I came and she just got up and left the room. First and only time it happened. Thankfully I haven't had to see much of her since that faithful night. But since coming back to Drogheda. I've back hanging around with her son Paul. And now I feel kind of bad"

"Hope you're not planning on telling him", was the first words out of Yvonne's mouth.

Jack sipped at his beer as he mulled that over, "I couldn't do that to him. Don't think he even knows about my parents being with her. He's a quiet fella. I reckon he's still a virgin. He never seems to get out of the house. Suppose you don't have any friends who would suit him?"

Yvonne let out a little laugh, "I doubt it. My friends are all a bit too mouthy for someone quiet. But I know were you're coming from, when it comes to a friend's parent making inappropriate advances. My friend Jamie's father, kissed me one night after a family barbecue. I was only sixteen and pissed drunk. He cornered me outside the bathroom. Thankfully I was able to think straight quickly enough and got away from him. But I never once went to another one of their parties after that. The look of guilt on his face ever since that day. He knows he did wrong"

Jack felt that Yvonne's story was bordering more on sexual assault, "have you ever been tempted to tell Jamie?"

Yvonne knocked the last of her drink off the head, "what good would that do. I'd end up just ruining my friendship and for what. Nothing. I'd just wreck my own life and his. It's not worth the hassle. Now, can I get another drink barman?", she handed him back her glass.

Jack filled it up again and gave it back to her. Yvonne took the glass and got up off the high stool. Making her way towards the large white leather couch that curved around like a banana.

Yvonne placed her drink on the glass coffee table, before kneeling onto the couch and leaning over the back, "I love the feel of this", she turned to look at him, as she lifted the back of her skirt to reveal her pink underwear, "always wanted to be taken across a couch like this"

Jack was already out from behind the bar. He couldn't believe how horny Yvonne was for sex. Even in her condition, she still wanted it more than most girls he had been with in the past. He opened his pants and kneeled onto the couch behind her. Sinking his cock deep inside her.

"Oh fuck that feels good", Yvonne moaned, before arching her back around to kiss him.

Jack began to pump away hard. Thrusting his purple headed warrior deep inside her tight wet pussy. He pulled Yvonne's top and bra up to play with her perky boobs. Jack knew he couldn't last long. But that didn't stop him from trying. Thankfully Yvonne orgasmed before he shot his sticky protein load deep inside her. Before both of them lay down on the couch for a much needed rest.

The tour continued around the house. Jack showing off the rest of the overly decorated rooms. As they turned onto the first floor, Yvonne noticed the attic door above them. She couldn't help but ask, "is that where it happened?"

Jack glanced up at the hatchway, "yeah. I try not to think about it, when I pass under it each time. But it's still there. It never goes, no matter how many years pass by. Can still see him hanging. I came up the stairs that day and I thought he was just standing here with his back to me. He was that close to the ground, that you'd honestly think his feet were touching. That's how well he planned it. Who even does that?. I've asked myself that question, so many times. Never makes sense to me. I was only aware that he was dead, when I noticed the leather belt wrapped around his neck. He'd even nailed it to the wooden beam in the attic. Just incase a knot would fail. I know I was suppose to be upset that day. But all my family's problems and stresses died with my brother. That sounds terrible. I know. But we'd all suffered with him up to that point. I know there's those who say the grieving afterwards, is ten times worse. Trust me, that couldn't be further from the truth. Life moved on and so did my family. My parents might have gone a bit off the rails since then. But they're happy", he thought about his last statement for a moment, "well, I hope so"

Yvonne's heart went out to Jack. She was even starting to regret asking in the first place. There had to be something else nearby, to distract him from his negative thoughts. Then she spotted it, "what's the pink unicorn for?", she walked over to the door and studied the artwork more closely.

Jack followed suit, "it's only been put up since I've been living in Cork. Been afraid to even dare ask, what's inside"

Yvonne tested the handle, "locked. You must be dying to know what's in there?"

Jack had learnt over the last few years, that ignorance was bliss when it came to his parent's private life, "not really. Besides, I don't have a key"

Yvonne threw him a cheeky smile, as she pulled a clip from her hair. She kneeled down beside the lock and picked it with ease. The door clicked open, "that was easier than expected"

Jack helped Yvonne back to her feet, "where'd you learn how to do that?"

Yvonne just shrugged her shoulders, "used to just practice it for the laugh. But it's come in handy loads of times. Especially when I've been locked out of my house at three in the morning"

Jack slowly opened the door and flicked on the lights, "holy fucking shite"

Yvonne gasped in disbelief, before laughing, "Jesus, your parents are fairly kinky"

Jack leaned on a chair next to him, as he tried to take in the full horror of his parent's sexual misadventures.

The walls were lined with sex toys. Dildos, whips, bondage equipment. The list went on. Against the far wall was a bed with, what looked like, a leather bottom sheet. And in the centre of it all, hung a rather complicated looking sex swing. It's leather straps attached to chains, that were firmly attached to the ceiling. The place would make even Mr Grey blush.

"I'll be honest. I love my sex and I've tried most things. But this is definitely way out of my league", Yvonne opened a nearby wooden cabinet to reveal a selection of condoms, lubricants and pills of various different colours, "look at this stuff"

Jack was still speechless and in much need of a sit down. He went for the chair next to him. But quickly jumped up as something large, jabbed him between the cheeks of his arse, "what the fuck", he glanced down to see a rather large dildo, connected into the middle of the seat.

Yvonne caught sight of what happened and fell to her knees laughing, "this gets better and better"

Jack was still rubbing the cheeks of his sore arse. Definitely put him off any plans of trying anal in the future, "I'm starting to wish that I hadn't come in here. I knew they were bad. But not this fucking freaky"

Yvonne playfully pushed the sex swing, "I'd love to try one of these. Looks fun"

But Jack was hearing none of it, "don't think I could even get hard, knowing my mother was already ridden on that thing. It just doesn't seem right"

Yvonne headed towards the door and took her hair clip out again, "okay then. Let's lock the place back up"

Jack opened a nearby cabinet and took out one of the tubes of lubrication, a couple of pills and another container called pussy rub, "these might come in handy later"

Jack followed her back out into the hallway and Yvonne locked the room back up. The door clicked shut and the job was done.

Yvonne got back to her feet, "will we continue the tour?"

Jack waved his hand out to lead the way, "ladies first"

Yvonne smiled at the compliment and proceeded on down the hallway. While Jack enjoyed the view of her beautiful ass along the way.

Chapter Twenty Eight

The evening had gone as planned for Jack. He'd showed
Yvonne the rest of the house. Toured the large garden
that surrounded it. He'd even attempted cooking pasta
for them both. Even setting up the large dining room
table for two. When everything was tidied away and
conversation had turned to kissing. He'd grabbed a bottle
of his parent's best champagne and they'd retired to the
main bathroom.

Yvonne was initially shocked by how large and pink the
whole place was, "fucking hell. It's big, pink and
soaking wet. Like a menopausal woman's fanny"

Jack popped the cork and filled two glasses of bubbly,
"I'm sure my parents would love your description. This
is another one of their favourite rooms. Not a bathroom
you'd use if they were home. Never know what you'll
walk in on"

Yvonne wrapped her arms around his waist, "bet you've
had a few girls in here over the years"

Jack pulled his T-shirt off to reveal his smooth chest,
"not as many as you think. Don't normally like coming
in here. You never know what you might find. But the
cleaner was in this morning. So I can guarantee you that
the place has been hygienically cleaned"

Yvonne pulled her own top off as well, "I like getting
dirty"

Jack could tell that Yvonne was well up for anything he had to offer. He turned on the taps and started to fill the four person jacuzzi, "this won't take long to fill", he popped one of the tablets he'd taken from his parent's sex cabinet. He wanted to be like a stallion that night.

Yvonne stripped off and lay her clothes over a nearby chair, before carefully climbing up onto the edge of the jacuzzi. Letting her legs and feet, dangle into the ever rising warm waters. She watched on as Jack pulled off the last of his clothes. His semi erect cock, swinging from left to right, as he grabbed the champagne glasses and got into the jacuzzi. The water level was already near the top.

Jack turned off the taps and handed Yvonne a glass of champagne, "are you not getting into the water?. It feels great"

Yvonne couldn't help but feel like a buzz kill, "I'm afraid to. I read before that it's not good for the baby. But I'm happy enough with just my legs in it. Don't be worrying. I'm enjoying the view from here", she glanced down at his wet naked body.

Jack flicked his erection up out of the bubbly water. It's tip breaking the surface, "we could play spot the submarine"

Yvonne was enjoying the sight of his growing erection, "I'd much rather play, how long can we hold our breath under the water while orally satisfying each other. But that ain't gonna happen. So tell us, what lucky lady did you last have in here?"

Jack was nervous about admitting the truth. It was years ago now and part of him felt that maybe sleeping dogs are better off left alone. But he wanted to be honest with her, "it wasn't a girl. It was this guy I used to hang around with in secondary school. Ended up taking a lot of drugs and drink that night. Then we came back here and for some strange reason we decided to try out the jacuzzi. Ended up giving each other blowjobs. I just went with it at the time. But when you wake up the next morning. That's when the horrible truth hits you. We were both naked in my bed and I wasn't even sure what happened after the jacuzzi. That didn't sit well with me. We grew distant after that", he'd felt that enough was shared on his side and hoped that Yvonne had her own similar story from the past, "what about you?. Have you ever gone off with a member of the same sex?"

Yvonne took a sip from her glass. Carful not to overdo it. She'd drank enough already that day and that tipsy feeling was growing, "not like a full on lesbian fest. But I did have a threesome with my friend Jamie. We both liked him and rather than fall out that night over who went home with him. We just said fuck it and both went home with him. It was a good laugh. We put on a show for the fella. Kissing and cuddling each other in the bed. We didn't go all the way. But my head was pretty close to Jamie's fanny a few times. Don't honestly know what men or women like about down there. At least when you have a dick. It's something visible. It's there for all to see", she opened her legs to reveal her own shaved pussy, "women just have two pink flaps and a patch of unruly hair. That's why I keep it shaved. Last thing I like to see down there is a crop of ginger pubes"

Jack leaned forward across the swirling water and opened her legs wider. He licked two fingers and began to massage her pussy lips gently, "I think you've got quite a spectacular fanny. Beautiful little pussy lips, that are just waiting to be spread, and for a firm, long tongue, to be thrust deep inside it", he played with her clit. Just to build Yvonne up towards her first orgasm, before he went in for the thrill.

Yvonne spread her legs even wider and thrust her head backwards as her body trembled. She grabbed Jack's head and forced it down between her legs, "get that tongue inside me. I want you to eat me out"

Jack happily complied, thrusting his tongue deep inside her. His index finger making its way up her asshole. Yvonne didn't fight any of it. She just lay back across the tiled surface and let her body go places it hadn't been in a while. She pulled him in closer. Not even the cold surface beneath her, could ruin the moment, "oh fuck, I'm coming", a little spout of clear bodily fluids, shot up into Jack's face. That only drove him onto satisfy her even more. Staying down there for the next half hour until she pleaded with him to stop.

The couple lay quietly for the next ten minutes. Yvonne still lying on her back. The foamy water running around her thighs. Jack sat back in the water. His erection still throbbing as he wiped the pussy juice off his face, "I'm fucking wrecked after that. Loved the way you spurted a little. It's like a little sign that I'm doing the job right"

Yvonne laughed, "remember when I was telling you about that threesome. Pour Jamie was close to that area when the fella made me cum with his fingers. She got a load of my fanny juice in the face. Never seen her run so quick for a shower. She still sneers me about it"

Jack stood up out of the water and kneeled between Yvonne's legs. His throbbing erection touching off her moist flaps. He pushed it gently inside her, "my turn now to shoot my load. You ready to get fucked?"

Yvonne stayed lying back on the cold tiles and let Jack take control of the situation. His hands groping at her boobs. Playing with each nipple gently, "I want you to fuck me hard. Don't stop. No matter how much I plead"

Jack didn't need to be asked twice as he thrust his cock in and out of Yvonne's wet pussy. His grip on her thighs growing. But her belly was throwing him off a bit. A constant reminder of the tender life inside her, "can you turn around and get on your knees. I'll be able to go harder at it"

Yvonne didn't need to think twice about it. She obeyed his request and turned around. Bending over the counter beside the jacuzzi. Her knees on the step under the warm water. Jack stood up and bent his knees. Sliding his cock deep inside her again. He began to thrust away once more. His hands clasped tightly onto her hips. It wasn't long until she reached her first orgasm. One of many that was to come, over the next three hours.

Chapter Twenty Nine

"It was unbelievable. We just fucked, drank and had a laugh for the last few days. Pity my parents came home. We could have gone for weeks like that. I think I love her", Jack had been mulling those words over in his head all day. It just seemed right.

Paul stared up at the stars above them, "does it still not play on your mind that the baby might still not be yours?"

Jack didn't like to think about that too much, "it does. But my feelings for Yvonne far outweigh all that. At the start I hoped to god that the child wasn't mine. Now I'm praying that it is"

Paul lit up another joint and sat up on the arc of the roof, "did your parents get to meet her, when they got back?"

Jack got up off the slated roof and moved up beside his friend, "no, I got her home before they got back. I'm not sure how it's gonna go, when they do meet. I told them about the baby. Ended up in an argument. They're not impressed that's I'm just accepting the child as mine. Reckon I'm being taken advantage of. Just because we are well off"

Paul couldn't help mentioning, one major detail, "take it you didn't tell them that there was a chance, that the child wasn't yours"

Jack wearily shook his head, "not a chance. Things are bad enough between me and my parents. No point in making it any worse. Besides, it's not just about the baby. Yvonne means a lot to me. Unfortunately none of that's gonna matter to my mother. Who is definitely not gonna like her. She'd prefer me to stay with Denise. Just because she comes from a good family. She even admitted to me, that she did the same thing with my dad. I kind of figured that was the situation. But it's just hard to hear her actually admit it. It's not right. You shouldn't marry someone for what you can get out of them. Am I being stupid?"

Paul awkwardly played with his fingers, "don't think I'll ever have the opportunity of finding out either way. Think I've been alone so long now. That I'd be happy for a girl to go out with me, even if it was just because I had money", he let out a nervous laugh, "but look at me. I live in my parent's house. I've no third level education. I don't hang out with anyone except you. And I'm still a virgin"

There was a long silence in the air as Jack tried to decide if he really just heard those words come out of his friend's mouth, "you serious?"

Paul took another long drag from his joint, "tried a few times in my teens to meet women. Best I ever got was this one called Bethany. She was on my bus to secondary school. She wasn't a looker or anything. Extremely overweight and thick glasses. Probably would have looked okay if she was thin. But anyway, she was pretty forward. Which helped a lot with my shyness. She was up for everything. Talked about having sex and all. You wouldn't believe how excited I was. Couldn't wait till school ended each day to meet her. It was the best time of my whole life"

Jack could sense there was a downside to this story, coming, "so what went wrong?"

Paul cleared his throat, "I couldn't get it hard. Didn't matter what she was doing to me. She tried to wank me off. Give me blowjobs at the back of the bus depot. Nothing would work. I was just too nervous. Which was weird because I'd get home straight afterwards and I'd wank off to her with ease. It was just fucked up. I tried to explain to her what was wrong. But she didn't believe me. Thought I had a problem with her weight. In the end, I caught her with another fella at the back of the bus depot. She was sucking him off. But what really poured salt into the wound. She seen me watching them, smiled up at me and said, this fella has no problem with getting hard. As you can guess, that was the start of endless bullying from everyone in the school and bus depot. They all knew my problem and were happy to sneer me about it. Don't know how I got through that time. You wouldn't believe how low I felt for a long time. Thought about ending it all", he realised that the last part, might not go down too well with his friend, "that's probably the last thing you need to hear with everything that your family has gone through"

Jack patted his friend on the back, "don't be worried about me. That's long in the past now. You just ended up with a bitch who made you uncomfortable. Don't let one bad experience affect the rest of your life. There is women out there for you. It's just up to you to go out there and find them. I know that probably sounds hard. But dating is a lot different these days. Most of it's done online. You wouldn't have to meet them in person until you felt comfortable. Don't base all women on your experiences with this Bethany bitch"

Paul handed his friend the joint as he mulled over the suggestion of online dating, "let's be realistic here. What could I honestly put on a profile that will make women actually want to click on me. I'm not even gonna have a good profile picture"

Jack laughed, "come on. You're not that bad looking"

Paul never could see it, "I look like Harry Potter's older and uglier brother. I wouldn't even embarrass myself by trying. Can we stop talking about this now. I'm just getting really pissed off, the more I think about that bitch"

Jack suddenly had an idea, "what's this Bethany one's second name?"

"Stewart", Paul replied.

"Not your typical irish surname. Might be easy enough to find", Jack pulled out his phone and began to search through social media for her. He could only find one woman with the same name, who was living in Drogheda. He held up the phone for his friend to see, "is that her?"

Paul studied the photo carefully. The woman still had thick glasses. But she was now stick thin, "she looks a lot better than I remember her. How's this suppose to be helping me?"

Jack flicked through some of her personal information, "she's a proud single mother of four kids. That really means that she can't hold up a relationship with anyone. She works part time in retail. That probably means she can only work while the kids are in school. Most likely on the tills. Oh, and she's a Scientologist. Looks like you had a lucky escape. So I wouldn't feel bad about it"

Paul sensed his friend might have been lying about the last bit. But it was nice to know that someone had his best interests at heart for once in his life, "thanks for trying to help. But I think I'm a lost cause. May as well get used to being single", he stared out towards the lights of Drogheda in the distance.

Jack so wanted to help his friend out. But finding Paul a woman, seemed like such a long shot. All he could do for now, was just be a kind ear to his friend's problems and hope that love would fall in his lap sooner or later.

Chapter Thirty

Jamie lay on Yvonne's bed, listening with interest to her friend's wild few days away with Jack, "fucking hell. You really landed on your feet there. Large dick and large house. Every girl's dream"

Yvonne was laying on the floor, with a yoga mat for comfort. Her back had been giving her hassle and this was the only way that she could get any relief, "it's more than just that. We get on great. I'm falling in love with him. You probably think I'm being stupid?"

Jamie began to search through her friend's handbag for chewing gum, "you're not being stupid. You're just lucky that he's rich and has a big dick. That's like the perfect man for me", she pulled out the jar of pussy rub and held it up for Yvonne to see, "what's this stuff for?"

Yvonne glanced up from where she lay on the floor and smiled, "you stick it on your clit and it gives you a nice warm tingle. You should try it. Really fucking heightens the intensity of sex"

Jamie jumped up off the bed, "fuck it. I'm gonna give a it a go now. Back in a minute. Just going the toilet", and with that, she disappeared out the bedroom door.

Yvonne briefly enjoyed the peace until her mother barged in the door. Her face was filled with concern.

Yvonne knew something was wrong, before her mother even spoke, "what's up with you?"

Sammy lit up a special cigarette, "Dermot brought his new girlfriend over. She's downstairs"

Yvonne struggled up to her knees, "and what's wrong with that?"

Sammy struggled to word her concerns properly. So just blurted them out instead, "she's black"

Yvonne shrugged her shoulders, "and what's wrong with that?", she'd slept with black fellas in the past herself. But that wasn't something to be shared with her mother right now.

Sammy pulled hard on her cigarette, "this is the same girl he only said the other day, that he could see himself marrying. Even have more kids with. That means half cast grandkids. I'll be the talk of the estate. We can't let him go through with this. You need to talk to him"

Yvonne held onto the edge of the bed and struggled to her feet, "I'm not the one that has a problem with it. So I'm not getting involved. I hope dad is at least being polite. You know what he gets like about stuff like that. He thinks they're all over here to leech off the social. Even though we're all on it as well"

Sammy was far from impressed with her daughter's attitude, "that's totally different. We're irish. We have the right to abuse the social. That lot just swan into this country and expect everything for free. You wouldn't see any of us going to their weird countries, expecting the same handouts. Probably be killed just for asking. They should be just happy that we even let them in. Let alone expecting freebies the whole way"

Yvonne was getting sick of her mother's backwards attitude and she still hadn't answered her question yet, "you never told me what dad thinks about all this?"

Sammy glanced out the bedroom window at the street outside, "he's not home yet. He's gonna be a nightmare when he sees her. You know what he gets like. Especially when he sees her hair"

Yvonne threw her eyes up in disbelief at her mother's attitude, "what's wrong with her hair?"

Sammy struggled to describe it, "you know that short black stubbly look, that a lot of them have. You'd think she'd wear one of those fancy wigs that they're well known for.

Yvonne was well aware of her parent's terrible attitude, when it came to different skin colours. Thankfully it could be mostly ignored. But Dermot had brought the problem right to their doorstep. Something Yvonne had avoided over the years. It hadn't been worth the hassle. And today just proved her right.

Suddenly a loud scream echoed from the bathroom. Mother and daughter ran across the landing to investigate. Sammy swung the bathroom door open, to be met with the sight of Jamie, with her jeans and knickers around her ankles, as she fired cold water onto her bald fanny. Her face was grimaced in pain.

"What the fuck is wrong with you?", Sammy wasn't in the humour for any more problems that day.

Jamie struggled to reply, "my fanny is on fucking fire. That pussy rub burnt the shit out of it", she turned to her friend, "how in god's name, can you say that turned you on?"

Yvonne ignored her mother's dirty glances and picked up the container of pussy rub, "how much did you put on?"

Jamie was still splashing water onto her fanny. A lot of it dripping down onto her jeans and underwear, "I stuck on a big handful. Wanted to get a good tingle off it. Like you were on about"

Yvonne held up the jar for her friend to read the instructions, "you're suppose to only put a tiny bit on your clit. That's all"

Jamie struggled to hide her annoyance, "now you fucking tell me"

Dermot rounded the corner with a stern look that reflected his mood, "what in Christ's name is going on up here ?. I'm trying to make a good impression on Julia. Can you lot not act normal for one bloody day". He tried to point incriminatingly at the lot of them, until he noticed Jamie with her pants around her ankles. Water still dripping from her crotch, "what's going on here?. And why the fuck have you an audience?"

"Piss off", Jamie slammed the bathroom door shut.

Sammy had bigger concerns at the moment, "why didn't you tell me about your girlfriend?"

Dermot had a feeling this was coming. But had hoped he would be proven wrong. Unfortunately not, "I was hoping that you'd just give her a chance. Sit down and chat to her for a while. Didn't hear you moaning when Yvonne was dating a black fella for a while"

Yvonne threw her brother a dirty look, before turning to face her mother.

This was the first Sammy had heard about this, "what black fella was this?"

Yvonne wasn't in the humour for long drawn out explanations, "it was years ago. We dated for a while. No big deal. I just wouldn't mention it to you and especially not dad. You would have been ten times worse than you are now with Dermot. But today is not about me. You two stay here and talk it out. I'm gonna go down and say hello to her. Make a good impression before dad gets home and fucks it up", and with that, she headed downstairs. Leaving the bickering behind her.

Yvonne stepped into the sitting room to find her brother's new girlfriend, examining the framed family photos that lined the mahogany sideboard. She coughed loudly to get her attention, "heya. I'm Dermot's sister Yvonne. Nice to meet you"

Julia turned and smiled politely. Putting her hand out to greet Yvonne, "hi, I'm Julia, nice to meet you. I was just looking through your family photos. I thought Dermot said there was just you and him. But there seems to be more kids in the photos"

Yvonne laughed when she heard the common mistake that was made by people who didn't know them, "my parents used to have all our friends over. Even bringing them on days out to the beach or the zoo. So they just seemed to end up in all the family photos. Kind of became a family joke. We probably have more framed photos of them. Than some of their own parents have", she attempted to throw the questioning back the opposite way, "are you from a big family yourself?"

Julia took out her mobile phone and flicked up a photo of her own family. There was eight kids in total. Standing around a grey haired couple who must have been her parents.

Yvonne studied the photo briefly, "big family. They all doctors and nurses as well?"

Julia put the phone back in her pocket, "my youngest brother is studying to be a surgeon. But the rest of my family went down different career paths. My sister Sofia is an artist. Had her work displayed in a few places around Dublin"

Yvonne couldn't help pointing out Julia's strong accent, "you'd definitely know you where from Dublin. Anyone ever tell you that your accent is pretty strong?"

"Your brother for starters", Julia laughed, "I just seemed to pick it up easier than the rest of my family. Don't know why. But I find it makes me stick out from the crowd and I like that"

That reminded Yvonne of someone else, "you sound just like my brother. Probably why you get on so well"

Julia smiled as she thought about the man who had brought her here, "he's definitely a live wire. Never met anyone like him. You know when you meet the right person. You can just feel something between you. A spark. Ever feel like that about someone?"

Yvonne's mind wandered to thoughts of Jack. It wasn't just a spark between them. It was enough to start a god damn forest fire, "never thought I would. But thankfully the father of this little bundle of joy, proved me wrong", she rubbed her swollen belly.

"May I?", Julia asked as she moved in for a feel.

"Go right ahead", Yvonne still found it strange at how many women wanted to feel her growing belly. Even some men. Which just creeped her right out.

Julia gently rubbed around her belly, "even in my line of work. I still never can stop being amazed at the creation of life"

Suddenly the sitting room door swung open and in fell Bernard. He was pissed drunk and staggering from side to side. He spotted the strange black woman, feeling his daughter's belly and got the wrong end of the stick, "sorry love. Didn't know you had the health nurse calling over. I'll leave you to it", he went to shut the door, to give them some privacy.

Yvonne quickly called him back, "dad, she's not the health nurse. This is Julia. She works in the Lourdes hospital"

Bernard's expression quickly went somber, "is there something wrong with the baby?"

Yvonne hated it when her father was this drunk. It made him impossible to talk to, "no dad. This is Dermot's new girlfriend. Remember he told you about her"

Bernard looked Julia up and down suspiciously, before announcing to her, "you wanna excuse my daughter. She thinks she's fucking hilarious at the best of times. So how's my grandchild doing in there", he patted Yvonne's belly like it was a piece of antique furniture.

Yvonne wanted to tell him to cop the fuck on. But current company didn't allow such an outburst to be possible, "I'm not joking dad. Now be nice and I'll go make you a strong cup of coffee", she turned to Julia, "would you like one as well?"

Julia gave her usual order of black with no sugar. The one thing that got her through most long nights at work.

As Yvonne opened the door to the hallway, she nearly walked right into Dermot as he marched in the door. She gave him a stern look and whispered, "keep an eye on dad. He's acting a bit of an asshole", she walked past him and caught sight of Jamie right behind him, wearing a pair of her white shorts. Yvonne grabbed her by the arm and dragged Jamie unwillingly into the kitchen.

Jamie was still protesting when the kitchen door was shut behind her, "what the fuck. I wanted to see Dermot's new girlfriend. I'm sure you can make the coffee on your own"

Yvonne began to fill the kettle, "my dad is pissed drunk and he's about to make a holy show of himself. I'm not getting involved. Dermot can deal with him and mam's not acting much better. And why have you got my shorts on?"

Jamie jokingly posed in the tight little pair. Showing off her ass in the process, "my jeans are soaked. But you can't deny that my ass looks feckin awesome in these. Way better than yours"

Yvonne was long used to her friend's attitude and just went with it at the best of times, "whatever floats your boat. But we're better off in here. That lot are gonna kick off and I'm not in the humour to get between them"

Sammy entered the kitchen, smoking one of her special cigarettes, "so this is where you two are hiding", she took a long drag, before exhaling a large cloud of white smoke into the air.

Yvonne grabbed the cigarette out of her mother's hand, "you can't be smoking that shit today. Dermot is trying to make a good impression"

Sammy snatched her cigarette back, "why do you care so much?. He didn't go out of his way with Jack"

Yvonne hated to admit that her mother was right. But no matter how badly her family treated her over the years. She'd still try her best to support and be there for them when required. Even if she rarely got any thanks for it, "that doesn't matter mam. Julia seems like a nice girl and I'm trying my best to help today go smoothly for him. I'd just wish you and dad did the same"

Sammy was highly insulted and struggled to hide it, "don't stick me in the same group as your father. I'm not as bad as him"

Yvonne was still trying to prepare the mugs for the coffee, "you aren't much better"

Jamie could see things were getting out of hand, "can we all not just smoke a bit of hash, chill the fuck out and go back in there with a big smile on all our faces"

But before they had a chance to answer. A lot of loud voices rang out from the next room. It was Dermot and Bernard having a verbal disagreement. Sammy rushed out to see what was going on. But she was met with the sight of Julia rushing out the front door, followed closely behind by a worried looking Dermot. Something had just gone terribly wrong and she had a good idea who'd just caused it.

Sammy stormed into the sitting room to find her husband pouring himself a large whiskey from the drinks cabinet, "what the fuck did you just do?"

Bernard kept filling his glass to the top, "I was just making a little joke and the young woman took offence to it. If she's gonna be around this family. She'd wanna grow a sense of humour"

Yvonne and Jamie stood at the open doorway, watching on. Dermot pushed past them as he exploded in anger. Punching his father in the face with his remaining good hand. Bernard dropped his drink and fell against the cabinet. He was briefly stunned for a moment. But quickly got his senses back and swung a punch at his son. It missed widely, before he fell to the floor in a drunken heap.

Dermot stood over him, "why the fuck did you say that?. What part of your small narrow mind made you think that was an acceptable thing to say?"

Yvonne had to ask, "what did he say to her?"
Dermot ran his fingers through his sweaty red hair, "he asked her did she ever hear about the signs they used to have in bed and breakfast windows, years ago in Britain. The ones that read, no blacks no Irish and no dogs. Julia said no. And dad here said, well at least times have changed. They don't mind the Irish. But they still don't want the blacks or dogs. And if that wasn't bad enough. He joked about getting the same sign for this house"

Yvonne couldn't hide her disappointment at her father's behaviour, "I can't believe you did that"

Sammy sat down on the couch. Still smoking her special cigarette, "doesn't surprise me. You know your father when he gets a few drinks in him"

But Dermot wasn't letting his mother off that easily, "you weren't much better. It was nearly a fucking interrogation with you. You'd swear you worked for immigration. Fuck this, I'm getting the fuck out of here. See can I even save what I had with Julia. Fuck the pair of you", he grabbed his jacket off the chair and stormed out. Slamming the front door behind him.

There was an awkward silence between everyone left remaining in the sitting room. Dirty looks being thrown around amongst them.

Jamie chose to be the voice of normality, "anyone still want a coffee?"

Chapter Thirty One

Yvonne hadn't been looking forward to this night. She'd done her best to get dressed up in a brand new maxi dress. Got her hair and makeup professionally done. Which cost more than usual. Thanks to the extra charge her hairdressers added for all the protective equipment they had to use during the procedure. Also, the repair work to her home hair dying wasn't cheap. But it looked fantastic when finished. She just hoped that it would make a good impression on Jack's parents.

The restaurant wasn't that busy looking. Probably thanks to the current restrictions on having to space everyone out around the large room. It was definitely somewhere Yvonne wouldn't have bothered with herself. All style and small meals. Give her a McDonald's or a kebab any day. But now wasn't the time to share her views.

Jack looked stressed enough as he stared at the menu. He'd been dreading this meeting the last few days and now it was really starting to show.

Yvonne reached out and grabbed his hand, "don't be worrying. It's all gonna work out"

Jack wished he had her positive attitude. But he knew his mother was gonna be a hard one to win over. She'd made her mind up about her son's future and that was a hard thing to change. Jack forced a smile to put Yvonne's mind at ease, "I'm sure it will. I just wish they'd let me pick the restaurant. I've never liked this place. All style and small portions. Last time I was here. I ended up getting a takeaway later that night. And the names of some of this stuff is a joke. I reckon they run the names of basic dishes through one of those online translators and see what comes out the other end"

Yvonne glanced through her own menu and quietly laughed, "like this one. Smoked fillet of fresh cod in a lemon juice sauce with finely cut, freshly picked potatoes. That have been fried in cooking oil. Isn't that just fish and chips?"

Jack leaned across the table so no one else could hear him, "it's fish and chips for snobby people"

Yvonne locked her fingers into his, "I love you"

Jack was taken by surprise at first. He wasn't expecting to hear those words from her so soon. But he was quick to return them, "I love you too. I'm just glad we met again"

"Me too", Yvonne pulled him towards her, "can I get a kiss?"

He leaned over and happily complied with her request.

The wine arrived at the table. Yvonne felt it was for the best if she turned down the offer from the young blonde waitress who looked like she should still be in secondary school. While Jack happily accepted. The waitress left the bottle with a smile and disappeared off into the kitchens.

"You not drinking tonight?", Jack kept his voice low.

"I want to make a good impression on your parents. They already think I'm not good enough for you. I just wanna prove to them that I'm not as bad of a person as they think I am"

"I love you no matter what they think. Nothing is gonna change how I feel", Jack replied.

Yvonne smiled, "you really love saying those words now"

"And I'm never gonna stop saying those words", Jack replied.

"Thank you", Yvonne couldn't help breaking into a big smile.

"See you two are here already", Michael stood next to the table with Ellen standing a little further back. Her eyes locked on the baby bump that Yvonne was sporting. Jack got up to greet them and Yvonne felt she should do the same. Michael went in for a hug with the young woman. But Ellen just went for a handshake instead. A strange look between them throughout. Finally they all sat down and tried to make conversation. Which came easier to some of them.

Michael grabbed the bottle of wine and poured his wife a glass, "see you went for your mother's favourite wine"

Jack was trying his best to make the night go by smoothly, "thought I'd save you time by ordering it straight away. Wouldn't mind a beer myself. Don't think they have any on draught though"

Michael perked up, "yes you can. We can go around to the pub and bring them through. I do it all the time", he turned to his wife, "you don't mind looking after young Yvonne here for a minute?". But before either women could complain. Michael and his son stood up.

Jack kissed Yvonne on the cheek and whispered, "don't worry. Might be a good thing to chat on your own for a few minutes. I won't be long", and with that, he disappeared off after his father. Leaving the two women alone. Both trying to find something to look at around the large restaurant. Anything to avoid eye contact.

"You may as well have this", Ellen lifted Jack's glass of wine and placed it down in front of her son's girlfriend.

Yvonne so wanted to drink the whole glass in one quick motion. But she fought the urge, "I can't drink alcohol. Not with the baby", she had to keep up the act for the Jack's sake.

Ellen filled her own glass with wine, "there's nothing wrong with a bit of alcohol. I used to drink a few glasses of wine each night, when I was pregnant on both my boys"

Yvonne figured it was only right to say something on the touchy subject, "I'm sorry about your son Oliver"

Ellen took a sip of her wine, "why, did you kill him?"

Yvonne froze and was lost for words.

Thankfully Ellen laughed, "I'm only fucking with you. You wouldn't believe the amount of people that have said that to me over the years. Now I just say that in retaliation. Makes it easier for me to cope. Think we all need that outlet. One day you'll know what I mean by that"

Yvonne took a much needed sip of her wine, "I suppose you're right. I've seen stuff like that, tear families apart. They fall apart. Rather than pull together. You three still seem very close"

"Me and Michael would be pretty close. We've always enjoyed each other's company, more than others. That's the sign of a strong relationship. But I was always worried about Jack. He pulled away for a long time. Him and Oliver hadn't a great relationship. Don't know if the few years in Australia was a good thing or not. When he came back to Ireland. He seemed to prefer to stay away from home. Moving to Cork for the last few years. Does he talk about Oliver at all?", Ellen's eyes were filled with hope for a positive answer.

Yvonne felt put on the spot. So quickly took another sip of the much needed wine, "they didn't seem to get on. That's what I got from the things he told me. Said that the last few years of Oliver's life was tough on you and your husband. I think he found it difficult to watch you both mentally suffer, as you tried to help Oliver"

"Did he mention that he found him?", asked Ellen.

"Yes he did. That couldn't be easy", Yvonne replied.

"It's gonna sound terrible. But I'm glad it wasn't me. Don't get me wrong. I didn't want it to be Jack either. I know he hides it. It was tough on him. But I don't think I could have dealt with seeing him dead. Even when I walk up the stairs to this day, I try to imagine what he looked like. I know Jack thinks I've moved on. But that couldn't be further from the truth. I've tried to stay strong for my husband and Jack. Michael has been struggling ever since. He might not show it. But it's still affecting him to this day. He's on antidepressants and seeing a psychiatrist. Jack doesn't know any of this. And I hope we can leave it that way", Ellen's stern eyes helped drive the point home.

"No problem", Yvonne thought it might be best to move the conversation on, "I'm sorry if you felt in any way deceived, when we met the first time in the supermarket. I honestly wasn't expecting to see Jack again. I'd plan to do things on my own. Be a single mother. What happened between me and him after that, wasn't at all planned. But I'm glad it did. Jack told me your feelings about me and how you preferred him to stay with Denise. I understand why. You only want the best for him and I'm far from that"

A sudden wave of guilt washed over Ellen as she listened to the young woman's words, "I'm sorry about that. I've been pushing so hard for Jack to have a bright future. That I forgot about his own happiness along the way. I didn't see the warning signs with Oliver. But I've got a habit of speaking before I think"

Yvonne nervously laughed, "I've got that problem as well"

"Then you're in good company. But I've been thinking a lot about life recently. And all I want is for my son to be happy and you do that for him. It'll also be nice to finally be a grandmother", Ellen smiled down at Yvonne's belly.

Yvonne felt a pang of guilt as the truth begged to be revealed to one and all. But she couldn't do it. Her relationship with Jack had come so far, that the truth would only tear that all down again. She rubbed her belly and forced back the guilt, "I can't wait to be a mother myself. Hopefully I can do even half of a good job as you did"

Ellen was delighted with the compliment. But her body language didn't show it, "thank you"

Out in the bar, Michael glanced at his watch, "do you think we gave those two long enough to get to know each other?"

Jack knocked back another shot of Sambuca, "I hope you're right about this dad. This could end up going either way"

"I know your mother better than you", Michael replied, "sometimes you need to put her on the spot to get results. Force her to face up to a situation. Then she's grand. So don't be worrying and have another shot"

Jack glanced down at the row of shot glasses that lined the bar. Only four were empty already, "you've over done it again. We'll be locked by the time we go back in. And I'm not carrying you to the taxi rank again"

Michael picked up a shot glass and knocked it off the head, "that was your eighteenth and you can't deny it was a fucking brilliant night"

"It was a great night. Now we better get this lot drank before mam sends out a search party for us, "Jack picked up another shot glass and knocked it off the head", his face grimacing as the burning effect ran down his throat, "I don't know how people drink these all the times"

"With great difficulty son. With great difficulty", Michael picked up the pace with his shots. Much to Jack's relief.

Back in the restaurant, the two women were getting on a lot better. They barely noticed when the men in their lives, wandered back in. A bit more worse for wear.

Michael sat down beside his wife and kissed her on the lips.

Ellen straight away tasted the Sambuca and seen the drunken expression on his face, "you're pissed"

Michael squeezed her bare thigh playfully, "pissed on love for you sexy"

Ellen kissed him back, "same here honey"

Yvonne leaned over and whispered in Jack's ear, "I hope we're like that in years to come"

Jack kissed her cheek gently, "same here"

Yvonne stared into Jack's eyes and knew he meant it. Their lips met and once again, they felt like the only two people in the room. Everything else didn't matter at that moment. Life was good.

Chapter Thirty Two

The hospital corridors were mostly quiet as Yvonne
snuck around the back of casualty, in a feeble attempt to
get in without security giving her shit. She had a face
mask on. Yvonne hated the bloody things. But she
hadn't much of a choice in certain parts of the hospital.

There was no one around the doorway into casualty and
she was straight in before anyone seen her. Now all she
had to do was find Julia. That was easier said than done.
There was loads of nurses with face masks on. Rushing
about in all directions. Which was strange since there
didn't seem to be many patients around.

Unfortunately the fairly new casualty building, was a lot
bigger than the old one. There was different rooms and
corridors going off in different directions. This was
gonna be a long night.

Dermot had given up hope trying to win Julia back. His
phone calls and texts falling on deaf ears. Yvonne had
noticed how withdrawn he'd gotten ever since that
disastrous meeting in their home. So it was left up to her,
to try and salvage his love life. Before he fell back into
old habits and started screwing anything with a
heartbeat.

An extremely tall porter in a blue uniform, blocked her
way down the corridor, with a battered looking
wheelchair, "are you looking for maternity miss?"

Yvonne knew she'd have to start lying her ass off, "I'm actually looking for a nurse. Her name's Julia"

"I'm gonna need something more than that to go on", the porter replied.

"She's black with short hair", for some reason Yvonne hated to describe Julia like that.

The porter looked around at the nurses rushing around the area he was in, "take a seat over there", he pointed at a row of seats against a nearby wall, "and I'll go get her for you. No need for you to be wandering around it your condition"

"Thanks very much", Yvonne took a seat and watched the porter head off in search of Julia.

It wasn't long until Julia appeared. Disposable gloves on her hands and a surgical mask across her face. She looked disheartened to see Yvonne, "why are you here ?. It's not safe for you. Especially in your condition"

Yvonne patted the seat beside her, "please, can you just sit down for a few minutes and listen to what I have to say. That's all I'm asking for"

Julia reluctantly took a seat, "go on then"

"My family are fucked up. I'm sure you could tell that from the carry on in my house. They've grown up in a different era. And I know that doesn't excuse their behaviour. But it's not them who you're dating. Dermot still isn't talking to them over it. He's broken hearted. I've never seen him like that with a woman before. He normally just fucks them and moves on", it was only then that Yvonne realised that she'd just said too much, "probably shouldn't have said that last bit. But I'm trying to be honest with you here. He misses you so much and I'm pleading with you to give him a second chance. You never even have to come near our house again. Wouldn't blame you either. You should see the shite that my fella has to put up with"

Julia had heard that story in full before. With several comments about Jack being a hard headed prick, when Dermot was trying to do anything sexual with her, that involved the use of his hands, "how are things going with you and Jack?. From what I heard, you two had a rather unique way of getting together. Bet that was a one night stand, that you didn't expect to blossom into a relationship and a baby"

Yvonne felt a little embarrassed about the full truth, "it wasn't even a one night stand. Just a quickie in a nightclub carpark. Wasn't expecting it to go anywhere. Then I ended up pregnant and things just snowballed from there. But it's all been good. Only met his parents the other day. It went better than I expected. I had my doubts that things would work out between us. But now there seems to be a light at the end of the tunnel. Been a long time since I had that positivity in my life"

"That's nice to hear", Julia replied, "a lot of my friends have given up on searching for love. They say it's not worth the hassle anymore. For a while I felt the same way. That was until your brother walked into my life and everything changed. But as I said already. It just seems like too much hassle"

"Please just ring him", begged Yvonne, "even if it's not to get back together. Just give him a bit of closure. That's all I ask. Can you at least do that for me?"

Julia avoided eye contact for a moment as she mulled it over, "I'm not sure. I don't think anything good is gonna come from it. But I'll do it for you. I can see how much you care about Dermot and I do still have a soft spot for him"

Yvonne was over the moon and hugged Julia tightly, "thanks you. You don't know how much this is gonna help"

Julia was surprised by the affection. But still returned the gesture, "wish my sisters cared about me, as much as you do with Dermot. He's lucky to have you to fight his corner"

Yvonne shrugged her shoulders, "that's what family are for. Sticking up for each other. Me and Dermot have had our disagreements over the years. But he's still the best brother that anyone could ever have", it was only then, that she realised how much her brother meant to her. Except Yvonne wasn't gonna tell him that, anytime soon. She wouldn't hear the end of it off him. Sometimes in life, the less that's said between two siblings, the better the relationship.

Chapter Thirty Three

A couple of weeks had past and things had been moving along smoothly. Jack had started to spend a lot of time in Yvonne's house. Staying in her bed each time. He loved to lie beside her naked body and stroke her swollen belly. It was hard to imagine that a small life was growing inside her. His hands couldn't help but move up to her boobs. His erection growing. Rubbing roughly between the cheeks of her arse.

Yvonne was half awake and hadn't slept very well, "I'm tired. Wanna wank yourself off over my ass?"

Jack didn't need to be asked twice and started to stroke his thick cock, while rubbing the moist tip of his purple headed warrior off her ass. It didn't take long for him to splatter his load all over one of her bum cheeks, "oh fuck, sorry about that. Have you any tissues?", he looked around the room. But there was none in insight.

Yvonne moved a little more onto her side. As much as her baby bump would allow, "why don't you lick it all off"

Jack didn't need to be asked twice and went down straight away. He licked roughly around her cheeks. Swallowing up his own cum as he went. Yes it was disgusting. No, it wasn't much of a turn on. But Yvonne wanted it. And he was happy to comply. As soon as it was all gone, Jack moved onto her asshole. Sinking his tongue deep inside that cute little tight ring of flesh.

Yvonne moaned with delight as his long tongue reached deep inside her. Moving around in her back passage, "that feels so good. Please don't stop"

Jack briefly looked up from the job in hand, "no fucking way", before sinking back down and licking away again. This was a job that he was happy to get done right.

Downstairs in the kitchen, Dermot was getting used to not wearing the sling anymore. His wrist was still strapped up. But thankfully he was starting to feel a lot better. The strong painkillers had a lot to do with that. He was in a good place these days. Julia has reached out to him and they'd worked things out. She just wouldn't come near the family home anymore. Something he could easily understand. He was struggling to be around his parents more and more. They'd tried to apologise or play down their previous behaviour and attitude towards his girlfriend. But it didn't change things. He'd grown up with them and was used to their narrow minded views about black people. That was something that just couldn't be turned off.

Bernard flicked through his daily tabloid. Spending way more time than normal on a double spread of Maura Higgins. He was already planning on bringing the paper with him to the bathroom. Only relief he was getting these days. He folded it up and tried to make conversation with his estranged son, "you going out today?"

Dermot was making himself a cup of coffee. Never once offering any to his parents, "I'm going out with Julia. You remember her. The black woman you talked shit to"

Bernard threw his eyes up. This was the start of another one of his son's rants, "how many times do I have to say sorry. I was pissed drunk that day. You should know better than to introduce me to someone like her, when I'm well fucked"

"Someone like her", Dermot tried to hold it together, "what the fuck does that mean?"

Bernard knew he fucked up. Dermot wasn't giving him an inch anymore, "look son, I'm trying. I know she means a lot to you and I'm trying to support you with that. It's just hard for me to change my views on things. But I am trying. I've even fancied black women over the year. That Mel B one was a fine thing in her day. Always said that if I was gonna go out with a black one. It would definitely be her"

The floorboards began to creak above them. Picking up speed over time. Bernard glanced up at the ceiling, "that sister of yours is really taking the piss. I know she's already pregnant. But does she have to keep bloody practicing so much"

Dermot finally turned to face his father, "at least they're happy and in love. Think you and mam lost that along time ago. I don't even know what keeps you two together anymore. Youse always end up fighting after a few drinks. Why do youse even bother?"

"Because I still love your mother and she loves me", Bernard replied, "that's something that doesn't just turn off over night. The wild days of partying will run out sooner or later. The sex will dry up over time. And conversation will become less and less because you both know what the other one is gonna say. That's what long term relationships are all about. Yes, I'd love to be back where you and Yvonne are in your love lives. Carefree and dreaming of a brighter future that will never appear. No matter how much you want it to. But what me and your mother have, is perfect. We have are ups and downs. A lot of arguments along the way. But we still love each other. I couldn't imagine my life without her. Someday you'll know what I mean"

Sammy has been coming down the stairs, when she heard her husband admit his love for her. She knew deep down that he never once stopped. But it was always nice to hear the words come out of his mouth. Even if it wasn't directly to her.

Suddenly the doorbell rang. Sammy could see through the stained glass panel, that it wasn't the guards, thank god. But it did look like someone who'd she'd rather not see. She opened the door and came face to face with Stewy. He was now on one crutch and his new tracksuit and countless gold rings, showed that the money was still rolling in for him.

Sammy folded her arms in defiance, "what the fuck do you want?"

Stewy attempted to push past her, "out of my way. I need to see her. That's my fucking baby inside her and I'm not being fobbed off again"

Sammy put her foot between Stewy's legs and sent him crashing down onto the hallway floor.

Stewy moaned in pain as his legs twisted slightly, "fucking hell. Why the fuck did you do that?. I'm bad enough already. Thanks to Yvonne"

Sammy leaned down beside him, "my daughter didn't do this to you. Your own drunken ass, walked out in front of a moving car. So I better never hear you saying that again. And as for the baby. That belongs to her boyfriend Jack. Nothing to do with you. So move the fuck on and get a life. Because there's nothing here for you anymore"

Stewy sat up and leaned against the wall. His legs still in agony from the fall, "you and I both know that's bullshit"

Dermot stormed out of the kitchen to see what all the noise was about. He spotted Stewy and seen red, "you little prick. I told you to stay away. Looks like I need to get the message across a little better", he grabbed Stewy by the neck of his T-shirt and dragged him to his feet with his good hand, "I'm gonna fuck you up worse than that fucking car did. And I'll only need one hand to do it with"

Stewy showed no fear for once, "do your fucking worst asshole. I'm not afraid of you and I ain't leaving without seeing her"

Bernard came out of the kitchen to see what was happening. He'd never liked the little shit and was happy to see him get a beating, "go on son. Bust the little prick's nose and see those that change his tune"

Dermot didn't need to be asked twice. Holding his prey in place with his bad arm and pulling back his fist for a good punch.

"Don't do it", roared Yvonne down the stairs as she tried to cover her naked body with a light dressing gown.

Jack followed after her wearing only his tight white boxers, which left little to the imagination, when it came to hiding his semi erect monster.

Dermot still had his fist raised to strike, "why the fuck shouldn't I hit him?. He fucking deserves it. Pain in the arse"

Stewy spotted Jack and his abnormally large package, "I can see fucking now why you left me. And you always said that size doesn't matter. What a load of bullshit"

Yvonne finally got her gown tied tightly to protect her modesty, "it's nothing to do with that. I love Jack and he loves me. I fucking loved you once. But you fucked that all up by shagging Sarah. Just go home and leave me be. You lost me a long time ago. Please accept that"

Stewy tried to move, but he was still pinned tightly to the wall, "and what about the baby?. I don't believe the child is not mine. You're just saying that to get me out of your life. You can't do that. I've got fucking rights"

Jack put his arm around Yvonne, "it's my baby, not yours"

Yvonne couldn't love Jack anymore than she already did at that moment.

Stewy still fought to free himself, "fuck you asshole. I'll fucking make you pay. The whole fucking lot of you. Just wait and see"

Dermot had enough and pushed Stewy towards the front door. Sammy opened it wide, as her son frog marched Stewy outside and fired him out the garden gate. The whole family watched on from the doorstep as Yvonne's ex struggled to his feet and balanced himself against the wall.

Stewy was fit to be tied, "you lot are gonna pay for that", he stumbled off on his bad legs.

Yvonne knew Stewy better than most, "I'm afraid he's gonna do something stupid to get revenge on us all"

Dermot wasn't so worried, "fuck him. The little prick is afraid of his own shadow. Don't be worrying about him"

Stewy turned the corner and pulled out his mobile phone. He dialled in a three digit number and waited for an answer, "hello, I want to report someone for holding a large amount of illegal drugs in their house. But you'll have to move fast because they're gonna be moving the stash soon. Time is of the essence"

Chapter Thirty Four

Jamie was feeling pretty fucking good in herself. She'd pulled two fellas the night before in the chippy and was now off to tell Yvonne about all the sexy details. She still couldn't believe it herself. They two fellas had been young, fit and well up for it. Unfortunately a repeat performance was out of the question because they were both married with kids. She still couldn't see what the big issue about that was. Wasn't like she wanted a relationship. She'd be just happy with the sex.

She turned a corner and nearly bumped into a red faced and sweaty Stewy. Jamie didn't hide her annoyance, "slow the fuck down, hop along Cassidy. You nearly hit me with that fucking crutch", only then did she realise that there was only one reason for him to be in that area, "please don't tell me you were harassing Yvonne again?. Get the fucking hint. She doesn't want you anymore and the child is not yours. Now fuck off and stay fucked off", she got right up in his face.

Stewy flashed a sinister smile, "none of that matters now. And I wouldn't recommend calling round there now. They're about to be paid a visit. And if I know Bernard as well as I think I do. I reckon he's got a big stash of drugs hidden in that house to get him a nice long prison sentence. Maybe even that Dermot prick as well. Two faced little bastard"

Jamie head butted him hard in the nose. Blood spurted all over both of them, before Stewy fell to the ground in agony. She stood over him, "you sneaky little prick. That's only for starters. Wait till I get you again", and with that, she ran off in the direction of her friend's house. The tight fitting tracksuit, seeming more like a mistake with each forward lunge she took.

Back in Yvonne's house, the family were now all dressed and in the kitchen discussing recent events.

Sammy was concerned most of all, "do you think that little prick will do anything?"

Dermot had heard rumours about Stewy's sneakiness over the years, "he's been blamed for fucking people over in the past. He always denies it. But I reckon he calls the guards on people he doesn't like", he stared over at his father, "are you holding onto anything at the moment?"

Bernard thought for a moment, "just a couple of kilos of heroin. Not too much. Do you think we should move it?"

"What's all this we business?", Dermot shot that one down straight away, "you brought the drugs into this house. You can feckin get rid of them and soon. I don't trust that little prick"

Jamie ran through the back garden and in the kitchen door. She was sweating profusely. Her white tracksuit top was now damp. She tried to catch her breath while pulling the top's zip down, "Stewy rang the guards. Told them you have loads of drugs here"

Yvonne's mouth dropped open, "oh fuck. What do we do now?"

Bernard ran past them and up the stairs to retrieve the packages, hidden under the floorboards.

Sammy started to panic, "what the fuck are we gonna do?. They're probably already on the way"

Bernard ran back into the kitchen and flung the shopping bag into his son's arms, "take that and run"

Dermot held up his damaged wrist, "'this is gonna be a cross garden run and I can't fucking climb over many fences in my condition"

Suddenly a car with flashing blue lights pulled up outside the house. Time had run out.

Jack didn't think as he grabbed the bag out of Dermot's arms. He ran towards the backdoor. But he spotted a full latex mask of a hairy gorilla, sat on the sideboard. He had no idea why it was there. Or what it had been used for. All Jack seen was a disguise. He pulled it on and ran out the door. Across the back garden and out into the alley. He skipped over bags of rubbish with ease. Before dodging two guards at the end of the alley, who had just jumped out of another car.

Back in the house, the family watched on as the front door got kicked in and the guards raided the house. One of the guards aimed a gun in their general direction and ordered them all to put their hands up. Everyone complied to his demands. Even Jamie who was smiling from ear to ear. The guard was cute and she was now glad that she picked a good sports bra that morning.

"This is a load of shite", moaned Bernard, "fucking harassment. You'll be hearing from my solicitor about all this"

Dermot wasn't so polite, "bunch of fucking inbred assholes. That's all you guards are. Coming in from the countryside and acting all hard. Fucking scum"

Yvonne knew better than to mouth off. That wouldn't help the situation. She was more worried about her baby, "can I sit down please. I'm nearly seven months pregnant. It's not good for the child"

The guard didn't seem impressed, "you'll be grand love. You don't look that bad to me. Just keep your hands up and stay quiet"

But Sammy wasn't letting it go that easy, "she's heavily pregnant you dick. She shouldn't be made to stand. And I'll make damn well sure that the papers hear about this. Persecution of the travelling community again. I can see the headlines now. Drug bust Garda says no to heavily pregnant woman's pleas for her unborn child. Wouldn't look good for you and your colleagues"

The guard threw his eyes up, "right then. Sit down on the couch over there and rest yourself. The rest of you stay standing"

Jamie threw the good looking officer a cheeky smile, "I'll do anything you like. I'm all yours to use and abuse"

Dermot shook his head, "you'd get up on fucking anything"

"Didn't hear you complaining", Jamie shot back.

There was a long awkward silence after that.

Jack was still on the run. Jumping across garden fences and walls as he struggled to get away from the pursuing guards. He could hear their demands for him to stop. He knew better than that. The fallout from being arrested would be too great. He had to avoid capture at all costs. Unfortunately the mask wasn't helping the situation. His head was sweating like mad and he could barely see out through the narrow eye holes that were poorly cut into the mask.

As he ran down another narrow alley, a patrol car blocked his exit on the other end. But Jack took a chance and slid himself over the bonnet and off the other side. Hitting the ground feet first and he was off again. He pushed past a gang of onlooking teenagers, as more guards seemed to come out of nowhere. Only escape route he had open to him, was down another rubbish filled alley. A smouldering car sat beside the entrance. He took off down it. Followed closely by three guards. Things weren't going well.

Coming out the far end, Jack was met with a large green area spread out in front of him. It gave him the opportunity to open up some much needed space between him and his pursuers. The far side of the green was lined with unruly trees and bushes. Jack threw himself into the lot of them. The branches cutting at his skin as he pushed himself through the dense foliage. Thankfully he reached the other side. He looked back to see that the guards weren't willing to follow. Two going along the right of the hedge and the other one went left. Most likely in search of another way in.

Jack knew he hadn't much time to dispose of the bag. He ran through the many cattle that seemed bewildered by this strange young man, running amongst them. He jumped a barbed wire fence. Barely clearing his crotch across the jagged metal. He looked around for somewhere to hide the bag. The only thing available was the drinking trough for the cattle. He stuck the bag up underneath a small bit of cover that housed the ball cock for refilling the trough with water. Wedging it tightly on top of the metal bar. He just hoped it would hold. Jack had an image of a load of drugged up cattle staggering around the field, out of their heads.

As soon as the bag was in place, Jack ran off towards the gate of the field. He pulled the mask off, before stepping out onto the quiet laneway. There was no one in sight.

When he got a bit further down the lane. He fired the mask into a nearby ditch. Jack just prayed this was the end of his troubles. A life of crime, just wasn't for him.

Chapter Thirty Five

Thankfully things had calmed down over the next few days. The guards never found the drugs. The cows didn't eat them and Bernard was able to recover his stash a few days later. He'd then promised to never hold them in the house again. Especially since they were soon to have a newborn baby join the family.

Dermot was still uneasy about bringing Julia to the family home. This had meant most of their nights together, had to be spent in her house. So when Jack offered them over for a mini house party. The couple jumped at the chance. Along with Yvonne, Jamie and Sarah. Jack had even invited Paul over to join them. His friend had been extremely nervous about the invitation. He wasn't great with people. But Jack had finally talked Paul around and persuaded him to bring a bag of his strong grass.

The group had been amazed at the size of Jack's home. He'd brought them on a tour of the whole house. Even his parent's special room. Jamie taking a major interest in the wall of different sized dildos. When all that was done. They retired to the western style sitting room and began to drink heavily. While Paul silently rolled up joints in the corner for them all. Yvonne decided to mostly avoid both substances. Sipping slowly on a vodka and coke. She couldn't wait till the day she could go a little wild again. But would that day ever come?.

"This is some size house" Dermot was mostly amazed by the room they were in. He'd never thought much about how he'd furnish his own house when he got one. But now he knew that he definitely wanted a bar in it.

Julia was equally impressed with the furnishings, "my parents were getting their house done up and dad wanted a bar in the sitting room. But my mother was dead against it from the start. I would have loved something like this"

Yvonne wasn't saying too much on the subject. Her eyes more focused on the many joints being passed around. She so wanted one. But even being in their presence, was getting her stoned. She could only imagine what she'd be like after smoking one. Let alone her unborn child.

Over at the bar, Jamie was attempting to make a cocktail for Sarah, who was watching on from a nearby stool. Paul was at the other end, concerned about his cigarette papers getting wet.

Jamie was swinging bottles around behind the bar. A poor attempt at trying to look like Tom Cruise in the movie cocktail. It was one of her mother's favourite movies and she'd watched it with her many times over the years. The bottle swinging looked easy enough. But the reality was a lot different, "fucking hell. This looked easier in the film"

Sarah could think of one major difference, "ever think that they were probably using empty bottles while filming those scenes?"

Jamie didn't wanna hear such negativity, "don't start you. Professionals do this all the time. Doubt they use empty bottles"

Paul finally piped up. Which was unusual for him, "Tom Cruise is pretty fickle when it comes to realism. I'd say the bottles were full for all his scenes. He wouldn't have it any other way"

Jamie suddenly found a new liking for the quiet young man, "thank you", she turned back to Sarah with a new found confidence in her views, "you see. I am doing it right", and with that, she threw another bottle over her shoulder. It swung clear and over. Unfortunately it went a little too far and missed her other hand. Smashing onto the tiled floor below her.

Sarah held her head in her hands. Embarrassed for her friend as always.

Jamie glanced down at the mess she just created and then over at a bemused Jack, "don't worry. I'll clean it up", she quickly rushed off towards the kitchen in search of something to sweep the glass up with.

Sarah felt she should try and make conversation with the very quiet Paul, "must be hard to grow your own grass"

Paul shrugged his shoulders as he sealed another tightly packed joint, "it's easy when you have a greenhouse to grow it in. But you can make stronger and more potent crops if you can grow them under strong artificial lighting. There's only so much sun and heat that you can get in Ireland. But when you have the plants constantly getting those kind of conditions. You'd be surprised at what height they can reach to"

Sarah was finding herself more and more intrigued by how much Paul knew. He was polite and friendly. Yes he was a bit shy. But that just made him kind of sweet in a nerdy way. Things hadn't worked out with her older man. The dirty old git had only gotten weirder with his sexual demands. It didn't matter how well off he was. She'd decided to kick him to the kerb in the end. Life was too short to let men treat her like a doormat.

"I'd love to see them sometime. Always wanted to try growing a plant of my own. Just haven't a clue how to get it started", Sarah found herself awkwardly playing with one of the beer mats. A nervous habit that never seemed to go away with age.

Paul threw caution to the wind for once in his life, "I'll give you one of my budding plants. It's only just starting off. So it'll be easy to get home without bringing any unwanted attention"

Sarah was surprised by the offer, "really. You'd actually give me a plant?"

Paul was slowly finding his confidence, "yeah, no problem. Jack said you're all staying over tonight. So if you want. Just call over to my house in the morning and I'll show you the best way to grow it"

Sarah got up and moved down the bar towards Paul. Taking the seat right next to him, "I'm up for that. Are you staying over tonight as well?"

Paul felt a little pang of nerves hit him. He wasn't sure if he was being hit on or not, "I'm just living next door. So I'll probably just head home"

Sarah threw him a cheeky smile, "maybe you'll change your mind before the end of the night"

Paul wasn't sure how to reply to that. So just smiled and nodded in agreement. He liked her. But at the same time, he felt slightly intimidated. He lit up another joint and hoped its strong effects would help him mentally jump those social divides with ease.

Yvonne had been in much need of fresh air. So Jack had brought her out to the back garden for awhile. Leaving Dermot alone with Julia on the couch. He ran his fingers though her short hair. As he stared deep into her eyes, "I love you"

Julia thought he was joking, "come off it. No way you love me already"

Dermot grabbed his drink off the coffee table in front of them. A weak attempt at hiding his embarrassment, "probably pushed the boat out too far with that one"

Julia noticed her mistake. He hadn't been joking at all. She put her arm around him and tried a quick attempt at damage control, "I'm sorry. I honestly thought you were taking the piss. I'm not saying I don't love you. But it's definitely heading in that direction with each day. It's just that I've been there before. Had my heart broken and all. So I promised myself ever since. That I'd be damn well sure before I say those words again. And trust me when I say this. I really want you to be the next person I say them to. I just want to be sure first. Is that okay?"

Dermot wasn't one to express his feelings so openly. So Julia's words had hurt him deeply. But he'd knocked many a woman back in his day. Toyed with their emotions for his own sexual needs. So he could understand that she didn't want to be hurt again. He'd done enough of that himself through the years.

He kissed her on the forehead, "I don't mind waiting. I'm sure my parents put our relationship back a few steps. But I'm happy to retrace them once more"

Julia held his hand tightly, "Same here", she kissed him on the lips.

Jamie strolled past with a dust pan and brush. She seen the couple getting passionate on the couch. Deep down she wished Dermot's hands were exploring her body.

Wanting her like no other man wanted her before. But he never seen her in that way. Thankfully she was getting used to it.

"Will you two get a bedroom before the clothes start coming off", Jamie joked as she headed towards the bar.

Dermot laughed slightly with embarrassment. Turning to Julia, "wanna go find a free bedroom for a while?. It's a big house. Maybe we could christen a few rooms while we're here"

Julia got up and pulled Dermot to his feet, "come on then. Let's satisfy the beast inside you", and with that, the amorous couple disappeared off down the poorly lit corridor. Hand in hand.

Jamie began to sweep up the broken glass. She noticed Sarah and Paul getting on better than expected. She knew from experience that her friend wasn't gonna make the first move. And Paul didn't look the type either. It was time to play Cupid once again.

"Have you seen the library in this house?. A whole fucking room filled with timber shelves, that are stuffed with books. It's a pyromaniac's wet dream. You like reading Sarah. Why don't you get Paul to show you it. Bet they have a few Danielle Steele books"

Sarah had a strong suspicion what her friend was up to and was quite happy to go with it. She turned to Paul, "what do you say?. Wanna show me this library?"

"Okay then", Paul jumped at the chance. Getting off his stool and leading the way with a new eagerness to satisfy her request.

Jamie watched on as another couple went off to be alone. She threw the broken glass in the bin and poured herself another vodka. Before picking up the bottle and going in search of the sex room. Jamie had a date with a ten inch vibrator and another go with that pussy rub. Just this time she was gonna use a lot less of it. Things were still a little tender down there. But she still had her sexual needs to satisfy.

Outside, in the back garden, Yvonne and Jack were sitting on top of the picnic table, admiring the stars above them. The night was pretty cold, so Yvonne had Jack's jacket wrapped tightly around her body, "thanks for tonight. Dermot hasn't brought Julia near either of my parents since her last visit. Wouldn't blame him either. He really wanted to show her that some of the people in his life were normal and I hope he proved that tonight"

Jack was struggling to pretend he wasn't cold, "I'm happy for them. They get on great. I'm just glad my parents went away again. They've gotten an addiction for hotels since they reopened for business. I reckon we could do more nights like this. What do you think?"

"I'm just happy to be in your company. Doesn't matter where we are", Yvonne kissed him gently on the lips.

Jack rubbed her ever growing belly, "I can't wait till we're a little family"

"Same here", Yvonne whispered gently in his ear.

Jack wrapped his arms tightly around her, "wanna head in yet?"

Yvonne looked up at the stars, "in a minute. I'm just loving this view. I haven't just stared up at the night sky in years. That all died off with my magic mushroom years. I forgot how beautiful it is"

Jack stared deeply into her eyes, "even more beautiful with you here"

Yvonne's cheeks reddened with the unexpected compliment, "thank you. I really needed to hear that. I've been feeling a little down with my figure going and all. It's not easy"

"I'm proud of you. And you're gonna be a great mother. I've no worries there", Jack replied with a smile.

"Thank you", Yvonne cuddled into Jack's chest and felt his heart beat close to her ear. She had never felt so safe in her whole life. She just prayed that things would stay that way forever.

Chapter Thirty Six

The heavy door was stiff and creaked loudly as Paul put all his weight behind it. The last thing he wanted was to look weak in front of Sarah. It had been a long time since he'd had to impress a woman. But he still knew that body strength was pretty important to most of them. His thin body definitely didn't help his image. But he hoped Sarah would look past that minor issue.

"My god", Sarah gasped as she turned on the lights to reveal a whole room lined with books. The centre of the room had more free standing bookshelves with a large desk sitting amongst them, "it's like the one in Buffy"

"The vampire slayer?", asked Paul.

"The one and only", Sarah wandered around the shelves. Looking at the many titles on display, "why have they got all these here?. This place is massive"

Paul sat up on the desk. Resting his feet on the wooden wheeled chair, "Jack's parents built it for his brother Oliver. They had a free room left over after all the renovation work. So they converted it into a library for him. He loved to study and read. Also, I reckon Ellen only put it in to show it off to guests at their parties"

Sarah found a little wooden ladder and moved it up beside one of the shelves, before climbing up onto it, "Ellen is Jack's mother. Am I right?"

Paul couldn't help but admire Sarah's beautifully curved ass as it pushed tightly against the material of her blue jeans, "that's right. He was the only one that really used this place. Supposedly he wouldn't be seen for days on end. Think the only one that comes in here now, is the cleaner"

Sarah moved some books, so that she could read the backs of them, "and what about your house?. Have you got a library as well?"

Paul laughed, "not a hope in hell. My father would consider that a waste of room. We do have our own sauna and jacuzzi. Maybe you'd like to come over some time to see it?", it was a long shot. But it was one worth taking.

Sarah turned around on the step of the ladder and threw him a cheeky smile, "bet you're just trying to get me into my underwear"

Paul looked away with embarrassment, "I was just asking. Sorry if that sounded a little too forward"

Sarah climbed down off the steps, "I'm only fucking with you. You seem pretty nervous around me. Do I make you feel nervous", she moved closer and closer to Paul. Her eyes staying locked on his.

Paul wasn't the best with the opposite sex in general. But women being flirtatious and forward towards him. Just made the whole thing even more difficult, "I've just never been great around women. Especially ones I like"

Sarah moved the chair out of her way and stood between Paul's legs. Resting her hands on either of his thighs, "does that mean you like me?"

"Yes I do", replied Paul nervously.

"I like you as well", Sarah gently bit her own bottom lip playfully.

"Can I kiss you?", asked Paul.

Sarah didn't answer him. Instead she went in for the kiss herself. Wrapping her arms around Paul's neck. Letting his inexperienced tongue probe deep inside her wanting mouth.

Paul nervously gripped Sarah's thin waist and pulled her closer. He so wanted to get this right. His mind overthinking every little part of the current situation. Sweat was already forming on his forehead and back. His mind constantly shouting at him, "you're gonna fuck this up"

Sarah sensed his worries and finally came up for some munched needed air, "tell me what's wrong?"

Paul looked down at the floor in shame, "I haven't been with many women in my life", he felt the full truth would sound even worse, "and I'm just afraid of getting this all wrong. I barely know what I'm doing. While you seem so…", he was starting to regret what he was about to say. But he'd gone too far now.

"Experienced?", Sarah finished the sentence for him.

Paul's mind was working overdrive, in an attempt to save himself, "yeah. That sounds really bad. But you just seem so confident. While I'm like a blind man at an orgy. Haven't a fucking clue where my hands are going"

Sarah wasn't one to expect too much from her lovers. Each one being a lot different to the last. She didn't have a type. It was always just who she fancied at that time. Paul was the total opposite of her last lover. In age, looks and experience. But she still wanted him.

"Have you not much experience yourself?. Not even with your last girlfriend?", asked Sarah.

"I didn't do that much with my last girlfriend", replied Paul.

"What about the one before that?"

"I've only ever had the one girlfriend"

Sarah eyed him suspiciously, "are you a virgin?"

Paul couldn't look her in the eyes as the guilt and embarrassment filled his soul, "probably sounds pretty fucking sad to you. A guy my age, never being with a woman like that. Think that's why I gave up trying"

Sarah kissed his forehead gently, "you wouldn't be here with me now, if you gave up. Stop being so hard on yourself all the time. There's nothing wrong with being a virgin. Kind of a turn on if I'm honest. I've never deflowered a virgin in all my years. You'll be my first. Now let me help you out"

Sarah unbuttoned his pants and put her hand deep inside. Feeling around for his erection. But all she could find was his shrivelled cock. She played with it gently, "is someone having a problem with nerves?"

Paul was surprised by the question. He had figured that Sarah would just give up hope there and then, "I don't know what's wrong down there. I can get an erection no problem. Especially if I'm ...", that didn't seem the right thing to say to a beautiful woman who was holding your dick at that very moment.

"Wanking", Sarah laughed, "stop worrying. This happens to a lot of fellas. It's totally normal. Girls can have similar problems. I knew a one who got that stressed about sex. Her fanny used to tighten up so badly, that her boyfriend couldn't even get inside her. She ended up having to smoke hash to relax beforehand. So please. Calm down and let me help you"

Paul was intrigued by her caring attitude, "how can you help me?"

It wasn't long until Paul found himself getting dragged into a large guest room. The lights flicked on to reveal a décor that looked like a clown exploded in there and nobody bothered to clean up the mess.

"Jesus Christ", was Sarah's first impressions of the furnishings.

Paul's eyes didn't care about anything around him except Sarah, "what are we gonna do now?"

"We're gonna get you stripped firstly and then into that nice big bed", she replied with a cheeky smile.

Sarah began to pull his clothes off. Kneeling down to help him with his pants and underwear. Slowly pulling down his boxers to reveal his flaccid cock. Paul couldn't help but be embarrassed.

Sarah sensed this and kissed the tip gently, "stop worrying. Just lie down on the duvet and enjoy the show"

Paul did as he was told and stared up at Sarah, who was now standing over him. She rubbed his bare chest, "I'm gonna put on a little show for you. And as you watch on. I want you to play with this little fella. Until he's ready for action". She turned on a nearby lamp and put the main bedroom light off. Pulling out her mobile phone, Sarah proceeded to find a slow, sexy song that would help set the mood.

Sarah pulled her T-shirt up and over her head to reveal a black lacy bra. She began to rub her breasts seductively through the light material. Cupping each breast gently in her small hands. Paul could feel a little tingle in his penis. Something was happening down there.

Sarah opened her tight jeans and turned around so that he could have a clear view of her ass. She proceeded to pull the denim material down slowly across her firm cheeks. Revealing a matching black thong that beautifully disappeared between the cheeks of her ass. Soon her jeans were down to her ankles and she kicked them off, before proceeding to rub her body suggestively with her finger tips.

Paul's erection grew harder. Not enough for sex. But enough to make him feel a lot more confident about the current situation, "oh fuck you're so beautiful", he blurted out mid wank.

Sarah got down on her hands and knees and crawled along the floor to the end of the bed. She grabbed one of his feet and ran her tongue up the base of his foot, before proceeding to lick and suck his big toe. She then moved onto each one in unison, "not many fellas like me doing this. I just love to suck toes"

Paul wasn't complaining. It wasn't his thing. But it was still nice to be touched by a woman in any kind of sexual manner, "I don't mind. Feels kind of nice, if I'm honest"

Sarah carried on for the next few minutes. Feeding her fetish. Until finally she ran her tongue up his leg, before reaching one of his hairy testicles and taking it in her mouth. Sarah sucked on it gently as he wanked at his cock. Finally she took his hand away and proceeded to vigorously wank him off. Licking the tip of his purple headed warrior with a big smile on her face.

Suddenly Paul exploded all over Sarah's face. The cum dousing her eyes and mouth with its salty goodness.

Sarah sat up and tried to wipe her eyes clean, "Jesus, I wasn't expecting that"

Paul was relieved. But at the same time, absolutely mortified. He'd definitely cum way too early, "I'm really sorry. I didn't mean for that to happen", he grabbed his T-shirt off the floor and handed it to her, "wipe your face with that"

Sarah grabbed the T-shirt and wiped her face. But the sticky cum was well and truly stuck into her hair. Thankfully she laughed it off, "that was definitely some load that you were holding back. At least with that out of the way. We can now get onto a nice long rampant sex session", she fired Paul's top back onto the floor, before climbing up onto his waist, pulling her thong to one side and sliding his still erect cock deep inside her wet wanting pussy. She moaned with excitement.

Paul had never been inside a woman before. If felt totally different from how he had imagined it. It wasn't as tight as expected. But definitely wet. He could feel Sarah's juices running down onto his crotch as she slowly bounced up and down on him. He was half tempted to ask about a condom. But feared she might take that up the wrong way.

Sarah pulled her bra off and grabbed his hands, positioning them tightly on her perky breasts. Paul gently played with her nipples as she writhed around on top of him. He never wanted this moment to end.

Suddenly Sarah moaned loudly. A gush of fluids ran out from deep inside her pussy, "oh fuck, that felt good", she moaned. Her body still riding him like a well experienced cowgirl.

Paul held on for dear life, as she picked up speed. More liquid gushed out on top of him. Sarah cursed loudly as another orgasm hit her.

Soon Paul couldn't hold off anymore and he exploded his sticky white load deep inside her, "oh fuck that felt good"

Sarah orgasmed once more and fell down on top of him. Her sweaty body rubbing tightly off his, "hope you enjoyed that", she struggled to get her breath.

Paul was exhausted as well, "enjoyed would be an understatement. That made my whole fucking life. God you're wonderful. Where have you been all my life?"

Sarah kissed him on the lips, "always nice to hear from a satisfied customer", she lay her head down on his chest, "now, I need a bit of a rest before we go again"

Paul smiled from ear to ear, upon hearing this. Looked like his insomnia would finally come in handy for something.

Chapter Thirty Seven

There was a very strange smell filling the corridors of the house. Somebody either was cooking or a weird scented candle had been lit. Jack reckoned it was the first option.

He stepped into the kitchen to find Jamie playing chef that morning. She'd mixed up something in a bowl and was now cooking it in a weird kitchen appliance that looked a bit like an omelette maker. Jamie had on one of Jack's mother's novelty aprons. The one he had both as a joke and his mother had refused to wear. Probably wasn't the best idea to get one with the body of a naked man, printed down the front. And to top it all off. It had a large fake willy attached were it should be. The long fluffy member, swung around as Jamie moved from counter to counter.

Sarah sat across from her, eating a small bowl of cereal. She spotted Jack, "morning. Hope you didn't mind us getting our own breakfast?"

Jack sat a few stools down from her, "not at all", he turned to Jamie, "what are you cooking?. It smells nice"

Jamie opened up a nearby appliance and popped the contents out onto a plate, which she placed in front of Jack, "they're egg waffles. Way nicer than the potato ones. Don't mind that lying shite, Aisling Bea. These are the feckin best ones going. Just add cream, strawberries or maple syrup and you've got a beautiful breakfast. And the ingredients for some kinky food sex afterwards. What would you like on yours?. Your parents have some fucking spread here. I found everything I needed. Even the fucking waffle iron"

"I didn't even know we had a waffle iron", Jack glanced around at the toppings that were on offer, "I'll go for the syrup please"

Jamie handed it to him and proceeded to pick up a few oranges from a nearby glass bowl, "want some orange juice with that?. Please say yes because I love using the machine you have for it"

"Go on then", Jack was starting to like her more and more. Jamie was a good laugh to be around. Always doing the unexpected. It always brought a smile to Yvonne's eyes. And that's what Yvonne needed most these days. The late stages of pregnancy was really getting her down.

Jamie began to run the oranges through the large machine that sat on the counter. It made a loud chopping sound as it devoured the oranges whole and spat them out the bottom as orange juice. She let the glass fill near to the top before handing it to Jack, "there you go"

"Can I get one as well?", Sarah asked.

"Coming up", Jamie was delighted at the opportunity to play with the machine again. She popped in more oranges and listened with interest as it tore them apart. The glass was soon full and she handed it to Sarah.

Jack was more interested in how his friend got on the previous night. But he had to approach this carefully. Just in case Paul had gone home and nothing happened, "so, how'd it go with Paul last night?"

Jamie didn't even give her friend time to answer, "Sarah here wore him out. Shagging the lucky little git all night. He definitely picked the right girl to lose his virginity to"

Jack nearly choked on his waffles, "he actually told you?"

A cheeky smile spread across Sarah's face, "he did. But I would have guessed it in the end. I'm glad I was his first. Poor fella just needed someone to break him in slowly. Bet he wouldn't have gotten that treatment off Jamie here"

Jamie looked up from her cooking, "excuse me. I can be gentle when I want"

Sarah laughed, "yeah right. We both know that's bullshit. Now let us try one of these waffles"

Jamie fired two fresh waffles onto a plate and held it just out of reach of her friend, "now, take that back and you can have the waffles"

"I'm sorry", Sarah jokingly replied, "now can I have my waffles?"

Jamie put the plate down in front of Sarah and patted her on the head, "good girl. Now eat up before it gets cold"

Dermot stumbled into the kitchen. He was dressed fully from the waist down. But he was still opening up his T-shirt to put on. The two ladies stopped what they were doing and turned to get a good look. Admiring his many tattoos and hairy chest.

Jamie's mouth was open and close to drooling, "think I know what I want to put my cream and syrup on"

"Unfortunately that's off the menu", Sarah joked.

"Morning everyone. Hope you all slept well", Dermot pulled his top on and fixed it down over his chest, "that was some comfortable bed. Way better than my shitty one. I really need to get a new one"

"Say you wrecked the springs on your one", Jamie joked.

"You should know all about that", Dermot fired back.

Jamie went red in the cheeks and smiled widely. It boosted her confidence to know that Dermot still remembered their particular energetic romp. Even if it was never gonna happen again.

Dermot took a seat next to Jack, "so what are we having for breakfast?"

Jamie placed a plate of waffles in front of him, "here you go. Make sure you cover them in syrup and whipped cream. It'll taste even better", she threw him a seductive smile.

Dermot totally missed it and just started eating, "grand thanks. I was doing a lot of thinking this morning. About that little cunt Stewy. He still has to pay for what he tried to do to us. Wanker didn't give a shit who'd end up in the Garda station that day. And the fact that he still thinks he's the father of Yvonne's unborn baby, just makes it even worse because he couldn't give a fuck if she got locked up and all. No way he's getting away with that"

Jamie enjoyed the idea of punching the head off the little prick. Her heart rate already rising at just the thought of it, "are we gonna fuck him up?. Because I'm well up for that"

Dermot held up his damaged hand, "I won't be fucking up anyone for a while yet". He nudged Jack's shoulder with his own, "thanks to this hard headed bastard here"

"And I'm still sorry about that", not as sorry as Jack pretended to be.

Dermot continued, "but that's not how we're gonna get revenge on him. That little bastard can take a beating better than most. He'd just walk away from it and move on with his life. I've got a much better idea. But I want to know first if you're up for this?"

Jack wanted revenge just as much. Mostly because of the hassle he brought to Yvonne's doorstep, "I'm up for it. Little bastard deserves to get taught a lesson"

But there was a problem with Dermot's plan, "we need at least one more person to help with this. I'd do it myself. But my hand is gonna let me down and there's a lot of climbing involved"

"Climbing?", Jack was totally lost now.

"I'll do it", Jamie blurted out, "I was always great on the ropes in gym class. Can fly up any climbing frame without falling. Even that tall one up in that park in Dublin"

"And she was out of her head, doing that one", Sarah added.

"Exactly", Jamie continued, "anything that involves getting back on that prick, I'm up for. Now what's the plan?"

Dermot was surprised at their eagerness to help, "right then. But there's only one thing we need to agree on first. No one finds out about this. Not Julia, my parents and especially not Yvonne"

Jack didn't like the prospect of lying to Yvonne, "I'm not comfortable with not telling her. And if something happens to Stewy. She's gonna put two and two together and know we had something to do with it"

Dermot held his hands up to stop Jack's babbling, "right then. You can tell Yvonne. Just after we've done the job. At least then, it'll be too late for her to talk us out of it. Is that acceptable?"

Jack wasn't sure what he was agreeing to. But he wanted to be part of it, no matter what, "that's grand. Now tell us this plan of yours"

Chapter thirty eight

The alleyway was in total darkness as Dermot reversed
the van back towards a large cargo bay door. Turning off
the headlights, he checked his surroundings and was
satisfied that no one was watching, "right you two. Time
to make a move", he jumped out of the driver's seat and
opened the back doors wide.

Jack got out, carrying five long cardboard tubes, which
had white plastic bungs on each end. He had one of his
dad's skiing balaclavas on and was dressed in a black
tracksuit, "hope you're sure about the alarm system?"

Dermot glanced up at the ladder that was built into the
wall above them. It only started ten feet off the ground
and led to the roof of the building, "it'll be grand. I know
the guy that installed it. Totally done on the cheap. Most
of the sensors and cameras are there just for show. So
you'll be in and out without anyone noticing"

Jack was still doubtful, "I hope you're right"

Jamie climbed out of the back, fixing a pink balaclava
over her face. It had a large fluffy white bobble on top,
that swung around as she moved.

Dermot tried not to laugh, "where the fuck did you get
that?"

Jamie fixed her tight fitting leather jacket, "I made it out of one of my old hats. I think it looks pretty fucking awesome. So don't start your sneering"

Dermot pulled out a long length of rope and began to wrap it around the cardboard tubes, "I'm only messing with you. It looks great. Now get up onto the top of the van and you'll be able to reach the ladder"

Jamie moves like a cat as she clambered up onto the top of the van and jumped with ease. Grabbing the bottom rung and pulling her body upwards. The two lads watched on. Mostly because she was wearing skin tight black horse riding pants, that left little to the imagination.

"That's one fine arse on that one", Dermot couldn't help but look.

"Definitely", Jack forgot himself briefly.

That was until Dermot gave him a sneaky dig in the shoulder, "but you shouldn't be fucking looking. Now get this rope tied tightly onto your belt and get climbing. We've only got an hour before the next security guard comes to check the building. He's managing a few places in the area. So even if he does show up. He won't check the place over properly. But I'll still have to move the van. So let's hope it doesn't come to that"

Jack climbed up onto the roof of the van and looked up at the high rung above him. It sounded easy, when the plan was explained to him, only a few day before. But now in reality, it looked a whole lot more difficult. He took a deep breath and made the jump. Grabbing the bottom rung with both hands. He forced his feet against the wall and pushed himself up towards the next rung. The rope still hanging from his belt. Dermot was still on the ground, guiding the cardboard tubes as they rose up into the air after them. The execution of the plan was out of his hands now.

Jack was making good time as he quickly caught up on Jamie. Her firm buttocks not far from his face now.

Jamie looked back down and flashed a cheeky smile at him, "hope you're not looking at my arse back there"

"Don't worry. I'm not looking at your arse", Jack was more concerned about the fall.

"Why?. What's wrong with my arse?. Most men would love to be in your position"

"I'm a bit more concerned about falling Jamie. Now please just keep moving"

Finally they reached the top of the ladder and Jack untied the rope from his belt, "we need to find the right skylight", he glanced around the large rooftop to see that there was about twelve of the bloody things, "we better spread out and start looking for it"

"Okay", Jamie lit up a joint and took off down one row.

Jack couldn't be arsed complaining about the joint and just went in the other direction. Still regretting ever agreeing to this plan in the first place.

They both stumbled around the rooftop in the dark until Jamie spotted the room they were looking for, "it's over here"

Jack couldn't help the natural reaction to look around. Just to make sure that nobody heard her. But there was slim chance of that. Since they were about twenty feet off the ground and far away from any busy pubs.

Jack peered down through the skylight and studied the large room below them, "think you're right. It's the only room with paintings in it", he noticed something directly below them, "what the fuck is that thing?"

Jamie took out her mobile phone and turned the light app on. She shone it down through the glass to illuminate a white cloth covered table with a pile of brochures on one end and a cardboard head and shoulders photo of Stewy, "this is definitely the right fucking place. There's a photo of the slimy little bastard down there. Now, how the fuck are we gonna do this?"

Jack tied the end of the rope around his waist tightly, "I'm gonna lower you down with the tubes and the rest is up to you"

Jamie picked up the other end of the rope, "I'm shite at fucking knots. It'll end up opening if I do it"

Jack hadn't time to argue, "right then. I'll tie the fucking thing. He took the end of the rope off Jamie and wrapped it around her waist tightly, before putting a double knot in it, "is that tight enough for you?"

Jamie threw him a cheeky smile, "always been a bit partial to bondage. You'd definitely make a great Mr Grey. Bet Yvonne loves it when you tie her up"

"We haven't tried that yet", replied Jack.

"Forget I said anything then", she turned and climbed up onto the arched skylight.

Jack figured it was best to let the topic go for the moment. But the thought of trying bondage with Yvonne, was definitely giving him a hard on. He struggled to push it to the back of his mind and get on with the job in hand. Climbing up onto the frame of the heavy glass. He searched around for a way to open it. But nothing was springing to mind.

"What about this thing?", Jamie moved further out onto the white PVC frame to investigate a small metal catch, that was screwed onto the side.

Suddenly the skylight they were standing on, tilted to one side and the two of them slid downwards. Both of them grasping at air, in the hope it would stop their fall.

Jack thankfully grabbed the rim of the window and stopped his decent. Jamie on the other hand, fell quickly towards the table below her. But suddenly, her body snapped to a stop a few feet from it. Hurting her stomach in the process.

Unfortunately the sudden stop had made Jack lose his grip and he fell down beside her. Slamming into the table hard. The sudden impact, made the whole table collapse, sending Jamie falling onto its contents and the whole lot spread out across the floor. Everything briefly went silent.

Jack groaned loudly as he looked up at the skylight above them, "this has all really gone to shit quickly"

Jamie forced her sore body up, "ain't that the fucking truth", she looked down at the large cardboard picture of Stewy beneath her, "dirty little bastard will never have the pleasure of having me in this position for real", she proceeded to punch his picture. Hurting her hand slightly. But it was well worth it.

Jack stumbled to his feet, "how the fuck are we gonna get out of here now?"

Jamie untied the rope from around her waist, "let's just get the job done first and then we'll worry about our escape", she grabbed the cardboard tubes and proceeded to open them up, before pulling out a load of rolled up sheets of paper.

Jack couldn't help but examine one of Stewy's paintings a little closer. It was framed with rather expensive looking varnished wood. But the picture definitely looked out of place. He wasn't sure if it was his own dirty young mind. But it definitely looked like a vagina.

Jamie was already spreading glue on another painting and putting one of the sheets of paper they'd brought with them, fully over it. She pressed down hard to make sure it stuck tightly.

Jamie noticed Jack was still examining the same painting, "can you please stop looking at that fanny and get on with the job in hand"

"So I'm not just seeing things. I definitely thought it was a fanny as well", replied Jack.

Jamie started on the next painting, "it's not just any fanny. That's Yvonne's. He's put the freckles all around it and all. She definitely must have left a lasting impression on him"

Jack didn't want to know how Jamie knew Yvonne's vagina so well, "oh right", and got to work with his own tube of glue.

It wasn't long until the whole room was complete and the only thing left to do was to fix the table in the middle and put all its contents back in place.

"What now?", Jamie asked as she picked up the empty cardboard tubes and fired them into a large bin in the corner of the room.

Jack noticed the long corridor the led off the gallery, "let's try down there", he rolled up the rope and led the way.

Jamie lit up another much needed joint, "hope you know what you're doing?"

Jack was starting to lose his cool with her, "I haven't a clue what we're doing. I've been winging it since you made us both fall through the feckin skylight"

"Don't blame this shit on me"

"Let's just gets the fuck out of here and we can argue about whose fault it is later"

At the end of the corridor, there was a disabled toilets. Jack opened the door and spotted a small window with no bars on the outside, "perfect. I can tie the rope around you and lower you to the street. You'll only be a few feet off the ground"

Jamie spotted one big flaw in his plan, "and how the fuck are you gonna get down?"

That bit Jack wasn't too sure of, "you'll have to get back to the roof and lower the rope down. Then I'll have to try and climb it"

Jamie stared at him doubtfully, "have you ever climbed a rope before?"

"No, but I'm sure it's easy enough", replied Jack.

"No it's fucking not. Trust me. I've done it loads of times before. So you're going out the fucking window and you can lower the rope down through the skylight for me"

Jack was feeling quickly emasculated by Jamie's strength and abilities.

Five minutes later, Jack was down on the ground again. Jamie fired the rope out after him and after a bollocking from Dermot for leaving her alone inside, Jack was back up on the roof and holding carefully onto the thick rope as Jamie climbed it with surprising ease.

Soon Jamie was back on the roof and the skylight was shut. She rubbed her dusty clothes down, "piece of piss"

Jack wanted to say something a little more colourful on the subject. But he chose to bite his tongue instead.

It wasn't long until they were all back in the van and on their way out of the alley.

Dermot was smiling from ear to ear, "that little prick Stewy is in for a nice surprise tomorrow", he turned to his battered and bruised passengers, "was his paintings any good?"

"Load of shite", Jack felt it was best not to mention the picture of Yvonne's anatomy.

But Jamie wasn't one to hold back, "there's a painting of your sister's fanny in there"

"How the fuck do you..", Dermot held up his hand to stop her, as he realised that some things are better off not being talked about, "please, for the love of god. Don't answer that"

The rest of the journey continued in mostly silence.

Chapter Thirty Nine

There had never been a day as important as this to Stewy. He was starting to believe all the hype that his hanger ons were filling his head with. So had decided to change his image a lot. He now wore thick, black rimmed glasses. He didn't need them. But Stewy felt he looked good and more intelligent with them on.

Even his dress sense had changed. Deciding now that pants and wooly jumpers were the way to go. Replacing his crutch for a fancy walking stick with a good clenched fist on the top of it. Just like the one out of back to the future. He definitely felt the part of a real artist, as he strolled into the Griffith's art gallery.

Stewy was quickly surrounded by his many fans and followers. All of them excited about the grand opening of his new pieces of art. He was so proud of them. Every piece had something to do with Yvonne. His love for her, splashed across every wall for her to see. His last ditch effort of winning her back. Some of the pieces included elements of their sex life. Other ones included childhood memories that she had shared with him over the years. While the last of the paintings tried to visualise the negative thoughts and feelings he'd been suffering since she had dumped him.

Sleeping with Sarah was the biggest mistake he'd ever made in his life. Mostly because she was the only one of many girls that Yvonne had caught him with. It had never bothered him over their relationship. But now looking back, he could see they had a good thing between them. Unfortunately it took two broken legs and being dumped, to finally see that.

Stewy arrived at the entrance to the gallery. A red ribbon ran across the large doorway. Photographers were already setting up for the grand opening. The mayor had even turned out for the event. This was gonna be spectacular.

As Stewy greeted many fellow artists and critics, the elderly owner of the gallery, Mr Griffith, hurried up along side him, "excuse me sir. May I have a word about some of your work before we cut the ribbon?"

Stewy loved to be asked about his art and this would hopefully be the first of many questions that day, "go on then. But make it quick. We're about to open up this whole exhibition to the public. Big day for me and you"

Mr Griffith looked nervous about carrying on, "it's just that some of your pieces aren't exactly what we expected for the event. To be honest, some of them are downright vulgar"

Stewy tried to contain his anger, "I thought you understood art. If you can't accept my brilliant creations. Then you shouldn't be in this fucking job. Now get the hell out of my face before I make a holy fucking show of you in front of all these nice photographers"

Mr Griffith glanced around at the many reporters and walked away. Fuming quietly.

A beautiful young blonde woman in a tight black dress, pushed through the crowd with a large set of gold scissors in her hands. She handed them carefully to Stewy, "its time for your big moment", she leaned in close to his ear, "thanks for last night. You really made it feel so special"

Stewy glanced down at her ample cleavage on show, "I'll paint you again tonight if you like?"

She made sure that no one was listening before answering, "just as long as this stays between us. Last thing I need is for my husband to find out"

"Your secret is safe with me", Stewy replied with a poorly concealed sleazy smile, before proceeding to get on with the job in hand. Opening up the scissors and placing the red ribbon between its blades, "okay everybody. I'm about to open my new baby up for your pleasure. Everything on show has a strong meaning to me. Parts of my life that has been seared onto my brain and stayed there ever since. This is my way of expressing those inner feelings", he spotted a familiar face among the crowd. It was Yvonne. He kept on talking. But his words were now directed towards her, "we've all been in love. All felt that hurt that comes with it. Some more than others. We make mistakes. Sometimes ones that can't be forgiven. But it's those mistakes that can haunt you for years to come. This collection of work is my way of begging for forgiveness. It's something I need most. But I fear I'll never get. Thank you", and with that, he cut the ribbon and the crowds began to filter inside.

But Stewy didn't care about that. He's eyes still locked on Yvonne. He pushed through the crowd towards her. He wasn't sure what to say first, "I'm glad you came"

"So you're not gonna apologise for nearly getting my father locked up?", Yvonne's stern face said it all.

Stewy tried to play it down, "I had nothing to do with that", it had been a total mistake. Mostly thanks to anger and alcohol. A weak point in his character since becoming an artist.

Yvonne wasn't gonna get into it now. She was already satisfied about the plan to get revenge on her ex. Only being told about the whole scheme that morning by a battered and bruised Jamie. Who had slept on her couch the previous night. Moaning loudly about her injured back.

At first Yvonne had been angry at their actions. But the more she heard about the paintings of her body parts and childhood memories. The more she wanted to make sure that no one ever seen them. Her life wasn't gonna be used by someone else to make a profit.

"Let's not play games here", replied Yvonne, "you tried to ruin my family. And if you really gave a fuck about me. You wouldn't have done that. You never loved me. I was just something you wanted to own. While you went around and fucked god knows who"

Stewy tried to defend his honour, "I never slept with anyone else except Sarah. And that was a total mistake. Don't know why I ever slummed it with her. She's not the best looking"

"Don't knock fucking Sarah. She is good looking and a nice person. She was just stupid enough to believe your bullshit", Yvonne was still trying to control her anger.

"Why can you forgive her and not me?. That makes no sense", pleaded Stewy.

"Because she's been my friends for decades now. I know her weaknesses. I know how she's easily led. That she follows her heart too much. I'm not throwing away a good friend because she made a mistake with you. But you're just a Johnny comes lately in my life. When I caught you in bed with her. I knew there and then that I had to move on with my life. Amazing when you finish a relationship, how many people come out of the woodwork to tell me about all the other women you were screwing behind my back. Funny how they won't telling you before that. You've lost me. So get over it", Yvonne went to walk away.

"What about the baby?", asked Stewy.

Yvonne thought she'd gotten her point across. But it looked like he was never gonna believe her about the child's father, "what about the baby?"

Stewy got right up in Yvonne's face, "we both know that child is mine. I don't believe all this shit about this one night stand being the father. You're just doing this to punish me. That's all it is. But I ain't going quietly. I'm gonna fight for joint custody. I've got the money now and the free time. So you can walk away all you want. But this won't end here"

Yvonne was truly sick of the little prick by now. It disgusted her to think that she ever let him inside her. The memory of some of her orifices being violated by his extremities, made her feel even worse, "what if you were the fucking father. What then. You and I both know you'd be a useless father. Think you forget that you told me about your other kid Adam. How often were you there for him?. You never gave his mother money. You only seen him by chance on the street. Have you ever bothered with him since?. Now, being fucking honest for once. When did you actually ever go out of your way to see him?. Do you even know anything about him?. What's his favourite colour. Who's his best friend?. Do you know any of that stuff about him?"

Stewy couldn't look her in the eyes, "the mother wouldn't let me see him"

"That's because you only tried to contact him after eight years. You left her to bring that child up on her own. I never told you this. But I ended up talking to her on a night out. She's a lovely girl. Said you dumped her as soon as she got pregnant. And then you had the cheek to say the child probably wasn't yours. If that's the way you treated your first child. Why would any other woman want you around your next?"

Stewy's face was filled with guilt. Her words touching an emotion that he'd long since buried.

But before he had a chance to answer. The young blonde rushed up and grabbed his arm roughly, "there's something wrong with the paintings. You better get in here now and sort it out"

Stewy glanced back at Yvonne. He just knew she had something to do with it.

Yvonne just smiled, "better go check up on your work"

Stewy hurried inside with the attractive blonde.

Yvonne figured it was time to leave. She grabbed a small booklet about the art exhibition off a nearby table and opened it up. She was met with a small photograph of the painting of her vagina. It was actually a good likeness.

Stewy rushed inside the gallery and was met with the sight of numerous crayon drawn pictures of erections, blowjobs and people having doggy style sex. On further examination. All the drawn characters were men. Big beards and willies hanging off every animated body, "what the fuck is this shit?", he bewilderingly moaned.

"It's a fucking disaster",Mr Griffith stood angrily to one side, as photographers and critics scrutinised every piece on show. The wheels had just fallen off, Stewy's gravy train.

Chapter Forty

"You really are a moaning shite", Jamie couldn't see what the big deal was about giving birth to a baby.

Yvonne was bent over the kitchen table as Sarah rubbed her back.

Sammy was making another hot water bottle for her daughter, "wait till it's your time Jamie. You won't be so bloody mouthy"

Jamie lit up another joint and opened the backdoor to let the smoke go out, "I won't be ever getting pregnant. Can barely look after myself. Let alone another little person. I'm happy the way I am. Shit like this just drives that point home"

Sarah had been bottling her irritation at Jamie's lack of compassion, "can you be a little more supportive. Yvonne's in a heap here. She's about to squeeze something the size of a watermelon, out of her fanny. She needs our support"

Yvonne's hands were clenched tightly onto the edge of the table, "saying that the birth is gonna be like pushing out a watermelon, is not fucking helping"

Sarah rubbed her friend's back a little harder, "sorry about that"

Dermot and Bernard were in the adjoining room, watching the football on the telly. The glass doors that separated the two rooms were wide open and the moans of Yvonne were starting to get in the way of their enjoyment.

"Can you keep it down sis. I can't hear the telly"

Yvonne wanted to lose her shit. But she was too fucking tired to shout, "fuck you. You'll never know this pain"

"Thank fuck for that", Bernard added.

Sammy shut the doors over before anything worse was said.

Yvonne had another painful contraction. She balled her fists and forced her tired body to take the pain, "fucking hell. Did you definitely ring Jack?. I want him here now"

"Calm the fuck down", Jamie was growing impatient with her friend, "I fucking rang him. He's on the way"

Sarah was starting to sense that her back massage wasn't helping anymore, "do you want me to stop?"

Yvonne tightened all her muscles as she waited for the next contraction, "no, please keep going. It's helping. Thanks"

Sarah was glad just to help in some small way.

Jack came running in the kitchen door. Panic plastered across his face, "is it already coming?"

Yvonne stared at him angrily, "no it's fucking not. It's gonna be feckin hours at this rate"

Sammy poured a whiskey and added a little hot water from the kettle. She placed it on the table in front of her daughter, "drink that"

Yvonne was getting sick of all the shitty help, "how the fuck is that gonna help me?"

Sammy shrugged her shoulders, "can't do any harm either"

Yvonne couldn't disagree with that point, so she grabbed the glass and knocked it off the head, before sitting down on one of the wooden chairs.

"They should show this to teenage girls in school. Definitely put them off getting pregnant", Jamie was supportive as always.

Jack sat down on the chair next to Yvonne. He kissed her sweaty forehead, "you're doing great. Won't be long now", felt like the right thing to say under the circumstances.

Yvonne suddenly stood up and held onto her sore lower back, "fuck it. Let's go to hospital. I can't go on like this. I need some decent drugs"

Jamie held up her lit joint, "will this help?"

Yvonne threw her eyes up, "I mean fucking proper drugs. Like that thing they stick in your spine. I need that shit and I need it now. Get us to the fucking hospital", she stumbled towards the hallway to grab her bag of necessities for the hospital. The rest of the family followed close after. Afraid to say anything that was contradicting to Yvonne's current needs.

Yvonne opened the front door, to be greeted by the sight of the pink BMW, "oh for fuck sake. Could you not have brought your mother's car instead?"

Jack took the bag off Yvonne and ushered her towards the car, "my mother's car would be too cramped for you. At least with the BMW, you can lie out in the back", he opened the back passenger door and led her inside.

"I'm coming", Jamie announced and jumped in the back beside her.

Sarah got in the front passenger seat and put on her seatbelt, "we better get going before the baby starts coming"

Jack jumped into the driver's seat and they were off in the general direction of the Lourdes hospital. With no time to waste.

"Fuck this hurts", moaned Yvonne as she held onto the top of the seats tightly.

"You'll be grand", Jamie's bedside manner needed work. She opened the passenger window and lit up a cigarette.

"Can you not hold off till we get to the hospital", Sarah unusually snapped at her friend. She'd been trying to stay calm for Yvonne's sake.

Jamie fired the cigarette out the window, "fine then. I'll wait till we get there.

Jack swung the car out of the estate at high speed. His father's BMW may have looked liked the inside of a vagina. But it had some speed under the bonnet. But all that was short lived as he turned another corner and slammed on the breaks. The one way street they had turned down, had a funeral procession, walking slowly towards a nearby graveyard. The crowds filled the entire road and footpaths.

"Social distancing is well out the window here", Jack went to put the car into reverse. But a number of more cars had pulled up behind them. The whole place was blocked up and there was no way out, "for fuck sake. We'll just have to wait until this lot clears", he leaned over the backseat and rubbed Yvonne's sweaty hair, "don't worry. It's gonna be okay. I'll get you there in time"

Yvonne wasn't so sure. Life had a habit of fucking her at any given turn. Why should this be any different.

Ten minutes later, they were still stuck in traffic, "for fuck sake", Jack so wanted to beep the horn at the extremely old pensioners who were stumbling along behind the hearse, "thought this lot was suppose to be self isolating"

"Nobody gives a shit anymore. Wouldn't blame them. If you're gonna die from a virus. May as well face it head on", Jamie now had the window wide open and was smoking away again.

Sarah was bent over the seat, holding onto Yvonne's hand, "how you getting on?"

Yvonne moaned loudly once more, "fucking hell. I think the baby is coming. What the fuck do I do?"

"Hold it fucking in. That's what you do", Jamie wasn't up for seeing a baby being born in her presence. She still had a weak stomach from a late night drinking, the day before.

"Get her knickers off Jamie", Sarah tried her best to take control of the situation.

"Excuse me", Jamie wasn't sure if she heard that right.

"Get her knickers off. She's gonna have the baby"

"Why do I have to take her knickers off. I'm sure she can do it herself"

"Just do it Jamie"

Yvonne moaned loudly, "please just fucking take them off Jamie. I'm fucking in agony here"

"Ah for fuck sake", Jamie flicked the last of her cigarette out the window and turned to take on the messy job in hand. She lifted up Yvonne's loose dress and grabbed her large knickers and pulled them off down past her ankles. She held them up for all to see, "at least she's still getting use out of her period knickers"

"Oh fuck, this baby is definitely coming. I can feel it coming out. What the fuck do I do?", Yvonne stared at her friend's faces. Hoping that they'd say something that might help.

Sarah rubbed Yvonne's sweaty forehead, "you're gonna have to start pushing"

"Fuck that", Jamie was having none of it, "I'm not delivering a baby"

Sarah threw Jamie a stern look, "well your bedside manner sucks. So you can stay fucking that end. All you have to do is guide the child out"

"Why can't Jack fucking do it?", protested Jamie.

Jack was trying to stay calm for Yvonne's sake. But it was getting harder and harder under current circumstances, "because I'm fucking driving the car"

Yvonne grabbed Jamie's hand, "you can do this. You've gotta do this. Please for the love of god. Just pull this child out of me", she lay back and moaned loudly once more. Her nails digging deeply into the leather seats.

"There's a fucking head", screamed Jamie, "a fucking head. What do I do now?"

"Cradle it gently and wait till some more of it comes out", Sarah was still trying to stay calm. She looked into Yvonne's eyes, "don't worry. I've seen enough hospital programmes to know that you need to give one big push. Then a break and another big push. So take a few deep breaths and we'll go again. You just tell me when you're ready"

"I'll never be ready", Jamie moaned as she cradled the baby's head.

Sarah threw her friend a dirty look, "it's not about you"

Yvonne breathed heavily as she readied herself for the next difficult part, "okay then", she began to push hard again.

"Oh my good god. There's more of it coming out. Jesus your fanny is taking some battering", Jamie cradled more of the baby's body.

"That's not helping", Yvonne just wanted this over.

Sarah wanted to shout at Jamie to stop saying unhelpful shit. But now wasn't the time. She stared into a tired Yvonne's eye, "just one more big push and that's it. Are you ready?"

Yvonne nodded and went for one big final push. Putting her whole strength into finishing the job in hand.

Jamie fell backwards against the car door, clutching the newborn crying baby, "oh my god. It's a girl", she was nearly crying herself from the whole experience. She handed the baby to Yvonne. Who cuddled the child into her.

Jack put the handbrake on and gave up trying to get to the hospital. He leaned over the back of the seat and kissed Yvonne's forehead, "I'm so proud of you", he proceeded to kiss the baby's forehead.

"Love you", Yvonne's eyes were filled with tears.

"Love you too", tears were also coming to Jack's eyes.

Sarah was crying as well.

Jamie glanced down at her bloody gunk covered, white T-shirt, "this is fucking ruined"

Chapter Forty One

It had been another while since they'd gotten to the hospital. But thankfully all the care that mother and daughter received after that, was outstanding. Jack's parents had paid for Yvonne to get a private room in the hospital. Yvonne hadn't been too impressed with the waste of money at first. But now that she had her own private toilet, it felt fucking amazing.

Yvonne's friends had gone off for a much needed drink in the nearby pub. Leaving her alone with Jack for the first time. All he could do was stare into the see through cot at their sleeping baby, "hard to believe that she was inside you"

"Can barely believe it myself", Yvonne pulled herself up in the bed.

"Any ideas for a name yet?", Jack had a few suggestions. But felt the decision was completely up to her.

Yvonne had always thought that she'd know exactly what to call the baby when it made an appearance. Now she wasn't too sure. Many names she had mulled over recently. But none of them suited her. There was Chardonnay, Chantelle, Loretta and many more. Yes, most of the names cropped up over a few drinks with family and friends. But none of them fitted now. Yet there was a completely different name that had only come to her, since arriving in the maternity ward. She'd seen it on one of the name tags of the staff, "I was thinking the name Katie might be nice"

Jack mulled the name over in his head, "that's a nice name. Where'd you come up with that one?"

Yvonne just smiled to herself, "it just came to me. How are you feeling now?"

Jack was still staring down at a sleeping Katie, "I feel great. We're a little family now"

Yvonne just hoped he was right. But she hid her own fears, "that we are"

A knock came to the room door. Michael and Ellen stood there awkwardly, waiting to be invited in. Jack got up off the edge of the bed and brought them in.

After much hugging and kissing, Ellen turned her attention to the newborn baby, "she's so beautiful. What have you decided to call her?"

"Katie", the name was still growing on Yvonne more and more.

"That's a beautiful name", Ellen played with Katie's little fingers, "you forget how small they start off as in life. So defenceless and vulnerable to the world. Reckon that's why I only had two. I was a nervous wreck at being a mother"

Michael rubbed her shoulder, "you were a great mother. You're always too hard on yourself"

Suddenly the room door knocked again and in marched Yvonne's parents.

Sammy straight away filling the room with her loud voice, "where's my new grandchild?", she glanced into the cot and nearly cried, "my god. Another little member of the family", she finally noticed Jack's family standing beside the bed, "hi, you must be Jack's parents", she hugged Ellen tightly, "now we're all family"

Ellen wasn't sure how to react. A strange bulky woman hugging her tightly, was not what she was expecting from new in laws. And she was pretty sure the woman's accent was bordering along the lines of the travelling community, "nice to meet you finally", she attempted a hug back. But it was weak in comparison.

Bernard shook Michael's hand firmly, "heard this was your first. This is my third one already.

Michael wasn't too sure how to take Bernard. He was scruffy and smelt of stale alcohol. He just hoped this wasn't a bad sign of what was to come, "third time lucky", he joked.

"Will be. Never see the first two ones", Bernard wasn't one to hold back and went back to admiring Katie.

Jack sat next to Yvonne on the bed and gently held her hand, "you see. Everything is gonna be okay. Our parents are getting on and we've got a healthy daughter. We have nothing to worry about from here on in"

Yvonne just agreed and wearily smiled back at him. But somehow she knew that things weren't gonna go that smoothly. They never did for her.

Later on that night, both families had finally gone home. Even Jack had to call it a day and went back to Yvonne's parent's house for a good night sleep, so that he could get to the hospital first thing in the morning. Yvonne was delighted that he was so dedicated to her and the baby. Even when there was still doubt over who the father was. She stared in at Katie. Her little bundle of joy was fast asleep in the cot. The long day of constant visitors, had totally worn her out. But still she couldn't see who the child looked like. Jack, Stewy, or even just herself?. Yvonne couldn't tell. And she didn't dare ask anyone else, for fear they'd realise that she was having doubts. That couldn't happen. Not now. Not never.

A knock came to the room door. Yvonne was snapped out of her worrying thoughts, as she glanced up to see Julia standing there, "heya"

Julia came in and sat on the chair beside the bed, "hope you don't mind me calling up?. Hadn't a chance earlier on. It's been mental all day in casualty", she looked in the side of the see through plastic cot and smiled like all women do, when they see a newborn baby, "she's beautiful. Heard you called her Katie"

"Thank you", Yvonne had a sneaky suspicion that there was more to Julia's absence earlier that day, "you weren't in earlier. Did that have anything to do with you avoiding my parents?"

Julia shifted awkwardly on the seat, "I didn't wanna be the first to say it. Don't get me wrong. Everything is going great with me and your brother. But your parents are a different story. Especially your dad. Maybe some day they'll be a little more accepting of me. But at least me and you are okay. That's something. I've always found sisters a hard one to win over in relationships. But you've been sound since the very start"

Yvonne was delighted with the compliment, "thanks. Would you fancy a drink?"

Julia held up her bottle of water, "I'm sorted, thanks"

"I mean a real drink", Yvonne opened her maternity bag and pulled out two small cans of vodka mixed with coke. She handed one to Julia, "join me for at least one"

Julia took the can and flicked it open, "just tell me if you see a nurse coming"

"I see one right now"

Julia quickly looked behind her as she hid the can from sight. There was no one there, "I don't see any nurses coming"

Yvonne pointed at Julia's uniform, "I was on about you", she laughed.

"Very funny"

The two of them chatted for the next two hours. Finishing off three cans each in the process.

Julia yawned loudly, "I better get going. I've got an early shift in the morning and I'm suppose to be going out with your brother after. Think we're going the cinema"

"Don't fall for that popcorn trick of his"

"What popcorn trick?"

"He sneaks his willy up through the bottom and waits till you get down to the tip. He's tried it on loads of girls in the past. Thinks it's fucking hilarious. If I were you. Bring extra packets of salt with you and dump the whole lot in. Teach the dirty git a lesson"

Julia was briefly lost for words as the image of her boyfriend's erection shoved up through the bottom of a box of popcorn, haunted her thoughts, "why does that not really surprise me. He was definitely fairly wild in his day"

"Still is. But I've never seen him fall for someone, the way he fell for you. I can see wedding bells down the line"

"We'll see", Julia tried to hide her embarrassment, "but I reckon it'll be you and Jack walking down that aisle. You get on great. And now you have a baby to finish off your little family"

Yvonne so hoped she was right. But doubts still filled her mind, "maybe one day"

They finally said their goodbyes and Julia headed off. Leaving Yvonne to get some much needed sleep.

But it didn't last long, as Yvonne was awoken from her mild slumber, by a tapping on her room door. She opened her tired eyes to see a nervous Stewy standing there. Yvonne quickly sat up in the bed with fright, "what the fuck do you want?"

Stewy held up his hands in a weak attempt to prove he wasn't a threat, "please Yvonne. I just wanna talk. That's all. I'm not here to cause trouble. Just please hear me out"

Yvonne was still struggling to trust him, but gave him the benefit of the doubt, "go on then. Say what you have to say and get out"

Stewy pointed towards the chair beside the bed, "can I sit down please?. My legs still aren't the best"

Yvonne couldn't see any reason to refuse him, "go on then"

Stewy limped past the cot with a sleeping Katie inside. He stopped briefly for a look, "she's beautiful. Reckon she looks like you. Don't you think?"

Some part of Yvonne felt relieved to hear that. Yet, she wouldn't show it. Especially not to Stewy of all people, "thanks. So why are you here?. And before you start. It better not be about you being the father again"

Stewy lowered himself awkwardly into the chair, "kind of. But not in the way you think. When you came to the gallery a few weeks ago. I was on my high horse as always. Couldn't see the woods for the trees. You wouldn't believe how much I wanted… what you call her?"

"Katie"

"Beautiful name"

"Thank you. Now get on with it"

"I really wanted her to be my child. It was more about my own ego. But I've been thinking about it the last few weeks and all that came to mind was my shitty father. I told you about him before. Fucked off on my mother and never darkened our door unless he was looking for money or a place to stay for a few days. And of course my mother would be stupid enough to give into his demands. You wouldn't believe how much I hated him. I don't want that for Katie here. The possibility that she might actually be my child is scaring me. I'd just be as bad as my dad. I just know it. And there's no way I can let another generation of my family suffer like that"

Yvonne felt she should say something. Even though there was a strong urge inside her, screaming not to, "you can't tar yourself with the same brush as your father. Just because he fucked up being a father. Doesn't mean that you will"

But Stewy was adamant, "even if that was true. You have a good thing going with that Jack fella. I don't wanna get in the way of that. At least you'll be a proper little family. You don't need someone like me getting in the way. And since I'm moving to Dublin in the next few weeks. You'll be seeing even less of me"

Yvonne couldn't believe what she was hearing, "why are you moving to Dublin?"

"I've been asked to teach art in a college up there. Still can't believe it myself. My career is going from strength to strength"

"But what about your last exhibition?. Thought we fucked things up for you", the guilt of her family's actions, was starting to get to Yvonne.

Stewy shrugged his shoulders, "it did a bit. The critics thought I was trying to express some form of deep rooted homosexuality. But I still sold a few of them. So you can thank Dermot from me. He's a secret artist and he doesn't even know it. I better be going", he got up to leave.

Yvonne couldn't help but feel sorry for Stewy, as he limped towards the door on his walking stick. He was becoming less of the person she hated.

Stewy stopped in the doorway, "did you get to see what the original paintings should have looked liked?"

"I did. Thanks"

"That was gonna be my last ditch effort of winning you back"

"I'm sorry Stewy. But you lost me for good a long time before that. But they were beautiful paintings. Pity they never seen the light of day"

"Maybe it was for the best. A constant reminder of you. At least this way I can move on with my life. And so can you. See you around sometime", and with that, Stewy disappeared out of her life for good.

Chapter Forty Two

The next two months had gone by like a flash. Bringing up a baby had been more work than Jack and Yvonne had expected. Thankfully they had no shortage of babysitters on offer to let them have nights out. They had talked about getting a place together. But Yvonne wasn't in much of a rush to move out. She was enjoying the constant help from her mother. Even Dermot had been known to change nappies and administer a bottle of warm milk.

That's why Jack had found it worrying when he arrived at Yvonne's home one day, to find Jamie holding baby Katie in her arms and making more bottles. Turned out Sammy and Michael had gone away for the night. Another effort of putting a spark back into their marriage. Yvonne had been teary that morning and had asked Jamie to mind the baby while she went for a much needed walk. It had been two hours and still no sign of her.

Jack had driven around for at least an hour, looking for Yvonne on the streets of Drogheda. But then something from their past sprang to mind and he headed towards the docks. And he was right. There she was. Sitting on the river's edge. Feet slung over the side and a cigarette in her mouth. He parked his dad's car behind Yvonne and sat down beside her. Already he could tell that she had been crying.

"What's up?", asked Jack.

"What makes you think there's something up?", Yvonne rubbed the stray tears from her eyes.

"Pretty much the red eyes and the fact that you're back on the fags again"

"Well, there's that alright. Just needed some time to think"

"About what?"

"Got some news this morning. Not what I wanted to hear. But I had to know for sure"

"Know what?"

Yvonne put her hand in her pocket and pulled out a crumpled letter, which she handed to Jack, "read that"

Jack opened up the folded page carefully, "what is it?"

"Just read it"

Jack did what he was told, "it's a paternity test. But I don't know what any of it means", but he was already fearing the worst.

"She's not yours", Yvonne broke down crying.

Jack found himself staring at the piece of paper in his hands. He couldn't believe that so few complicated words, could ruin his life so easily. He tried to fight back the tears. But they flowed freely down his cheeks, "I thought we agreed not to find out?. I thought we were just gonna carry on being a family and this was never gonna matter"

Yvonne wiped the tears from her eyes, "I needed to know. It wouldn't be fair to any of us. Especially Katie. What if one day she hears something about Stewy. That he might actually be her father. If that time ever comes. I'd want to be able to tell her the truth. I know this is hurting you. But I couldn't go through my whole life without knowing for sure. I'll understand if you wanna break up with me. I don't deserve you. You've been my rock all this year. While I've just torn your perfect life apart. And here I am doing it again. You should have stayed with Denise"

"I never loved Denise. And just because I'm not Katie's father. That doesn't make me love her any less. And I don't love you any less either. I know we didn't get together under the most normal of circumstances. But I wouldn't change anything about it. This last year has been a turning point for me. I didn't know what I wanted until I met you. Now I can't imagine my life without you", Jack suddenly remembered something and jumped up from beside her, "back in a second"

Yvonne watched on as he opened up the booth of the car and began to rummage around the contents, "what are you looking for?"

"Just one second", Jack finally found what he was looking for and sat back down next to her. He held up a small black box and flicked the lid open to reveal a rather expensive looking diamond ring.

Yvonne's jaw dropped at the sight of it, "are you serious?"

"Will you marry me?"

Yvonne tried to smile. But the recent revelation was still echoing deep throughout her thoughts, "why would you wanna marry me now?. I messed up your future. I've dragged you away from a better life, for a child that's not even yours. My family is a total disaster. And I'm not much better", she grabbed the letter out of his hand and held it up for him to see, "you can't still want to marry me after seeing this"

Jack took the letter out of her hand, "this means nothing to me. I want to be Katie's dad. Please let me. I don't care what this says. I might not be blood. But I already feel like her father. Now I want you to be my wife. Please say yes?", he held up the ring for her to admire once again.

Yvonne went silent for a moment as her thoughts ran wild, "you're probably gonna regret this"

"I've never regretted a single day I've spent with you"

"Then you're a dope"

"A dope that wants to marry you"

Yvonne took a deep breath, "okay then. I'll marry you"

Jack couldn't believe his luck as he took the ring out of the box and placed it on her finger, "and that's where it belongs", he kissed her gently on the lips.

Yvonne treasured that moment for all it was worth, "I love you so much"

"Not as much as I love you", Jack got to his feet and helped his new fiancé up, "now, why don't me, you and Katie go off somewhere nice for a few days. I think we deserve a breakaway. What do you say?"

Yvonne wrapped her arms around his neck. The tears still running down her cheeks, "it's sounds perfect"

Neither noticed as the letter was caught by a freak gust of wind and was blown out far into the river Boyne, where it quickly soaked up water and disappeared from existence.

Chapter Forty Three

"What do I have to do?", moaned Jamie as she tried to
fix her cleavage into the extremely tight fitting red dress.
She'd already given the poor elderly priest an eyeful
when she bent over to fix her high heel and he got a
good look at her lack of underwear.

"You just have to stand beside the baptismal font and
look holy", Sarah was quite the opposite in her long
flowery dress.

"What the fuck is a font?", Jamie lit up another cigarette.

"It's a small marble pillar with a bowl on top, filled with
holy water, "Paul had made an effort for the big day.
He'd finally bought his first suit. Even his hair was tidy
and his face clean shaven. Being with Sarah had made
him want to make a bigger effort when it came to
personal grooming. The feeling of just having his arm
around her thin waist, was giving him a minor erection,
that he was fighting hard to keep down. But he was
failing badly.

Dermot was around the side of church, kissing Julia up
against the cold wall. His hands exploring her body a
little too eagerly for public display, "fuck, I love you so
fucking much", his lips exploring the smooth skin of her
neck.

"You love me?", this was the first time that Julia had
heard those words from his mouth.

"I do"

"Same here"

"Well then say it"

"You say it first again"

"Okay then, I love you"

"I love you to", Julia leaned in for another kiss.

They were lost in the moment when Dermot's parents passed them by.

"You two should get a room", Sammy joked as she fixed her cleavage back into the long but tight fitting blue dress.

"Did I hear the love word being thrown around?", Bernard was wearing his best black suit. It was nice to get it out of the wardrobe for something besides funerals and court appearances.

Dermot rubbed his head awkwardly, "indeed you did dad", he clutched Julia's hand tightly in his, "I love her and she loves me", he stared lovingly into Julia's eyes.

Bernard nodded his approval, "I'm happy for the two of you. And sorry for being a dick in the past. I'll be more careful with my mouth in future"

"I'm glad to hear it", Dermot hoped this was the end of any awkwardness, "we better get inside before this starts. Don't wanna miss out on being the godfather"

Yvonne, Jack and guest of honour Katie, arrived at the front of the church with Jack's parents. They parked the pink BMW and got out. As they approached the large door, they met Yvonne's family coming around from the side of the church. It was only then that Ellen realised that she was wearing the exact same dress as Sammy.

"Penney's?", Ellen joked.

"The one and only", replied Sammy, "great minds think alike"

Ellen interlocked Sammy's arm in her own, "we'd be better off making an entrance together"

"I like your thinking", replied Sammy, and with that, the two of them marched into the church proudly.

The rest of the family followed.

Yvonne briefly stopped before entering. Jack fixed Katie in his arm, before holding Yvonne's hand gently, "everything okay?"

Yvonne wearily smiled, while wiping a tear from her eye, "are you still sure you want to spend the rest of your life with me?. To be Katie's father?"

Jack kissed her cheek, "I've never been so sure about anything in my whole life. Now let's get in here and do this"

Yvonne hugged him tightly. Being careful not to put too much pressure on poor Katie in the middle, "I love you so much"

Jack was lost in the smell of her beautiful perfume, "I love you to. Please never forget that"

"I won't"

"Now let's go do this"

"Okay"

The young family pushed the doors open. Ready to start another phase in their life together. A life full of love. A love that would never die.

Printed in Great Britain
by Amazon

72742137R00220